THE BRIDE

JOHN NICHOLL

Boldwood

First published in Great Britain in 2023 by Boldwood Books Ltd. This paperback edition published in 2024.

I

Cover Design by Head Design Ltd

Cover Photography: Shutterstock

A CIP catalogue record for this book is available from the British Library.

Paperback ISBN 978-1-83561-893-6

Large Print ISBN 978-1-80426-399-0

Hardback ISBN 978-1-80426-400-3

Ebook ISBN 978-1-80426-397-6

Kindle ISBN 978-1-80426-396-9

Audio CD ISBN 978-1-80426-405-8

MP3 CD ISBN 978-1-80426-404-1

Digital audio download ISBN 978-1-80426-401-0

Boldwood Books Ltd
23 Bowerdean Street
London SW6 3TN
www.boldwoodbooks.com

For my family.

1

My name is Daisy Earl; just twenty-three years old, an expectant mother and already a widow, haunted by events, counting the cost, struggling with painful reality day after day. And I'm writing this book primarily for the child inside my womb as my due date fast approaches. I need her to know the truth – my truth – as I've lived it, as it's happening to me. There's been so much mindless speculation since my arrest, so much online abuse, a media frenzy, and so many lies. Some people seem to see me as a monster – fools who've never met me, trolls who don't know the facts. But I'm so very far from that. I'm a victim of events. A survivor innocent of any crime. That's the reality, whatever the haters say.

I want to give my unborn child a chance to read this when she's old enough to understand. I want her to know what *really* happened in *my* words if I don't get to tell her myself. Her lovely father disappeared before he ever had the chance to meet her. That's when I learned what grief is. She lost him before her birth. And now she's in danger of losing me too. Not because of anything I've done. Not because of any fault on my part. But due to an imperfect justice system that sometimes gets things wrong. I wouldn't be the first to be wrongly convicted. I'm the only reliable source of information, but will the court believe me? I have no way of knowing. People make mistakes. All I can do is hope.

I'm keen to write my story for all the reasons stated. But I'm not devoid of insight; I know the telling won't be easy. Even now, a part of me finds it difficult to accept what's happening to me. My previously happy existence was blown apart, mercilessly destroyed in a way I could never have predicted. And that all seems crazy, even to me.

Yes, real life can be stranger than fiction. It can change in the blink of an eye. Everything we know, love, trust and rely on can be turned on its head at a blinding, wrecking-ball speed we can't hope to resist. And that's the way it has been for me. Bang! An irresistible tide. Suddenly, I'm the central figure in a tense drama not of my making. A high-stakes game it's impossible for me to control. So much has changed in such a short time as my life continues to spiral out of control, faster and faster, never to be the same again.

There are no women's prisons in Wales. And so I find myself remanded and incarcerated in the South West of England, over 100 miles from home, charged with an alleged murder that was nothing of the kind. I'm sitting alone in my cell with a notepad on the small table in front of me and a plastic biro in hand. Not exactly the most salubrious accommodation for an innocent young woman expecting a baby, but it's where I'm forced to reside. A concrete box, bars on two square windows, a steel door, graffiti scratched into the four stained walls, and a bright electric light above my head that highlights every inch of this awful place. I've seen so much suffering in this world within these walls, so much unhappiness. And time passes slowly. Oh, so very slowly. Minutes can seem like hours, hours like days. I've been here for six seemingly never-ending weeks already, with another three weeks until my trial. That's quicker than usual, apparently, or so I'm told. I wish I'd started writing sooner now. But if I work hard and put in the hours, I'm sure I can finish in time. It's not like I'm doing anything else. I've given a flavour of my situation and opened a window just wide enough to peep in. But I'm getting ahead of myself. I may have said too much already. I need to start at the beginning if this is going to make any sense.

2

I'm a very ordinary woman who had an unremarkable childhood, a girl-next-door type, the kind of person people can trust, not a scheming shrew like some idiots like to think. No one could ever have guessed what was coming down the line. Not me nor anyone else.

I grew up in a happy home close to an estuary beach in beautiful west Wales, the daughter of a schoolteacher father and a bookkeeper mother, who loved me from my first day of life. I went to the local primary school where my father taught, just a short walk from our modest bungalow on the edge of the village. It was a happy time, yes, *happy*; I think that's the one word which best sums it up. It wasn't perfect, of course, but then whose life is? My parents had their issues like everybody else.

There was sometimes a tension in our home, an atmosphere. Mum and Dad often argued about the same issues, seemingly without resolution. Never about anything major, just silly things. Things which mattered to them.

'I wish you'd stop taking those pills, Delyth,' my dad often shouted. That was a regular theme. 'They're doing you no good at all. It's time you had another talk with the doctor. I'd throw the damned things down the toilet if it were up to me.'

I can remember it all so very clearly. And it often comes to mind. 'Oh, be quiet, Tim,' Mum would reply. 'I've got anxiety, you know that. Why I keep having to tell you, I don't know.'

'I'm just trying to help you, Delyth,' he'd say, almost pleading. 'I'm concerned, that's all.'

But she wouldn't listen. She'd shake her head, glaring at him, or storm off full of indignation. It wasn't always easy for me to listen to. But I got used to it. And most of the time, things were wonderful. So I don't want to over-stress the negatives.

I know Dad worried about Mum, and now that I think about it, he worried about me too. I think that's worth mentioning. It's strange the way the memories flood back as I write. Maybe things weren't always as happy as I thought. I sometimes had nightmares for no apparent reason. Awful dreams that woke me in tears. I remember, early one morning, Dad rushing into my bedroom with Mum close behind.

'Are you okay, Daisy?' he asked, wringing his hands, a concerned look on his face. 'You screamed out loud. You sounded scared.'

I recall wiping my eyes as my lovely mum sat beside me on the single bed.

'I had a bad dream,' I mumbled as Mum hugged me tight.

'Another one?' Dad asked. 'What about this time?'

I don't think I remembered anything about my dream that morning, or at least not that I can think of now. And anyway, I don't think it's worth focusing on that aspect of my life any more than I have. Because I was lucky to be loved in a way not all children are. And I was fortunate to enjoy our rural idyll's freedoms as I played with my young friends. I've lost touch with them all now, but we were close then. I feel sorry for children who live in large cities. I realise there are benefits, but they miss out on so much, growing up too fast. I was blissfully naïve, unaware of the dangers lurking in dark shadows. That would come later as fate sank in its fangs. Back then, I felt safe and secure, the bad dreams apart, just as every child should. A fantasy, perhaps, but one I'm glad I lived.

I went to the local comprehensive school at eleven, travelling the eight miles by train each morning to the pleasant market town of Carmarthen on the River Towy, or the *Afon Tywi*, as it's written in the lyrical Welsh language.

I remember that first morning, the fearful apprehension as Dad drove me the short distance to the station.

'Everything is going to be fine, Daisy,' he kept repeating, full of good intentions but with only limited positive impact.

'Is it, Dad, is it?' I said in reply. Wanting to believe him, but not quite.

'Of course it is. There's nothing to worry about. You're a big girl now; you'll be fine.'

His words offered solace, but being the youngest child in the first year of a much bigger school still came as a shock. However, the anxieties of that first day were soon tempered by experience as I settled into my year group, mixing mainly with an old primary school friend initially but soon making new ones. Sadly, those friendships didn't last into adulthood either, something I've had to accept. People move on. Things change. And I guess it's no great loss. Such is life.

I began enjoying my lessons, particularly English, history and art, as the weeks passed. My marks were good, better than expected, and close to the best in my class. I remember the beaming smile on my dad's face when he read my first end-of-term report. It seemed he could hardly contain his excitement as he informed my mum of my newfound success, his musical, singsong voice rising in pitch and tone. He was expressive, brimming with emotion. I hadn't seen him like that before, never once. He seemed to come to life. His eyes lit up. He glowed. As if, at that moment, all of life's burdens had melted away.

'She's done wonderfully well, Delyth. A chip off the old block if ever there was one.'

My dad laughed at full volume and then continued talking, now in full flow, communicating with repeated hand gestures as well as words. He pointed at the report on my laptop screen. 'Look at those marks, brilliant! An average of over 80 per cent. She's almost as intelligent as her father. Not quite, of course, but not far off. Maybe she'll be a teacher, too.'

'Thanks, Dad,' I said and meant it. I was grateful. The praise felt good. I wasn't the most confident child in the world. And even now, when I think back to that day, it fills me with pride. It bubbles up, filling my chest. My dad's opinion mattered to me as a child, and it seems it still does. That's one thing that hasn't changed when so much else has. I'll try to give my child that same encouragement if I ever get the chance.

James Robin Earl entered my life when I was just fifteen, a few weeks before my sixteenth birthday. He was about a year older than me. I later learnt he'd moved to our quiet Welsh coastal village from the Greenwich area of London with his parents after his father was given the opportunity to work from home as a successful architect. They moved from their small end-of-terrace property close to the Thames to a large detached mock-Tudor house fronted by impressive gardens with a glorious sea view. It seemed like a good deal to me.

James appeared shy when I first saw him at the local village youth club, slightly diffident, much like me. But I found an intelligence about him and a quiet strength too. I later discovered he was a lover of books, again, like me, not the typical teenager, and our friendship largely stemmed from that. I particularly enjoyed Agatha Christie back then, despite my youth, and I still do. The extremes of human behaviour have always fascinated me. In my current circumstances, the irony isn't lost on me.

James and I said nothing to each other on that first evening at the youth club. As I recall, he sat at the edge of the room, saying very little to anyone. He'd entered a new world, an alien society in rural Wales with a different history, culture and customs. No wonder he was silent. But we talked when I next saw him, this time seated cross-legged and alone on a grassy knoll close to the sea one warm May evening. He glanced in my direction, raised a hand and waved as I strolled past with our family dog, and then he said hello in his English accent.

'Hi, Daisy, isn't it?' he called out with a grin.

I found myself pleased to see him. I turned towards him, nodding with a smile, rather than hurrying on by as I likely would have had one of the local Welsh lads approached me. One or two tried their luck, but I was never receptive to their clumsy advances. With James, it was different. There was a mutual attraction right from the start.

'What's your dog's name?' he asked, his second question. I could tell he was keen to talk, and I was happy to reciprocate.

'Polly, she's a retriever.'

He picked up a small stick washed up by the tide and threw it, studying me the whole time, never looking away. 'Have you done something different with your hair?' he asked, question number three. And so unusual for a boy of his age.

I looked away, averting my gaze to the sand, shifting my weight from one foot to another. 'Just a wash and cut, that's all.'

Another smile lit up his boyish face as I raised my eyes. 'It looks great, really suits you.'

I felt myself redden. I must have blushed crimson. I pointed to a well-thumbed paperback on the ground next to him, keen to change the subject but flattered. 'What are you reading?'

He picked the book up, stroking the dog with his free hand and pushing the animal away when she licked his face. 'It's, er, it's a thriller recommended by my mum.'

'Any good?'

'Yeah, it's great. You can borrow it when I finish if you like?'

I nodded again, not wanting our exchange to end. 'Okay, thanks, I will.'

James flashed another smile. 'I hope you don't mind me asking. Do you fancy going out sometime, just you and me?'

It wasn't something I had to think about. In my head, I was already shouting: *Yes!* I couldn't get my words out fast enough. 'Yes, yes, I would.'

And that was it. We arranged a first date. It all started with that conversation. James was an individual who didn't follow the crowd. I liked that about him; he stood out. I stopped to talk because I liked him; instinctively, it felt right. That came as a surprise. It wasn't something I'd experienced before. I was comfortable in his presence. It was almost as if I'd known him all my life. As if our meeting was written in the stars. I'm not over-romanticising the past. I realise some may think that. But it's really how it was. I can't say I loved him from that moment, but there was a connection. I knew our meeting was significant right from that day. I later told my mum that I'd won the relationship lottery. I felt so lucky, so fortunate to be that girl. If only it had lasted longer than it did.

I can picture James back then as if it were yesterday. The years melt away as I cast my mind back, pictures playing behind

my eyes as if in real time – large, bright and bold. I can see his
lightly tanned, freckled, sixteen-year-old face, topped with a
tangle of shining jet-black curls, his bright blue eyes, his slightly
uneven white teeth, and his long, slim body, dressed in faded
jeans, a loose white cotton T-shirt and open-toe sandals, the
type popular with surfers. Thinking about him, it's almost as if I
can reach out to touch him, take his hand in mine and feel the
warmth of the blood flowing in his veins. Almost, but not quite.
He's always just out of my reach. I can never quite grasp him,
however hard I try. If I call his name, there's no one to answer. If
I search, there is no one to find.

James pecked my cheek before we separated that evening,
something I'll never forget. It was as if my heart had missed a
beat. I felt an energy surging through my body, a spark, an elec-
tric current like I'd never experienced before. It was one of those
magical moments that stand out in life, a high point. We already
had a bond that I believe we both recognised and appreciated. It
was meant to be.

I looked back and waved when I finally stood to walk away
about twenty minutes later. I'd never felt so self-aware. I was
desperate for him to like me as much as I liked him. And I
believed he did. I really did. Everything had changed. My world
seemed a different, better place. I didn't want to leave him. I
could have stayed there forever. A tad overdramatic but true.

We went to the cinema the following Friday evening, travel-
ling to Carmarthen by train and then walking hand in hand
from the station. We sat near the back, ate sweet popcorn, and
kissed, sensual, lingering, for the first wonderful time. It was all
about our connection. The film didn't matter. I can't even recall
the title. It was a mindless comedy I don't think either of us
particularly enjoyed. We had that in common, too. I wrote all
about it in my diary when I got home, not about the film, about

him, the kisses, how his erotic touch made me feel. Two pages of joyful, happy writing decorated with small hearts coloured with a red felt-tip pen. I pictured James touching me, fantasising as I put out the light, too excited for sleep. There were no bad dreams that night. It was as if my entire existence had finally found meaning, the most romantic, delightful development. I cry when I read those pages. That's how our love began.

3

'I've been looking forward to this,' James said with a grin as we sat together at a secluded riverside spot, well away from potentially prying eyes on a sunny September afternoon. I was sixteen, and he was seventeen. And we were in love. I remember our first time so very well.

I nodded once as James squeezed my hand, looking into my eyes. I was a virgin. What we were about to do was a big deal for me. Hormones were surging through my teenage system. But there were still nerves.

'Have you got the condoms?' I whispered after James kissed me insistently for a second time, unzipping his trousers.

And that was all it took, no more words. I like to think James was gentle, patient and caring, as well as passionate. Within a short time, two became one. We were lovers as well as friends.

I'm so very glad I can hold onto that memory. It's a place I often visit in my mind's eye. Because memories are the one thing I have left of him. I sometimes think nothing matters more.

My parents were initially less than enthusiastic about our growing commitment. But that all changed as they got to know him better. I recall my dad smiling shortly after James left the bungalow one dark autumn evening.

'You've got a good one there,' Dad said in his singsong voice. 'He's a bright lad. And he's not frightened to express an opinion. I like that. Quite impressive for someone so young.'

'Do you like him, Dad? Do you *really* like him?'

He laughed. 'I said so, didn't I?'

Mum didn't say anything in support, but I'm sure she was thinking along the same lines. Because James's intelligence shone out. He knew so much about so many things. And I was glad my parents approved. I saw it as another milestone. One less thing for them to argue about. Another hurdle overcome on my way to long-term happiness.

James entered the sixth form a year before me. And I wasn't in the least bit surprised when he achieved three A-stars at A level two years later.

'I'll be studying history at Swansea,' he told me, an announcement rather than a discussion. We'd talked about our future studies and shared a love of learning. But the reality of his going still felt a shock. Ferryside to Swansea is only about forty minutes by train and a little longer by car. So I told myself things could be a lot worse. I tried to look pleased as we sat talking, but my true feelings were written all over my face.

'What's up, Daisy?' he asked. 'Come on, I know there's something.'

'No, it's great; I'm delighted for you,' I said. 'It's the course you wanted at the university you wanted. What's not to like?'

James reached out, touched my face, and wiped away a tear. 'What are you *really* thinking?' he asked. 'Come on, you know you can tell me anything. You're not crying for no reason at all.'

And then it poured out of me, an emotional torrent. Everything I'd been thinking. All the things I'd dared not say.

'What if you meet someone else? A more intelligent girl, perhaps, or someone prettier, someone who grew up in a big city like you?'

'That's not going to happen.' A quick reply.

I wanted to believe him, but with me, there were always doubts. 'I know you're attractive to other girls,' I said. 'I've seen them looking.'

He looked away, I think suppressing laughter, but I can't be sure. 'Oh, come off it, Daisy,' he said. 'You're being ridiculous. It's you I love. I could have gone anywhere. I've got the grades. But I chose Swansea because of you.'

Why on earth did I let my anxieties get the better of me? James did love me. He spoke the truth. I would lose him, but not yet. He was as committed to me as I was to him. Even after leaving for Swansea, he was so very caring, ringing or texting me often, sometimes ten or even fifteen times in one evening on the rare occasions I went out.

'Where are you, Daisy? What are you doing? Who are you with? What time are you going home?'

He repeatedly asked the same four questions, I think needing reassurance I was safe and well. That's the sense I make of it. Yes, I was truly loved for as long as our relationship lasted. Later on, I saw a lot in my role as a nurse. Some might say too much. Not everyone is nearly so lucky. Some never experience love, let alone true love, at all.

James usually came home every two or three weeks during term time. And I occasionally made the journey on those weekends he didn't get back. Although, of course, he sometimes had to prioritise his studies.

'I've got too much work on, Daisy,' he'd say as I cried and pleaded. 'You can come next week or perhaps the week after. Stay in with your mum and dad, concentrate on your revision, and I'll let you know once I'm free. You've got no idea of the pressure I'm under. It's a really full-on course.'

I didn't see as much of James as I'd have liked. But I understood. He explained it often enough. And his first year of higher education passed surprisingly quickly despite my angst. I applied for a place at the same university to study nursing, and I worked even harder now, ensuring I gained the results I needed, two As and a B. It wasn't so much the course that attracted me, although I was interested in nursing. My primary motivation was being with James. Work matters, careers, success and all the trappings that go with them are all very well, but they're not life, not what really matters when we look back to evaluate our lives. Experience has taught me that. Life's trappings can all seem so very important until a real crisis hits, bang, and then, in an instant, they don't matter at all. I realised that even at eighteen, although I couldn't have put it into words back then, not as I have now. That's glaringly obvious from reading my diary. The comments are simplistic, clumsy even, but the foundations are there. I talk of the course briefly, with no particular passion I can identify, but so much more of my scribbled, girlish writing was directed towards James, almost to the point of obsession. I feel sure the depth of my love made the future loss I didn't see coming all the harder to bear. That seems obvious. How else could it be?

We rented a small flat in the Uplands area of the sprawling Welsh seaside city two weeks before my first term began. James had worked at a local bar during the evenings to create a deposit, and I contributed a small amount from my savings. The flat was basic, a little faded, badly in need of decoration, and expensive for what it offered. But we were together, and for all the flat's many faults, that was good enough for me. There were still anxieties. But life felt exhilarating as a new chapter dawned.

I couldn't wait to get on with it. Maybe I shouldn't have been in such a rush.

Even if the flat wasn't beautiful, I like to think our relationship was. We made love that evening for the first time in our new home. We had sex often, three, maybe four times a week, and sometimes more than that. What can I say?

'Oh God, you turn me on, Daisy.'

'I'm coming, I'm coming, don't stop, please don't stop.'

I can recall the electric touch of his hand, the heat, the heady emotion as he embraced me, fully erect, rhythmically moving his lean body with gradually increasing speed until I reached a climax with a throaty groan.

I always came, every time. There was so much love in him. If I close my eyes, it's almost as if I'm there, as if I can reach back in time. There's a pleasure in remembering, picturing the scene, a sweet sorrow. I wouldn't ever want to forget what we had together. But sometimes, the memories in my current single state are almost too much to bear. They hurt; they sting as well as please.

We were so close, the two of us. And we rarely argued, not in a heated way as my parents had. James and I sometimes disagreed. Of course we did. What couple doesn't? It wasn't all lovemaking. And it seems we always disagreed about the same things, repeated themes. When we disagreed I sometimes thought it was because he loved me almost too much.

'You need to stay in to concentrate on your studies,' he'd insist if I wanted to go out.

'But *you* socialise. You always go out,' I'd reply. 'I never meet *any* of your friends. And I haven't got friends of my own. If I ever go out, it's always with *you*.'

He'd look hurt rather than angry. 'What's wrong with *me*?'

'Nothing, I didn't say that, *nothing*.'

'Well, what are you worrying about then? Why the fuss? Why the big deal?'

'Can I come with you tonight?'

'Ugh,' he'd sigh, make a face. 'It's a lads' night; no girls allowed. We'll go for a curry on Friday. To that place you like. You'll have your essay finished by then.'

That was usually the end of it, as far as our discussions went. And then he'd go, closing the flat door, leaving me alone. I'd feel guilty for saying anything at all. James was brighter than me. He didn't need to work so hard. Why was I so needy? I should have understood.

I found lipstick on his shirt collar once when he arrived home late. I remember staring at it, pointing, and asking, 'What's that?' while resisting the impulse to vomit.

But he laughed it off. 'It's nothing, hah; one of the lads was messing about. He's an idiot. He had his girlfriend's lipstick with him. His idea of a joke. He thought he'd wind you up.'

It unnerved me at first, feeding my insecurities. But in the end, I believed him. James could usually convince me of his point of view. And disagreements never became personal. There were no verbal attacks. That was important to me. I like to think we were happy most of the time, those few disagreements apart. If only it could have stayed that way. Such things are fragile, so easily lost.

James finished his course a year before me, easily achieving his degree. He'd decided to become a teacher, like my dad, although James chose secondary education, something to which I thought him entirely suited. He had an easy confidence by then, so unlike me, and he was a good communicator. Words came easily to him. And he loved his subject, too. He used to say that if we didn't understand history's lessons, we were doomed to repeat past mistakes. I didn't give his wise words much thought then, but I now realise it's true. I'm a lot more careful now, not so ready to trust, a hard lesson learned, the hardest of my life.

We stayed in Swansea for another year after that, living in that same rental flat, enabling me to complete my nursing course while James travelled to Carmarthen by train each weekday, studying for a PGCE in secondary history at the town's Trinity College. He said he was sure he'd made the right choice, that teaching was definitely for him. All was good, and things continued to go well for us. We didn't see the storm clouds coming our way.

Within a year, we were both qualified and ready to join our chosen professions, having built up a heavy burden of student debt. There was a shortage of qualified nurses, so I obtained a post at Llanelli Hospital relatively quickly. I applied online, provided references and was shortlisted. Two pleasant female managers interviewed me a week or two later and offered me the job that same day.

It was another milestone, another change, but a welcome one. The future was calling. I was a grown-up, ready to embrace the adult world. And the money would be very welcome. There was that too.

I remember giving James the good news. It was *me* doing well for a change, and it felt good.

'But where are we going to live?' he asked as if he wasn't pleased at all.

'I'd really like to go back to Ferryside,' I said. 'Somewhere close to the beach. Ideally with a view. Although anything there would do.'

'What about the travelling?'

I took a deep breath. 'Dad's offered to lend me enough for a car. I know fuel costs will be high. But it's doable. And I can transfer to Carmarthen once there's a suitable vacancy.'

'Are you sure?'

I'd never been more sure. 'It's what I want, James. We were happy there. And it will be good to be near our parents. What does a bit of inconvenience matter?'

There were a couple of seconds of silence. 'Okay... let's do it.'

And that was it. I could have cheered. And maybe I did. I bought a shiny black Nissan Primera a few days later. Our quality of life seemed more important than money, although it didn't always feel that way when the inevitable bills arrived.

James and I moved into a 300-year-old stone-built rental cottage owned by close friends of my parents about two weeks after I got my job. It was ideally located on the quiet B road from Ferryside to Kidwelly, with a lovely lawned front garden bordered by flower beds, and an excellent view of the estuary from the two first-floor bedrooms at the front of the building. For me, it was a dream come true. I'd always loved that cottage. It's picture-perfect, with pink roses around the front door. I fanta-sised about living there when I walked past it as a child. And now it was mine, albeit on a rental basis. We both hoped to buy our own home at some future date, and I really wanted it to be the cottage. But we weren't financially able to achieve that even if the owners were willing to sell. I prayed that one day I'd find a way.

James didn't find work as easily as I had. He applied for jobs in local schools when a rare vacancy arose, but sadly without success. He was called for several interviews but no more than that. In all honesty, he could be opinionated, forthright, and a little obstinate when the mood took him. I wondered if that could be a factor. But, of course, I never mentioned it. And in the end, after about four months of unemployment, James accepted temporary defeat. He started working at a council-run leisure centre near Carmarthen, where he trained in first aid and qualified as a lifeguard, amongst other things. He didn't dislike the job fundamentally; he was a fit man and a strong swimmer, but it wasn't what he'd studied for four years to achieve.

'At least it pays the bills, Daisy,' he'd sometimes say.

But there was an unmistakable sadness about him whenever he left for work. He tried to hide it, but it was always there. He never gave up on the idea of becoming a teacher. But sadly, it never happened for him. That still brings a tear to my eye. It does now as I write these words.

I was content living with James as a partner, but marriage seemed the logical next step. I'm not sure why it mattered to me, but it did. I'd been hinting at marriage for months, less than subtly, pointing at rings in local jewellers' windows, talking about other couples we knew who'd made it official, all older than us. James couldn't help but get the message, and I knew he was planning something. He wasn't good at keeping secrets. Or, at least, that's what I thought. When I found a receipt from a local Goldsmiths in a trouser pocket when doing the washing, I knew it was happening; just a matter of time.

James proposed the following Sunday at lunchtime, down on one knee in our cottage kitchen, looking up at me with a boyish grin, about a year or so after we returned to Ferryside.

'How about we make it official?' he asked with a grin.

'Of course I want to marry you,' I said, giggling. 'Yes, yes, *yes*!'

He took a ring from his pocket, a single solitaire diamond in a platinum mount on a yellow 18-carat gold band.

'Oh my God, it's beautiful,' I said. 'And look at that, it fits perfectly.'

He kissed me. 'Glad you like it.'

I was proud to wear it on my finger, glad to have something

that proved James was mine. And he wore a ring, too, not to show ownership, but mutual commitment. It felt as good as I'd imagined so many times that it would.

We celebrated our engagement that evening with red wine and sex. And I made a special effort to mark the occasion: expensive French perfume, black mascara, smoky eyeshadow, bright red lipstick, shaved legs and bikini line, even a matching push-up bra and lacy red thong with an enticing satin bow at the back. Oh, and stockings, I wore a lace suspender belt and glossy black stockings. I think the first time I ever had. And it all got the reaction I'd hoped for; I created a male fantasy for James because I loved him. I could see his eyes light up as I unfastened my bra, dropping it to the lounge floor, swaying rhythmically on my four-inch heels as a soulful music compilation played in the background. I stripped slowly, and what I like to think was gracefully, in the light of scented candles, as James focused on me, aroused and lustful. His reaction made me feel sexy, attractive and desired. I'd never seen James more turned on, making for a memorable night as we enjoyed each other's bodies. I do like sex, and I'm happy to acknowledge that. And with James, it was a joy. But I won't share any further details of our lovemaking because they're mine. That's as much as I'm going to say. Readers can use their imaginations if they choose to. That's something I can't control.

4

James and I were married the following January on the second of the month at the small, picturesque church in Llanddarog, a nineteenth-century stone structure dedicated to St Twrog, a Celtic saint. Both my parents grew up in the quiet rural village, only about thirteen miles from Ferryside, where they spent most of their adult lives after Dad got his job at the local school. So the location of the wedding wasn't James's or my choice. But we were happy to go along with the arrangements. It seems there was an assumption on my parents' part that that's where we'd get married, as they had many years before, and so we did. It's a beautiful church with impressive stained-glass windows in a pretty Welsh village surrounded by rolling green hills even in winter, and so I had no objections. Sometimes it's best to go with the flow; life's easier that way and less contentious. And it pleased my parents, which in turn pleased me. They'd always put me first as a child. This time, I did the same for them.

Our wedding day went reasonably well in the main, or so I thought at the time. It was a cold, wet winter day, not exactly ideal for a marriage ceremony. But it was January. And several of my nursing colleagues were there, friends of my parents, and my relatives, two first cousins, one with a three-year-old son, and my auntie and uncle. So the climate hardly mattered, not as much as you'd think. One thing that disappointed me was that very few people came on James's side, just his parents and a few male friends from his university days. I thought it strange, but it seemed it wasn't something he wanted to discuss at any length. He simply reminded me he had a small family and left it at that. I guess I trusted him, taking his word at face value because I loved him as much as I did. I'm a little older now, more world-weary. I see red flags where I didn't before. My love hasn't changed, but my perception has.

When my dad led me up the aisle I felt beautiful, dressed in a stunning white lace dress with a veil, to the sound of rousing organ music, to where James was standing waiting together with the vicar near the altar, wearing a new navy Italian suit, shiny black leather shoes, and a dark-red silk tie with a Windsor knot. The vicar performed the ceremony with practised ease, and within a short time, we had made our vows; James had kissed me gently on the cheek, and we were pronounced man and wife.

One person turned up at the church, who I was surprised but pleased to see. Oliver had spoken to me a few times on campus and was always friendly. He'd even bought me coffee once in the student union, something I've never told anyone until now. I knew James knew Oliver, too, but I couldn't recall seeing his name in the invites. He was a tall, slim young man with shoulder-length brown hair parted in the middle, and a slight limp, as if he'd injured himself or one leg was slightly shorter than the other. But none of that detracted from his attractiveness. He was a good-looking lad with a relaxed demeanour who was easily liked.

Oliver approached me with a warm smile outside the church

to congratulate me on my marriage as I made my way back to the waiting wedding car with a sizeable white golf umbrella held high above my head. I'd heard his voice before, of course, but I still I couldn't place his accent, English, London maybe, certainly not Welsh. It wasn't unlike James's, but I thought not quite the same. He was still standing there in the cold and rain, waving, getting gradually wetter as the car drove away with James and me seated in the back. James appeared to ignore him completely, which I put down to his focus on me. I knew I hadn't invited Oliver to the ceremony, but I assumed James must have, despite not saying anything to me. It was a supposition, no more than that, I didn't give it much thought, and I didn't ask. But our wedding was announced in the local paper, something else my parents arranged, just written words, no photos. And I'd mentioned the ceremony on social media more than once, something James never did; he had no accounts. So, looking back, Oliver may have found out in one of those ways and decided to come. He didn't attend the reception. If he had, there wouldn't have been a seat for him at any of the tables. It might have caused an awkward scene. Oliver must have realised that because he wasn't a stupid man. I don't think I gave it much thought, not really, not on that day, if any at all. That came later. It seemed less important back then as Oliver sat alone at the back of the church, watching as James and I made our vows and exchanged our gold rings.

The wedding reception was held at Ferryside's Three Rivers Hotel, by the sea, surrounded by beautiful, unspoilt countryside, with stunning views of ancient Llansteffan Castle across the water on the other side of the estuary. We enjoyed tasty local food with our guests, fresh salmon, greens, and potatoes, listened to speeches, and then danced late into the night as the alcohol continued to flow from the well-stocked bar. It was all memorable and enjoyable, living up to my expectations in every way. The venue arranged by my parents did us proud, and I'm grateful for that. Another milestone was reached, I hoped one of many as we grew together, James and I. And I was pregnant. Now, that does bring a smile to my face. I hadn't told James yet. I hadn't told anyone.

I'd only just found out myself. I knew I was late, and had been feeling a bit queasy. So I did the test on the morning of the ceremony before putting on my dress. I remember my nervous anticipation of awaiting the result and excitement about seeing the two blue lines appear in the small plastic window, confirming my expectations. And all tinged with slight anxiety at the thought of such significant changes, marriage and now a child, too. A rollercoaster of strong emotions swept me along like an irresistible tide. I was desperate to tell Mum, I knew how much she wanted a grandchild. But I knew I had to tell James first. I was already anticipating telling him, choosing my time, my words, when I thought the moment exactly right. We had once talked about parenthood, but it wasn't something we'd planned nearly so soon. And I think, in truth, I was keener than him. But I very much hoped he'd be as pleased as I was when he finally found out.

I was tired but still excited as James and I left the hotel that night to return to our Ferryside cottage home. I felt blessed, happy and content with my life. I had many plans and dreams, some of which were already coming true. Or that's how it seemed at the time. There weren't very many happy days to come after that. Nothing lasts forever, not in this world, not in this life. I didn't know it then, but the clock was ticking, tick tock, tick tock.

I've still got our wedding day photos in a brown velour album. They'll still be at the cottage unless Mum has moved them. I recall the images were taken by a short, fat man with a receding hairline and perfectly round, gold metal-framed glasses, who worked part-time for a local paper. My parents had arranged that too. I recall thinking the glasses didn't suit the shape of the photographer's plump red face as he arranged us into varying-sized groups to take one predictable, unimaginative photo after another. It's strange what sticks in our minds, things that really don't matter at all. I looked at the photos occasionally before my arrest, although not so often as I once did, as the happy images of smiling people, me, James, family and friends, some still with us and others not, tended to make me cry.

The past is captured in that album. Twenty celluloid images, all reminders of a happy day before everything changed forever. James always insisted the photos were ours, not to be publicly shared, online or anywhere else. He said that applied to all our photos. Because they were special and private, there was no other reason. I believed him back then. I didn't have the life experience to question his motives. I only saw good in James, no more and no less. I had no idea that our time together was already running out.

I must open the wedding album again sometime soon when I summon the courage, if I'm released. It's been several months since I dared look, now that I think about it. And I should show the photos to my unborn daughter one day in the future if I ever get the chance. I think she'd appreciate that. Such things can't be avoided forever. The past shaped her life as well as mine.

5

James woke me up surprisingly early on the morning after our wedding despite the late-night celebrations, not exactly the start to married life I'd hoped for or expected. He had an unlikely and infuriating smile on his face as he shook me awake, the ceiling light shining bright above the bed, the electric glare making me wince as I narrowed my eyes almost to slits, screwing up my face. I resisted the impulse to swear loudly and crudely as I turned my head, peering at the alarm clock on the small bedside cabinet to my left.

Every part of my body ached, and I'd never felt more exhausted, I think probably due to my pregnancy. Although I'd slept fitfully, with those vivid dreams I often experienced. It seemed James, in dramatic contrast, could hardly contain his energy as he skipped across the bedroom floor, throwing open the scarlet curtains, first the left and then the right, almost as if it were a theatrical performance on a West End stage. I was amazed to see he was already cleanly shaven and dressed in a smart but casual outfit, navy chinos and an olive-green needlecord shirt, confusing at best given the hour. I genuinely didn't have the slightest clue what was going on.

It was still dark outside. And I could hear the wind howling off Carmarthen Bay, the heavy rain hitting the single-glazed bedroom window. I shivered at the sound of the weather. The central heating wouldn't be coming on for another hour. I buried my head in the pillow, pulling the duck-down quilt around myself to combat the winter chill. My white wedding dress was hanging on the back of the wardrobe door. I glanced at it before quickly looking away. I've no doubt that when I spoke, my tone conveyed my irritation. I couldn't always control my mood, however hard I tried.

'Put the light off, James,' I said insistently. 'For God's sake, it's not even six, and my head's splitting. We haven't had much sleep.'

He pulled my quilt back, annoying at best. It wasn't like him to be so seemingly thoughtless. His voice rose like an excited child on a Christmas morning.

'Come on, up you get. I want to be driving away at seven sharp.'

'Oh no, James,' I said. 'What on earth are you doing? I need to rest.'

He reached under the quilt, squeezing my big toe and shaking my bare leg before I pulled it away. He seemed even more cheery now, as if nothing I'd said had registered.

'Come on, Mrs Earl, up you get. Have a nice hot shower, and get yourself dressed into something comfortable for travelling; breakfast is already on the table. You'll be good to go after a bit of food and a couple of soluble aspirins. You need to power through.'

I sat up, gently massaging the back of my neck, accepting temporary defeat but not ready to rise just yet. I held my hands out wide, palms up, fingers spread. I couldn't figure out what he was playing at. It seemed there was no logic to his behaviour, nothing that made any sense. He was usually as keen for a lie-in as I was, more so if anything. So why so different that morning? I knew something was going on. I just didn't yet know what.

'What are you talking about, James? We're going to Cardiff Bay for two nights. We can't even book into the hotel until twelve at the earliest. It's an hour's drive at most. Why the rush? We'll still have plenty of time if we leave after eleven.'

He sat beside me on the edge of our double bed, taking my hand in his. He had one of those faces that were so easy to read. I could tell there was something he was itching to say. He couldn't get the words from his mouth fast enough. I loved him for that, his boyish enthusiasm. I still do.

'I thought you might fancy a bit of winter sun. Picture it, me and you on the beach, swimming in the sea, cocktails in the evening, dancing, Spanish food.'

I opened my bleary eyes wide, my head still pounding for lack of sleep, my teeth badly in need of brushing. I could taste my breath. I thought back to the evening before, glad I'd avoided alcohol. 'What are you talking about?' I said.

'One whole week in Lanzarote, in our private villa with a pool and sauna. On top of a hill with a sweeping view of the surrounding countryside. It's all arranged, booked direct with the owners, a Swedish couple, as recommended by Laura Kesey, you know, that police detective I mentioned who teaches karate at the leisure centre. She says it's wonderful. The nicest place she's ever stayed. And now we're going to be staying there too. It's going to be brilliant, and I can't wait to get there.'

'Really?' I was still slightly drowsy. It was all I could think to say. I sat there listening as his response poured out of him. His excitement was infectious, but it all seemed too good to be true.

'We need to be at Cardiff Airport by 8.30a.m. at the latest,' he said in that London accent of his. 'We're taking off at 10.30. I've found our passports, printed off the boarding passes, and got a couple of hundred quid in euros; everything's sorted. You just need to get yourself ready. That's all you have to do. I've taken care of everything else.'

I was almost fully awake now, logical thought tempering my thrill, unlike James, who didn't stop grinning. I'd never felt more conflicted. Who doesn't love a holiday? It sounded like my perfect honeymoon. But at such short notice and in our circumstances? Was it even possible? I've always been cautious by nature. I really didn't think it was.

'We were over a grand overdrawn last time I looked. And the gas tank is half empty. That's going to be at least another four hundred quid we haven't got. How on earth can we afford a foreign holiday?'

He beamed, the smile lighting up his face.

'It's all good, nothing to worry about; my mum and dad are paying the full cost. It's a wedding gift, their treat.'

I climbed out of bed, stretching on autopilot, my lower back stiff. I'd been neglecting my yoga. I yawned, smiling for the first time that morning. And then it hit me, work, what about work? Oh, for goodness' sake! I felt my heart sink, my gut twist, the disappointment crushing.

'That's all very well, very generous of them, and I'm very grateful, really I am. But I can't just fly off at short notice, however much I want to. I'll be back on the ward on Wednesday. I haven't booked leave. I wish you'd told me. What were you thinking? It's a nice idea, but we can't go. Don't you get that? Not if I want to keep my job.'

He started to laugh, seemingly amused by my reaction. I

could have slapped him, but, of course, I didn't. It was a momentary impulse, passing frustration, no more than that.

'I spoke to your senior sister weeks ago. She knows all about the honeymoon. It's all sorted. Your leave's booked. Your team even collected some spending money for us, almost sixty quid. It's in a card on the mantelpiece in a red envelope next to the clock. I put it there last night before heading to bed. You're not expected at work until the day after we fly back.'

It all came as such a surprise, my mind racing, one thought after another. I was already feeling slightly better, probably due to the adrenaline.

'Really?'

'Yes, *really*!'

I did a little dance of delight. I could have cheered. I still wished he'd told me sooner, but the fact he hadn't was easy to forgive. It wasn't one of his bad secrets. It came from a good place.

'Oh my God, that's brilliant,' I said. 'I can almost feel the warmth on my face. I've never stayed in a villa before. I'm a villa virgin.'

James laughed again. Just as I like to remember him. 'I've seen the photos. It's a lovely property. You're going to love it.'

'I need to pack,' I said, rushing my words. 'We haven't got a suitcase, not a decent one, only that crap old thing we bought in the market with the broken zip. Maybe we should borrow one from my parents. I could give them a ring now. Maybe Dad would bring it to the cottage. I'm sure he will if I ask nicely.'

I could smell James's musky aftershave when he leant towards me, pecking me on the right cheek with tenderness and love.

'Relax, we're only going to need hand luggage. It'll be warm, and there's a washing machine at the villa. I'll give you some help with the packing once you're ready. It won't take us long.'

I hugged James tight, my headache already fading. A luxurious hot shower with scented soap and I was ready for breakfast, which, as he'd said, was already prepared and waiting, laid out for me on the kitchen table. And bless his heart, he'd made a real effort with our best crockery, cutlery, a blue paper serviette, and even a crystal glass. And the meal was delicious. Fresh chilled orange juice, aromatic Italian roast percolated coffee, toothsome wholemeal toast, and sweet local golden organic honey bought from a nearby farm in the warmer summer months. It was perfect and very much appreciated. I drank the juice but left the coffee, pouring it away when I knew he wouldn't see. It really couldn't have been a better start to the day. James was fantastic. That was typical of his kindness. Such things typified our relationship. Or, at least, they did for a time.

I didn't take the aspirins he'd put out for me. And by the time we drove away from the cottage just before seven that morning, with me sitting in the car's front passenger seat next to my new husband, I was feeling much better than I had on waking. I was looking forward to the happy honeymoon week ahead of us. Sun, sea and sex, what's not to like about that idea? I'm not a fan of surprises. But that was a good one, the best of my life. The next wouldn't be nearly as welcome. But that was for the future. Not so very far away.

6

The approximately four-hour mid-morning flight from the Welsh capital Cardiff to Lanzarote's César Manrique Airport passed without incident. By the time we had settled in our seats, fastened our seat belts, listened to the inevitable pre-flight safety advice, and played an overly competitive game of Scrabble on my iPad, we were already well on our way as the miniature world passed far below.

I didn't really know what to expect of the island. It wasn't somewhere I'd ever considered visiting. I knew it was a Canary Island popular with tourists, located off the coast of West Africa, where they spoke Spanish. But not really any more than that. Fortunately, James had bought an illustrated travel guide on Amazon, which I read with interest once he tired of Scrabble, giving me a better idea of the island's various attractions. The scenery looked very different to anywhere I'd ever been before, almost like another planet, with volcanoes, lava fields, and red and black earth that contrasted dramatically with whitewashed houses, a deep blue sea and the violet-blue sky. And it seemed there were many beaches dotted around a rocky coast, some popular with tourists and others much quieter, off the beaten track. More my sort of destinations of choice, some nudist, others not, places I was keen to go, great locations for a picnic, a stroll, or a refreshing swim. The climate isn't scorching in winter, unlike the summer months, but it is significantly warmer than the UK, with very little rain, which I decided was okay with me. Locals call the winter visitors 'swallows' after the migratory songbirds. They seek the sunshine, too. I was glad James brought the book. It informed me, gave me ideas, and whetted my appetite for what was to come.

We landed a few minutes earlier than scheduled, the island appearing before us as we peered through the cabin window. We left the plane with green plastic luggage in hand, negotiated customs without delay, and then collected the white diesel rental car arranged by James, and again generously paid for by his parents, another wedding gift we very much appreciated. James did the driving, as he had on the way to Cardiff Airport. That's how it usually worked with us. He enjoyed driving, whereas for me, it was a necessary chore, so the arrangement worked fine. We played to our strengths, him usually in charge but working as a team.

James had brought detailed email directions on his phone, provided by the villa owners, so he didn't need to use a sat nav. He was confident about finding our holiday villa without any problems at all. As we made our way, I noted the island's scenery was very much as I'd seen in the guide's photos but even more dramatic when viewed with my own eyes. I remember describing Lanzarote as a rock, but a beautiful rock. There's a strange attraction about the place, a mystery. I loved the island then and still do now. I think that sums my feelings up well enough. I'd like to take my child there one day if I'm released. To visit the places James and I went to on our honeymoon. Another sweet sorrow, my lost love haunts those places too.

James and I stopped to buy provisions at a supermarket a few miles beyond Arrecife, the island's pleasant coastal capital, before we continued our journey towards Nazaret, a small inland village of white-painted buildings, well away from the busy seaside tourist resorts so popular with British travellers. The narrow red earth and stone-strewn track leading off the public road and directly to the villa was a challenge, steeper and rougher than anticipated. But we were both relieved and delighted when we first saw the villa. It was perched on top of a prominent hill at a high elevation, with incredible panoramic views that were truly impressive in every direction we looked. We smiled as James drove through the tall metal gates and up the cactus-lined, black lava driveway towards the entrance. It all looked so very welcoming, so impressive. As if it had been built only for us. As if it was waiting to welcome us in. As if the building had a soul.

Within minutes, we'd retrieved the keys from the key safe, unpacked, which didn't take long, and explored our new holiday home room by room. It was every bit as comfortable as James had promised. We enjoyed a glass of chilled local grape juice on the terrace next to the pool, taking it all in. I refused his offer of wine for reasons that were obvious to me. But I still didn't explain why and James didn't think to ask. In truth, I was putting my announcement off. Waiting for what I thought was an optimum time to break the news.

I placed my empty glass down within minutes, ready for a swim. It was as if I wanted to do everything as quickly as possible, fearing someone might snatch it away. As if I realised even then just how fragile our temporary idyll was. That may well be me rewriting the past. Memories can be so unreliable. They

don't come in straight lines. I may not have thought those things
then. Perhaps I did, or maybe I didn't. I'm not sure either way.
But as I lie awake at night in my cell, waiting for dawn's welcome
light to creep over the prison walls, it often seems I did. As if I
had a hunch as to what was to come. As if some unforeseen
force was telling me to make the most of what I had while I still
could. Everything ends with loss. And it did for me a lot sooner
than it should have.

We didn't bother with swimming costumes. There was no
need for them. We were the only people there. The villa really
was that private. We stripped off our clothes and jumped right
in. The water was chilly but pleasant enough once I got used to
it. I was just happy to be there, relaxing, exchanging sweet noth-
ings as the winter sun shone down from an almost cloudless
pale-blue sky. After a few hours of travelling, our world had
changed so much. I still hadn't told James about the baby. And
neither James nor I really mentioned the wedding. That would
come days later. In fact, now that I think about it, we hadn't
talked about the wedding at all.

I felt sure it was going to be a wonderful week. And I'm
certain James thought the same. We couldn't have hoped for a
better start to married life, or so it seemed. If only it had stayed
that way. If only, if only, what's the point in even thinking it? Fate
was already conspiring against us. That's the only way I can
interpret what happened. Monsters come in human form. Be
careful who you trust. That's my advice. I loved my life with
James. How did I not realise it could end?

7

Our Canary Island honeymoon passed all too quickly, each new day as memorable as the one before. We enjoyed a wonderful holiday of warm sun and gentle sea breezes, so very different to the winter storms of Carmarthen Bay. We'd left Wales in the deepest winter and arrived in Lanzarote in what seemed an eternal spring. And we very much made the most of it, fully appreciating the opportunity James's parents' selfless generosity had provided. We did the usual things holidaymakers do, visiting tourist spots, exploring the island in our rental car, swimming in the ocean, picnicking, and doing a little shopping. And we spent time at our lovely villa home, relaxing, reading, and making love. We swore we'd come back together one fine day, but sadly we never did. I so wish we had.

I told James of my pregnancy on our second evening in Lanzarote. We'd spent the day at Famara, a nearby beach popular with surfers, a sweeping five-kilometre stretch of pale sand and wild white-topped waves backed by dunes, located between an atmospheric fishing village of white-painted low-rise buildings and impressive high cliffs, which seemed to reach up to touch the sky.

We had stopped at a pleasant vegetarian eatery in the small town of Teguise earlier that afternoon before we returned to the villa. It was a restaurant we both loved right away, located on a quiet corner, comforting and welcoming, and run by lovely people who were easy to like. It reminded us of a similar café in Carmarthen, though it's now sadly closed. We'd loved that place too.

James and I drank fresh fruit smoothies and ate delicious vegan raspberry dream cake while the attractive female chef prepared generously proportioned mixed salads for us to take away in brown cardboard receptacles made for the purpose. She was even kind enough to give us a half-full bottle of gluten-free soy sauce to use as a dressing. I'm coeliac, so the kind gesture was very much appreciated.

I cooked tofu later that evening with olive oil and fresh garlic, accompanying the salads perfectly. James opened a bottle of chilled local wine from the fridge, but again I declined, unusual for me, on which he commented with a frown.

'Are you sure you're not going to have some?'

I remember smiling nervously and saying I just wasn't in the mood for alcohol, that I didn't need chemical stimulants, and that I was high enough on life. And I was. I'd come to love the idea of being a mother more and more as the days passed. But how would he react?

We sat opposite each other at the dining room table in a comfortable room with a picture window overlooking the volcanic landscape and a dramatic star-dotted dark sky. The full moon looked so big, so bright. I really couldn't have hoped for a better or more dramatic location to share my announcement. But I was still apprehensive, butterflies in my stomach. It was such big news, such a game-changer. I was praying for a positive response but, in all honesty, I felt close to panic. I'd read that not all newly expectant fathers are pleased. Some are angry, others disappointed or even disinterested. The responsibility can be too much. Some men don't want children at all.

I'm sure James knew something was up; no doubt he sensed it. And he may even have guessed what I was about to say before I said it. But either way, when I did tell him, his face paled. A mixture of tension and inquisitiveness dominating his handsome features. He asked me one question after another, rushing his words as he reached across the table to grip my hand.

'You're pregnant, really? You're going to have a baby? How? How long have you known?'

And so I told him about the pregnancy test I'd done on the morning of our wedding. That I'd done a second test that same day, just to be sure, and, of course, with the same life-changing result.

'How did it happen?' he asked. 'I thought you were on the pill.'

'I must have forgotten to take it. What with all the preparations for the wedding.'

'Why didn't you tell me before now?'

'I wanted the time to be right.'

He let go of my hand, sitting back in his seat. 'Do you want to keep it?'

He was surprised. I get that. But the question stung. 'Yes, absolutely I do, don't you?'

'But what about work?'

I felt close to tears. 'I can take maternity leave. And I'm certain Mum will help out.'

'Have you even asked her?'

'Not yet,' I replied. 'I wanted to tell you first. But I'm sure it will be okay.'

He lifted an open hand to his face, covering his mouth. 'It seems your mind's made up. You've got everything worked out.'

It wasn't exactly the reaction I'd hoped for or dreamt of. But the news was new to him. So I consoled myself with that. 'Are you glad, James?' I asked. 'Are you pleased? I know it's not something we planned, not so soon, but it is good news, isn't it?'

James gripped my hand again, not letting go. I could feel him trembling ever so slightly when he spoke. 'It's done, you want to keep it, so we'll make the best of it. It doesn't seem there's much of a choice.'

I still needed reassurance. 'Really?'

'God, yes, *really*! It's a surprise, that's all. Do you know if it's a boy or a girl?'

I remember laughing; such a ridiculous question. My tension was melting away.

'Not yet, James. It's far too soon for that. But it will definitely be one or the other. That I can promise you.'

I'd hoped it would make him laugh, but there was just a thin smile.

'Right, I want you to go and sit in the lounge,' he said. 'Choose some nice relaxing music for us to listen to, and I'll be with you once I've washed up. I need a few minutes alone to process all this. I thought it would be *years* before this happened. It's going to be one hell of a change.'

I did exactly what he asked, giving him space to think. But we talked baby names later that evening and then long into the night. After much thought, we reached the happy conclusion that a Welsh name would be perfect, something I welcomed and appreciated, particularly given that James was English. I wasn't as confident at speaking the language as my parents. But you can't live in Wales and not pick some up. And I'm proud of my roots. I asked James if he was sure, and he replied in the affirmative, saying our child's name should reflect the land of their birth. We looked at lists of names online, finally settling on Dylan for a boy, after the iconic poet and writer, or Deryn for a girl, which translates to English as bird. Looking back, I think, in reality, I did most of the talking and James let me choose. He didn't make it obvious, but that's how it was. He allowed me to guide the conversation and then agreed, saying he liked the same prospective names as me.

James never will meet our little bird when she's born, not even once, but I feel sure he'd have loved her every bit as much as I will. James would have been a truly wonderful father once he got used to the idea. I've never been more certain of anything in my life.

We visited that same windswept beach the following day, not to swim, the currents are too strong, but to walk along the breezy seashore and enjoy a shop-bought picnic in a sheltered spot with a dramatic view of the towering cliffs, nature's majesty at its glorious God-given best. We strolled into the small nearby village at about eleven that morning to enjoy a hot drink in one of several pleasant cafés that line the main street, a peaceful, unpretentious area with a strong surfing vibe. And then it happened, there he was, as I looked through the café window, a man who looked remarkably like Oliver, the same height, the same build, but with shoulder-length, straw-blond hair, not brown. Was it Oliver? It had to be, didn't it? I looked across the table and saw that James had noticed him too. James was staring at the man, as I was, but he said nothing, and then he suddenly turned away from the window as if he hadn't seen him at all. I focused back on James, looking him in the eye.

'Isn't that Oliver across the street?'

I got the distinct impression that James was trying to look relaxed, but the contours of his face had changed. In reality, all of a sudden, he wasn't very relaxed at all.

'Um, I suppose he looks a bit like him,' he said. 'But no, I don't think it's him.'

I looked again as the young man stopped to read a fish restaurant menu written on a blackboard in white chalk and then walked on, passing us on the other side of the sandy road, dressed in a body-hugging navy-blue wetsuit and carrying a yellow surfboard with a single sharklike fin. It had to be Oliver, didn't it? I asked myself the same question again. It seemed so unlikely that the same person would turn up at our wedding and now on our honeymoon. It seemed far too much of a coincidence, not just the same place but the same time. But the more I looked, the more confident I was it was Oliver. I was sure I wasn't mistaken. And I couldn't understand why James couldn't see it too. Okay, so the man looked a little different, but hair could be dyed. And he was walking slightly awkwardly along the uneven pavement; surely that was a giveaway. I continued watching the man until he turned a corner, leaving my sight. I still thought it was Oliver, that hadn't changed. I was confused more than anything. How could James not recognise a man he'd seen so many times before? Could I be so wrong? I really didn't think I was.

As we made our way back toward the villa later that day, James at the wheel, negotiating the quiet roads with ease, I raised the subject, much to James's obvious consternation. I don't think he would have wanted to talk if I hadn't said something. But then our conversation became really ridiculous. I clearly remember James insisting that everyone had a look-alike, a doppelgänger, somewhere in the world, even me and him. He'd read it somewhere, or so he claimed.

I turned my head to look at him as he continued focusing on the road. 'What on earth are you talking about, James? You don't even seem convinced by your own argument. You're not making any sense.'

He sighed, seemingly tired of our conversation. 'I'm saying it wasn't Oliver, that's all,' he began. 'He had the wrong colour hair, apart from anything. And you didn't even have your glasses on. We don't have to agree on everything. Surely you can accept that. You're not always right.'

I wasn't ready to let it go just yet.

'I've got my contacts in, as it happens. And the man had a limp. What about the limp? That's a very distinctive feature. Just because he had blond hair doesn't mean a thing. It's just not like you to be so stubborn.'

I could tell from James's tone that he was losing patience when he responded. A side of him I hadn't often seen. It wasn't like him to be so obstinate, particularly with me. Then, all of a sudden, he changed tack.

'What does it matter?' he said. 'It's not a big deal. If it was him, why do you care? The man means nothing to us. Let it go.'

I was beginning to think there was something James wasn't telling me. I surmised there might be things he was avoiding saying. And if there were, I needed to know what, for no other reason than I was interested. Maybe James had invited Oliver to the wedding and then fallen out with him for some reason he didn't want to talk about. Just a theory without any evidence. My mind was doing overtime.

'So, you accept it could have been Oliver?' I said.

His voice softened, I suspect trying to appease me, one way to shut me up. 'Yes, okay, it could have been. I'm far from convinced, but there's always that slight possibility. I know he's always been into surfing. And I think he may have mentioned the island once. Happy now? Can we please change the subject? This is getting boring.'

His reaction was starting to concern me. I could see he wasn't telling me the whole truth. That had become increasingly obvious. And for once I stuck to my guns. 'I think you *know* it was Oliver,' I said insistently. 'Come on, James, it isn't like you to be so obtuse. What on earth is this all about? If anyone is making a big deal of it, it's you.'

He didn't reply this time. I waited a few seconds for a response but then spoke again when one didn't come. 'How well did you know Oliver at university?' I asked.

James signalled, manoeuvring the rental car to the centre of the road, passing a group of Lycra-clad cyclists on racing bikes.

'Why do you ask?'

'I'm interested, that's all. Indulge me.'

James pressed his foot down hard on the accelerator, speeding up the hill towards Teguise. Five more minutes, another roundabout, past the petrol station on our right, and we'd be there. When James next spoke, his tone had hardened. He seemed so unlike the man I knew so very well. Just for a passing moment, something had changed.

'Okay, if it makes you happy. I saw him in the student bar a few times. I remember we played pool, and he bought me a few pints. He was an acquaintance more than a friend. We didn't talk much. Just the odd time, now and then. Happy now? Can we leave it at that?'

I could see that James's expression had darkened when I turned my head to glance in his direction. If anything, that made me even more suspicious. There was something James was hiding. I felt certain of it. I couldn't let it go. I felt I had to ask.

'So are you certain you didn't invite him to the wedding? I don't mind if you did, honestly, just tell me. It's not a big deal. I'd just like to know, that's all. The man turned up, and there he was, sitting at the back of the church. I'd like to know why.'

And then it poured out of him like a torrent.

'No, for God's sake, I've told you. How many times do I have to say the same thing? I don't particularly like the bloke. He isn't the type of person I'd want as a mate. I didn't want to see him at the wedding, and I didn't want to see him here. Why do you think I didn't talk to him at the church? And what the hell is he doing here, anyway? I only told a few people we were coming. And obviously he wasn't one of them. I'd be happy if I never saw the bastard again.'

I opened my eyes wide, surprised by his acknowledgement and the tone and intensity of his statement.

'It's just a coincidence – he's here, and we're here; it happens,' I said.

'I'm not so sure.'

I reached across, touching his knee.

'Where on earth is this coming from? If there's something upsetting you, just tell me. Whatever it is, I'll understand. You're really starting to worry me now.'

James blew the air from his mouth with an audible whistle. He was silent for a second or two as if considering his response, and then he blurted it out, spitting out the words. 'He said he fancied you.'

I resisted the impulse to laugh. It seemed so ridiculous. Was that really what this was all about, the male ego? 'What? He fancied *me*?'

'Yes, you, Daisy, *you*!'

I giggled now, no longer able to suppress it. I shouldn't have, but I did. It just wasn't what I'd been expecting. It was the last thing I thought I'd hear. James didn't react well. My fault, I guess, no, definitely my fault.

'What's so funny?' he said, his tone harsh.

'Oh, come off it, James, why all the drama? If Oliver fancied me, so what? It's not unheard of, and lots of girls like you. I've got to put up with that.'

James mumbled his response. 'I didn't like the way he talked about you.'

Finally, I thought I was getting somewhere. 'Such as?'

'He was crude, disrespectful.'

I felt my entire body tense. 'Tell me more.'

James sighed as if I'd said the craziest thing in the world. 'Do I *really* need to spell it out for you?'

I folded my arms across my chest. 'Yes, I think you probably do.'

He manoeuvred into a parking place close to the café, switched off the engine, and pulled up the handbrake. 'Okay, if that's how you want to play it. He said you had a great arse and nice tits. He told me that he...' James paused, took a breath, clearly uncomfortable about what he was about to say. 'That he would love to screw you. I didn't react well. That was the last time I spoke to him before he turned up at the church. The twat seems to think we're friends. I never want to see the bastard again.'

'Was he pissed? When he said all that, had he been drinking?'

James took the key from the ignition and put it in his pocket.

'Yeah, we both had. It was a cheap cider night in the student bar. He was smashed.'

I was beginning to think that maybe the two knew each other much better than James had made out. That was my interpretation. Both history and his reaction suggested that to me. I wasn't shocked by what James had told me. I'd heard a lot worse. I'd lost my naïvety long before then. I didn't appreciate the language, but confession time, I decided to take it as a compliment. My confidence was almost non-existent. I thought being fancied, even in those crude terms, was validation of sorts. Sad for me to admit, pathetic but true. I've changed now, matured. I see it for what it was, objectification, bordering on misogyny. But then, no. I've committed to honesty, so there it is, warts and all. And there was something about Oliver, despite his dishevelled and slightly gawky appearance. He wasn't unattractive to me. I'd never have told James that, not in a million years. Some things are best kept to yourself. But it's the truth, nothing but the truth. Again, not something I'm proud of, but there it is. We all have our flaws. I'm only human, after all.

'Isn't that the sort of thing men say to each other when drunk?' I asked.

James gripped the steering wheel with both hands, his knuckles white.

'Not to me, not about you; it was as much as I could do to stop myself from punching his lights out. He's such a git. I had to hold myself back.'

It was the angriest I'd ever seen James. He spewed out his words. I didn't think he was capable of violence. Even hearing him talk of it came as a shock. I paused for a beat, choosing my words with care. I was beginning to wish I'd said nothing at all. But now that I had, I felt I had to say something more to try to put things right. It felt a bit like being at work, addressing a needy patient's problems. I should have been better at it than I was. And to some extent, I felt flattered by his apparent jealousy.

'Okay, I understand,' I said. 'Please, let's leave it at that. You've explained, and that's enough. I'm sure Oliver being here is just a crazy coincidence. I get it. We don't need to ever talk about him again if you don't want to. Now, how about something to eat? There's a piece of dream cake with my name on it. Please, he's not important. Let's not let him spoil our day.'

James nodded once, and no more was said. I noticed he was sweating. There was a sheen on his face. And he was breathing deeply and, I think, actively calming himself. I could see the slow rise and fall of his chest as he sucked in and blew out the warm island air. I recall thinking his body language said so much. And his reaction still surprised me.

We entered the café, and once seated, we talked of other things, anything but Oliver. I was keen to avoid any further conflict. Arguments were the last thing I wanted. And I think I can say with relative confidence that James felt much the same. No relationship is ever perfect, but I was in love. And once again, that was good enough for me. James complained of a headache that evening due to the stress of the day, which seemed a bit over the top, but after a glass or two of local wine and a full-body massage from me, he was soon his usual chilled-out self again. Such a relief; things were back on track. Our talk of Oliver had seemed to irritate him much more than I could ever have antici-pated. Was it simply that Oliver fancied me and had spoken out of turn as James described? I thought, maybe, but I still wasn't entirely persuaded. I still thought there might have been more to it, but I let it go. I avoided the subject in the interests of our relationship. I was, I fully accept, opting for an easy life when maybe I should have asked more.

I kept an eye open for Oliver after that day. I was half expecting to see him again. He'd turned up at the wedding and was now on the island. That seemed entirely implausible but there he'd been. I thought he might make another appearance. But he didn't, not that I saw in Lanzarote or on the plane home. That would come later. I would see him again. But that time had not yet come.

8

Our return flight to Cardiff took off at 3.40 p.m. on a cloudy but warm Canary Island afternoon. There'd been a few spots of rain the night before for the first time that week, and the landscape had already greened slightly. I think that's something the locals must celebrate because water brings life. I was sorry our island honeymoon was over; a few days longer would have been nice, but home was calling. Neither of us was looking forward to returning to work, particularly not James, for all the reasons I've already explained. But there were positives; it wasn't all bad, and the inevitable end of holiday blues didn't truly take hold. I was looking forward to getting back to the cottage, preparing my nest. And the Welsh winter would pass, spring would soon arrive, the countryside would burst into life, and then summer – the best of all seasons for me. There was much to look forward to, too, as my pregnancy would progress. And within months, I'd be a mother; there'd be my baby to look after – happy days. There was much to arrange in preparation for that.

James and I were both in a buoyant mood, joking and laughing as we prepared to land, our seat belts still securely fastened around our waists. I'd beaten James at Scrabble again, resulting in a good deal of amusing banter, me taking the mickey and him accepting it with good humour. And I was keenly anticipating telling my parents about the baby. I wasn't going to wait till the end of the first trimester to tell anyone, like some people choose to. I knew in my heart I wouldn't lose this child. I had briefly considered phoning or texting them from the villa, but then had decided I wanted to tell them in person.

My mum was desperate for a grandchild. She'd made that perfectly clear more than once in the unequivocal language I couldn't fail to understand. And I knew my dad would be pleased too. He was a people person; family mattered to him. And so giving them both the good news would be a big moment for all of us. I wanted to see the reaction on my parents' faces, give them an affectionate hug, and hear the excitement in their voices as they celebrated.

James agreed to give his parents the news after that. We'd discussed it, and the plans were made and agreed, although I think, in reality, he was letting me take the lead. It might be that he just wanted me to be happy, or perhaps the whole notification thing was a much bigger deal for me than it was for him. I've given it much thought while locked in my prison cell, but I still can't be sure. Either way, we planned to visit my parents that evening after our return to Ferryside, I'd share what I was there to say, and then we'd do likewise with James's parents. None of it worked out that way, not as I'd hoped or planned, but I'll come to that in good time. There's so much more to say before then.

We landed on time, disembarked, quickly made our way through customs, and within twenty minutes or so, we were in the car, preparing to make the approximately seventy-five-mile journey back to our west Wales home. It was already dark by that time, but there was a clear, starlit sky, and the moon shone brightly as a late evening frost began to form. There was a beauty, a stillness. I love nights like that; so much better than rain. The cold doesn't really bother me at all. All one needs to do is wrap up warm. I once heard that there's no such thing as bad weather, just the wrong clothes. Billy Connolly, I think. One of my dad's heroes.

Unusually, I did the driving, with James seated next to me intermittently dozing. He'd had a drink on the plane, was likely under the limit, but I didn't want him taking any risks. We listened to Radio Wales, our favourite station, as we travelled west along the M4, with me carefully adhering to the speed limits after a £100 fine and three endorsement points on my licence two months before. I'd just finished singing along to a melodic soulful ballad when I said I planned to stop at the next service station. We were less than an hour from home, but I badly needed the toilet, my bladder close to bursting, and a cup of sweet tea would also be very welcome. Within ten minutes or so, I'd signalled, pulled off the motorway, and was parking the Nissan under the boughs of an overhanging tree in a dark corner of the car park, a couple of minutes' walk from the service station building. The temperature was still dropping as a faulty external light buzzed, hummed and popped. We were wearing jumpers but not coats, which were in the boot, silly really, given the time of year. I was shivering, and I think James was too. I really don't know why that's stuck in my head, there were far more important things to note on that cold winter evening, but it has. Memories don't always focus on the big stuff. I guess life could prove unbearable if they did.

James turned towards me as I locked the car with a click of a button. 'I'm going to have a bit of fresh air, Daisy,' he said, holding an open hand to his forehead. 'I've got a bit of a headache. You go in, order me a coffee, and I'll be with you in a couple of minutes.'

I threw him the keys. 'I think there's some paracetamol in the glovebox if you need them.'

'Okay, ta.'

I performed a quick rhythmic dance, my bladder uncomfortable, a sense of urgency in my mind. 'I'm going to have to go.'

He waved me away. 'Yeah, yeah, just get me a coffee and I'll see you in the café.' He called after me as I walked away, 'And a packet of smoky bacon crisps if they've got them.'

Such an ordinary conversation, nothing that truly mattered, nothing profound, nothing of any particular consequence. I find that so very regrettable. It brings a tear to my eye now as I write these words. Had I known what was coming, I would have said something different. I'd have said I adored him, that I'd be a good mother to our child, and that James was the love of my life, never to be forgotten. But I didn't know. And so I said none of those things. It seemed an inconsequential moment. We don't see the future. That's not the way it is. We can't see around the corner what's awaiting us. Not for a single second did I think there was anything out of the ordinary. How wrong could I possibly have been?

I glanced back in the semidarkness before rushing away, appreciating the warmth as I entered the brightly lit building, quickly heading for the women's toilets to answer nature's urgent call. I was queuing in the café after a few minutes, standing behind five or six fellow travellers of no particular note until I was finally served by a young woman with multiple tattoos, ordering a pot of tea for myself and a coffee for James. They didn't have the flavour of crisps he'd asked for, so I bought plain. I looked around with plastic tray in hand, located a comfortably cushioned seat, poured my tea and waited, allowing it to cool.

I was still sitting there, reading a discarded copy of the *Western Mail* newspaper and sipping my second cup of tea when I looked up to glance at a wall clock to my left. Another ten minutes had passed and James still hadn't appeared. I looked at my watch, confirming the time, placed the paper to one side, and then continued sitting there alone for another five minutes or so, waiting, frustrated at first, impatient certainly, cross even, but with a growing concern. I rang his mobile once, then again, but with no reply. I kept ringing, again and again, but with the same negative results. It wasn't like James not to answer. It wasn't something he ever did, not before then.

The longer I waited, the more concerned I became. Where on earth was he? My mind was racing now, one unanswered question after another coming to mind. The car was only a couple of minutes' walk away at most. Why hadn't he joined me? I stood, looking around me, turning in a slow circle, glancing in every direction with keen eyes, but he was nowhere to be seen. I looked in the shop, thinking he might be in there, carried away looking at one magazine or another, but he wasn't. I spoke to the red-haired woman at the till, showing her a photo on my phone, but she was adamant she hadn't seen him. He wasn't in the men's toilets either; I asked one of the male staff to look.

I could hear the man call out James's name, once, then again, more loudly the second time, but with no reply. There was just a cruel silence which seemed to mock me. I think it's fair to say I was feeling close to panic by that time, trying to hold it together with only limited success. I was totally stressed. I was starting to think something was very wrong. It was as if fear was reaching out, gripping me, beating me down as my anxiety levels soared to a new and savage high.

I was close to tears as I made my way out into the service station car park, looking to left and right as I hurried towards our car with quick-moving feet, covering the distance in significantly less time than I had in the opposite direction. And there the Primera was, exactly where I'd parked it. I peered through the windscreen, making use of my phone's torch feature, and then checked the front number plate; it was our car, all right. I hadn't made some stupid mistake and gone to the wrong vehicle. But as hard as I looked, there still was no sign of James.

As I glanced around me, first one way and then another with rapid, jerky movements of my head, I'd never felt more alone. It was as if, in that instant, I was the only person in the world. I'd never felt such confusion or uncertainty. A nightmare had come true. I felt like screaming, stamping my feet like a petulant child. It was as if the cold hand of fate was resting on my shoulder, sardonic, cynical, digging in its claws. Finding James was all that mattered. Everything else was entirely unimportant. I tried to be positive, to look on the bright side, telling myself he'd turn up at any moment, full of apologies, but deep down, I knew that wasn't true. I shouted his name loudly at the top of my voice, but no one answered. What to do? What the hell to do? Standing there looking around me to no good effect was achieving nothing. I knew I had to do something, but what?

I wiped away my tears before urgently ringing James yet again with the touch of my finger. It was the only potentially productive thing I could think to do. And then I froze, statue-like, rooted to the spot as the sound of an all-too-familiar ringtone hit me in the gut like a physical blow. I dropped to my knees on the cold, hard Tarmac, peering under the Nissan to see James's phone. Oh my God, there it was, no, please, no. No wonder he hadn't answered. How could he?

I ignored the pain emanating from a bruised, grazed knee as

I reached out to grab the phone with frantic fingers, then sat up, staring at the cracked screen, not wanting to believe the evidence of my eyes. My entire body was trembling now, as much from fear as cold. The phone was in perfect condition when I'd last seen it in its protective case not long before, but not any more. The entire screen was shattered, as if someone had stamped down on it with the heel of their shoe or boot. It was remarkable it was working at all. I held it in front of my face, staring, my tears flowing freely as I gasped for breath, sucking in the cold Welsh evening air. I think it was at that very moment that panic truly set in. I leant forward, supporting my weight on my free hand, let out a wail, eyes wide, and then threw up repeatedly until there was nothing left but green acidic bile.

9

I didn't contact the police, not then, not as I should have. I rang my dad. I'm not entirely sure why. I'm not always logical. My choices can sometimes be questionable, particularly in a crisis, not at work but in my personal life. I think it may be the intense emotion that affects me, muddling my mind. And for some reason, contacting my dad felt like the right thing to do. Looking back, that's the only conclusion I can reach. If I could turn back time, I would probably do things differently, ring 999, but I can't. I rang Dad, and that was it; that's what happened. It may be that I wanted to hear his reassuring voice. I'd relied on him so often as a child. I might have thought he'd come rushing to my rescue like a knight on a white charger. As if he could somehow resolve my plight in a way no one else could. A fantasy, of course, a fairy-tale, but one it seems I clung onto as if for dear life, at least for a time. And he did help; he tried his best and did everything he could in impossible circumstances. I'm grateful for that and happy to put my gratitude on record. I think he thought he let me down, but he didn't. I didn't believe that then, and I still don't now. I wish I'd told Dad that before he'd died. So much went unsaid. He really couldn't have done more.

I stood shaking outside the service station entrance in the light of the building for almost an hour before I finally saw my parents' Volvo estate car entering the car park and stopping in a disabled driver's space no more than sixty feet from where I was standing. I could just see Dad in the driver's seat in the half-light, but my mum wasn't in the car. I later found out that my maternal grandmother had been admitted to hospital after a fall. Mum was there at her mother's side, although Dad didn't tell me that on the night. Another family crisis, which, as it turned out, was less serious than mine. I suspect Dad thought I had more than enough to worry about without that additional burden. I just assumed Mum had stayed at home waiting for a phone call. Something else I'm grateful for; Dad really was a thoughtful man.

In two short bursts, my dad beeped the car's horn, flashed the headlights, and then waved, confirming he'd seen me standing alone in the cold. It was such a huge relief, a spark of reassuring hope. Time had passed so very slowly until that moment, each waiting minute seeming like an age that would never end. I was still desperately hoping James would turn up at any moment. That he'd suddenly appear, call out my name, hug me close, apologise and explain where he'd been. But I think, even then, I knew that wouldn't happen. It was a feeling more than anything else, and then there was his phone, which told its own story. All my optimism was gone. The savage black dog of depression was snapping at my heels, predatory, ruthless, some-thing I'd never experienced before, not to that extent. It was as if I was caught in a bad dream I prayed would soon end.

My relief on seeing my dad getting out of the car and walking towards me was almost palpable. There was a stiffness to his movements, his arthritic knees no doubt complaining as they often did in the winter months. Time hadn't been kind, and declining health had taken its inevitable toll, but he looked like a hero to me. His arrival in that service station car park gave me new hope where before there was none. I wasn't alone any more, which offered reassurance of sorts. It didn't entirely relieve my angst, it was so far from that, but it helped.

I ran towards my dad, eager for his comforting touch, throwing my arms around his thin body, pulling him close, not wanting to let go. He took a single step back when I finally released my grip. His voice was faltering when he spoke. There was an urgency to it, a concern I don't think he could have hidden even if he'd tried.

'Still no sign of him?'

A straightforward question that said so very much.

I shook my head, silent tears staining my face as I met my dad's oh-so-familiar eyes with what I can only assume was a pleading look.

'It's... it's been almost t-t-two hours, Dad,' I stuttered, the stress too much. 'It's, it's like I said o-o-on the phone. I was, I was waiting in the café, James was supposed to follow me in. He, he wanted the painkillers for a... for a headache. And I was sitting there, just sitting there, waiting. It should have taken him five, maybe five m-minutes at most. But he... he never... he never came.'

My dad let out a deep sigh; I think a loving response to my distress. I so wanted him to take control, to relieve my burden of responsibility. And that's precisely what he did. There was a determination about him now, a confidence that may or may not have been faked. He was good in a crisis, like I usually am.

'Right, first things first,' he said. 'You're freezing, you're shivering like a leaf – let's get you into the warm. We'll have a quick chat, and then I'll have a good look around. We'll take this one step at a time. James has got to be somewhere. We've just got to find out where.'

I forced a thin smile that I'm sure was far from convincing before he took my arm, leading me back into the service station, where I sat no more than a few feet away from where I'd sat before. Dad insisted on buying me a warming cocoa before we talked. I tried to argue, but it seemed he didn't want to hear it. I suspect he was worried about my welfare. I get that now.

I could see Dad glancing to the left, to the right and back again with repeated subtle movements of his head as he returned to our table from the serving counter, doing much the same as I had some time before. Like me, I suspect Dad was also hoping he'd spot James. That the evening's drama would soon be over and explained. That all would be right with the world.

He placed our hot drinks on the table, handed me a clean paper tissue taken from a coat pocket to wipe away my tears, and then sat, letting out a slight groan as he lowered himself into his seat. He'd done that for as long as I could remember. I don't think it was an age thing. He was the first to speak as we met each other's eyes, mine still filled with tears despite the tissue.

'I don't want you to take this the wrong way, *cariad*, but I have to ask: have you and James argued? It happens. No couple is perfect, not even me and your mum. You know how we go at it sometimes.'

Cariad was a name Dad called me as a child. It's the Welsh word for love, a term of affection. It was almost as if I was a little girl again. I desperately wanted him to understand that my situation was serious. I needed to drive it home, so I chose my words with care, speaking with passion, overwhelmed by the emotion of it all. I needed him to *know* that James's leaving wasn't some ridiculous inconsequence that had gotten out of hand.

I dropped my chin to my chest, head in hands, and then looked up, looking him in the eye, not looking away. 'No, Dad, we have *not* had an argument,' I insisted. 'That's not what's happening here. Do you think I'd be sitting here tearing my hair out if we had? I wish we *had* argued. At least then I could make sense of it all. We had a lovely holiday, and we've never been closer. James smiled when I left him at the car. He was in a positive mood despite a headache. We both were. And then... and then he was gone.' I checked my watch, a birthday gift from James, pushing up the sleeve of my grey wool jumper. 'It's now b-been well over two hours. I'm scared, Dad; I can't just sit here doing nothing. He could be anywhere. What if he's hurt? What if he needs my help?'

My father paused, then sighed. 'Has he ever done anything like this before?'

'No, Dad, never, never once, nothing like this,' I stressed. 'He wouldn't disappear for no good reason at all. Something has happened; something is very wrong. Please believe me. Please help me decide what to do. I'm relying on you. We can't just sit here doing nothing at all.'

Dad made a face. 'Come on now, Daisy, let's not jump to conclusions. Give James another ring. And then, if he doesn't answer, we'll have one last really good look around. I've got a decent torch in the car. Come on, you never know; maybe he'll answer his phone this time. It's got to be worth a try.'

With a trembling hand, I took James's mobile from a jeans pocket, pushing it across the table as my dad drained his cup, head back, Adam's apple bouncing. He placed his cup back on its saucer and then stared at the phone without touching it, screwing up his face. He paled as if, all of a sudden, he was worried, too.

'Is that... is that yours or James's?'

I wiped a tear from my face; stating the facts seemed to make them seem all the more real. 'It's his. Now do you get it? It's *his!*'

My dad's expression darkened. For the first time, I think he was almost as concerned as I was. I could hear it in his voice when he spoke. His jaw looked tighter. There was a tension.

'Was it already broken?'

'No, no, it wasn't. Not before tonight. I found it like this.'

His eyes narrowed.

'Where?'

'Under our c-car in the car park about an hour b-b-before you arrived. Look at the state of it. And how would it even get there? It looks almost as if someone smashed it on purpose. Why would James leave it, even if it was broken? There's no way he'd do that. He's only had it for a few months. He loves that phone. And it still works; I've tried ringing it. I'm frightened, Dad. What the hell's going on? None of this m-makes any sense at all.'

My dad stood immediately, using the tabletop to assist himself to his feet. I don't think he'd ever seen me so scared. Not even after the worst of my nightmares. But he didn't comment; instead, he focused on the task at hand.

'Okay, let's both have one last really good look around,' he said. 'You look in here, I'll look outside with the torch, and then if we haven't found him in ten minutes, we'll meet at the entrance and decide what to do next.'

'Such as?'

'Let's cross that bridge once we come to it. But as of now, I think we'll have no option but to contact the police.'

10

We travelled west in my parents' comfortable car, my dad driving and me seated next to him in the front passenger seat, repeatedly tapping a foot against the floor as we sped along the M4 motorway, sometimes faster than was sensible. Dad drove with the urgency I believed the situation warranted, and I was glad of that. I didn't feel there was a second to waste. We'd decided to make our way directly to Carmarthen Police Station to speak to an officer in person rather than use the phone. Looking back, I think it was my idea rather than Dad's, although he didn't object, not that I can recall. He may have tried to convince me otherwise, but I really don't think he did. And even if he had tried, he wouldn't have succeeded. I was convinced that as Detective Inspector Laura Kesey knew James, she was my best option. More likely to take my concerns seriously and act on them in the way I so desperately wanted. James's disappearance wouldn't just be another case to her; there'd be a personal connection. Finding James would matter to her. Not as much as it mattered to me, of course, or to James's parents, who didn't even know he was missing yet. But it would matter nonetheless.

In short, I thought Laura was the best person to help and that, given her relatively senior rank, she'd have influence.

Dad parked the Volvo close to the modern red-brick building and then led me into the small reception, where he told me to sit on one of several metal seats secured to the floor before repeatedly knocking on the glass reception screen with the knuckles of his right hand. He took the lead again, for which I was grateful because, by that time, I was close to falling apart, a blubbering mess. Thankfully, we didn't have to wait very long. And when a blue-uniformed female officer of about thirty years of age with short black hair and metal-framed glasses appeared a few minutes later, it was immediately apparent that Dad knew her. He later told me she'd visited his school, although he didn't mention it at the time.

He introduced the officer to me as PC Kirsty Whitlock and then explained the reason for our visit. She looked at me from behind the glass screen with a sympathetic expression when I started to cry again, still seated a few feet behind where Dad was standing, allowing the counter to support his weight. And then PC Whitlock spoke directly to me, speaking in a soft west Wales accent much like my own. There was comfort in the familiarity. She had a friendly but efficient persona that went some way to put me at my ease, or as much as possible in the circumstances. She didn't seem in the least bit fazed by what Dad had told her. It seemed events hadn't come as a shock to her as they had to me. But then why would they? She was a professional, used to dealing with one crisis or another. And James was the love of my life, not hers. To her, he was a stranger. I asked to speak to DI Laura Kesey, but she wasn't on duty. Although disappointed initially, I quickly decided that the pleasant and efficient female officer was an acceptable next-best option. I'd been half expecting PC Whitlock to say James hadn't been missing for long enough to justify police involvement. But she didn't; she took mine and my dad's concerns seriously, for which I was grateful.

PC Whitlock unlocked and opened a door to our right with the press of a red wall-mounted button, then led us further into the police station, away from reception, finding a free interview room and sitting us both down on the opposite side of a small table facing her. Before sitting herself, she'd taken a notepad and a yellow plastic biro from a desk drawer. She looked at each of us in turn, first my dad and then me, before speaking again, slowly, calmly, clearly enunciating each word. By that point, she was focused entirely on me.

'Okay, I think I've got the picture. You've done the right thing contacting the police. I'm going to do everything I can to help. I'll ask you a few questions, Daisy, and then, if it's all right with you, we'll get something down on paper. I need to be sure I've got all the relevant information and that it's accurately recorded. It's worth taking some time to ensure *everything* is properly covered, but we'll do it all as quickly as possible. How does that sound?'

I could feel my heart pounding in my chest as if it was attempting to burst from my body. As if I'd run a marathon. But I could see the logic in her approach despite my distress. And I was keen to cooperate. To do anything and everything I could to make her job as easy as possible.

PC Whitlock listened as I spoke through my tears, my eyes red, puffy and inflamed. She poised her pen above a blank page of the pad. For some reason, I noticed that her fingernails were cut short. I've no idea why. I guess it was the most practical style for her role. There was a clock on the wall behind her, black numbers on a white face. Another little detail that's stuck in my mind. It was such an unremarkable room, office-like, as we discussed things that were so far from ordinary. 'What do you n-need to know?' I asked.

'Let's start with your husband's full name, address, date of birth and contact details.'

I swallowed hard and blew my nose. And then I provided the information as requested, rushing my words, keen to move things along as speedily as possible.

'Okay, thank you, Daisy, that's very helpful. Now please tell me *everything* that happened from the time you arrived at the service station until you left to come here. Your father gave me a useful summary in reception, but I want the detail. I need to hear it in *your* words. Tell me even the little things you might think seem unimportant. Sometimes the seemingly most insignificant detail can break a case wide open. Do you think you can do that for me?'

I hadn't thought of my predicament as a case before, and for some reason, the term stung. My entire body tensed. It was as if James was reduced to that one word. I nodded once with a jerk of my head and then began telling my story, much as I had to my dad earlier in the evening. But this time, I left nothing out, just as she'd asked, picturing events in my head and then sharing them with her as moving pictures played behind my eyes. I was back in that service station in my mind's eye, reliving every awful second as if James had disappeared all over again. I could clearly see that the officer's concerns were growing with each new detail I shared. She looked shocked when I mentioned the phone, just for a fraction of a second, before she composed herself again. She had one of those faces that betrayed every emotion. Or at least that was my interpretation. I liked her a little more after that. Her concern was reassuring. Her reaction made her all the more human, a person like me despite the blue uniform. And I clung to that; it gave me hope.

'So, where is your husband's phone now?'

I took it from my pocket and held it out.

'Just put it on the table, please. I don't want to touch it without gloves. There may be evidence to find, fingerprints, forensics.'

I gripped the edge of the small table with both hands as my dad reached out, silently placing a reassuring hand on my shoulder as the officer continued talking. She pointed at the phone's smashed screen, keeping her finger a few inches away, never touching it. I noticed her nails again; how utterly ridiculous of me, another inconsequence. In truth, the talk of forensics unnerved me. It was the sort of thing I'd heard mentioned in TV detective shows. If there were forensics, James might have been hurt, or even worse. Oh God, please, no. I think I was trying to focus on anything but that. I listened as the officer asked the next question.

'Are you *absolutely* certain the phone wasn't already damaged like that before this evening?'

I was quick to reply. 'Yes, I'm certain.'

She looked less than persuaded. 'Can you tell me why?'

I nodded twice. 'We looked at some of our holiday photos on the phone, on the plane. We were together almost the entire time after that, other than when he popped to the toilet at the airport. I'd have seen the phone being damaged, or James would have said something. It's not the sort of thing he'd have kept to himself.'

'Okay, I understand.' She paused for a beat before talking again as if considering her choice of words. She opened her mouth as if to speak and then closed it before finally asking her next question. 'Did you and James argue at all before he went missing? I need you to be honest with me. If you had any disagreement, however seemingly trivial, I need to know about it.'

I felt the tiny hairs rise on my arms and neck, standing to attention. I'm sure my tone must have betrayed my irritation. I realise now she was simply doing her job. But at the time, it didn't feel like that to me. 'Why does everyone keep asking me that? My father said the exact same thing.'

'It's important, Daisy. It's essential I know. The more details you can give me, the more things we can rule in or out. One of our sergeants says it's like a jigsaw. We put the pieces together, and then, hopefully, a picture emerges. I'm following a set procedure because it works. I know some of my questions are uncomfortable, but I have to ask them because they're important. You need to bear with me. Do you understand?'

I felt my jaw tighten. 'Yeah, okay, sorry, I do,' I said.

'So what's the answer? Did you argue or not? Was there any sort of upset, anything at all? It's no bad reflection on you if there was.'

I shook my head to left and right. 'No, no, no, absolutely not! There was no argument, no heated words. We had a lovely honeymoon, and everything was fine between us. James was smiling before I headed into the service station. He was... he was just having some fresh air. He was going to follow me. Where the hell is he? What's happened to him? None of this m-makes any sense at all.'

She didn't answer my questions. How could she? She focused back on what she needed to know. I think most would say she was good at her job.

'Thank you for the information, Daisy. Now, this is something else I have to ask. Does James suffer from any form of mental health issues? Depression, anything of that kind? Do you think there's even the *slightest* possibility that he may have harmed himself?'

I held a hand to my heart, looking PC Whitlock in the eye. 'James is a happy, optimistic person. And I'd only recently told him I'm pregnant. We have everything to look forward to as a couple and as a family. He's as excited about the future as I am. There is not even the *slightest* possibility he's harmed himself. You can rule that out 100 per cent.'

My dad's mouth fell open at that point, but he didn't say anything; congratulations on my pregnancy came later. The officer moved on with her interview, making notes as I spoke. For some reason, she wrote in bold capitals with surprising speed. I could clearly read the words, even upside down. That's not something I'd ever seen before or since. On to the next question, in fact, two questions in one.

'Does James suffer from any physical illnesses? Is he on any form of prescription medication?'

It was straightforward to answer. James couldn't have been fitter or healthier. He was one of those fortunate people who are rarely ill. 'No, he's in great shape; there's nothing like that. He gets a bit of hay fever in the summer, but that's it. I don't think he's seen a doctor for years.'

'Any financial problems?'

I think I sighed when she asked that, my shoulders rising and falling ever so slightly. But even then, in the heights of emotion, I could still understand the reasoning behind the question. I'm sure a lack of money causes issues for many people, but that didn't apply to us. Not to the extent that it could have been significant. I wanted to make that crystal clear, not mentioning the overdraft. I kept that little detail to myself. 'We're both in good jobs with decent salaries,' I stressed. 'And Mum, Dad and my in-laws helped with the wedding and the honeymoon costs. James disappearing has got *nothing* to do with money. That's something else I'm certain about. You can rule that out, too.'

The officer nodded once, slightly lowering and raising her head before turning to the next page of her notepad. Her unusually large script filled the pages quickly.

'One more question before we move on to a description.'

What now? I thought. For God's sake, look for him. Please, please, get a move on. 'Okay, I'm listening.'

'Do you know of anyone with a grudge against your husband? Please think carefully. Is there anyone at all?'

I laughed, not amused but incredulous. Oliver did come briefly to mind. But one ridiculous drunken argument, as described by James, seemed inconsequential and unimportant. No one would call that a grudge, would they? Two pissed students rowing over a girl. The very thought seemed laughable. So what if Oliver turned up at the wedding? So what if he was on the island, too? That had to be a crazy coincidence. He couldn't have been at the service station, could he? I could be so stupid back then, so horribly naïve. More fool me. I made a quick decision not to mention Oliver at all. The last thing I wanted was to misdirect the investigation.

'James is one of the nicest people I've ever met,' I said. 'He's intelligent, kind, loyal and generous of spirit. There is not a single person I know who doesn't like him. He's a lovely guy. I'm sure my father would say the same.'

I glanced at Dad, who mumbled his agreement. And then I returned my attention to PC Whitlock, who seemed ready to continue. She'd accepted what I said and moved on, an opportunity lost, not her fault, but mine, definitely mine. I feel guilty about that now. I let James down.

'Right, let's move on to a description. Let's start with a recent photograph. Something taken in the last few days that clearly shows his face.'

I flicked through the many honeymoon photos on my phone, left to right. I soon found one I thought perfect, James smiling just two days before in the warm Canary Island sunshine. PC Whitlock looked at it, nodding her approval, holding my phone in her left hand.

'Yeah, that one will be ideal,' she said. 'He's a good-looking lad. I'll send the image to my official police email address and then get it widely circulated as soon as we've got a full description to share with other officers.'

Only seconds passed before she handed my phone back to me. And I felt we were finally getting somewhere. For me, the notification couldn't be sent soon enough. Any further delay seemed crushing. It was a huge relief when she asked me her next question. Those seconds passed so very slowly, time playing its games. She checked her own phone. Confirming the photo had arrived, which it had.

'That's great, Daisy, perfect; am I right in thinking his eyes are blue?'

I could easily imagine James looking at me with his lovely eyes. Momentarily, it was as if he was in the room, not lost in some unknown place; God only knew where. 'Yeah, they are. They really stand out, pop against his tanned skin.'

She looked at his image again, studying the screen. 'Yes, I can see that. Does he ever wear glasses?'

I shook my head. 'No.'

'Contact lenses?'

Why would that be significant to his description? Why the hell was she asking that? 'No, never. I do, but not him.'

'How tall is James? Feet and inches or metric. Either would be fine.'

I wanted to be as specific as possible, to get everything precisely right. I was terrified of making even the slightest error. It seemed like the most important thing in the world. 'He's six foot and three inches without shoes.'

She made a hurried note of my reply, again in capitals. 'And his build?'

I pictured James's lovely body, naked from head to foot. 'You can see from the photo. He's slim but well-muscled. He works at the leisure centre. A little over twelve and a half stone. He eats healthily – we're both plant-based, actually – and does a lot of exercise, swimming, yoga, that sort of thing.'

'And you say he works at the leisure centre, is he a gym fan? Has he ever used steroids? A lot of lads do these days. It can change their behaviour, aggression and paranoia. If James is a user, I need to know.'

I was more than a little irritated by the question. And I hated the implication, her questioning his integrity, but I answered anyway, again keen not to cause further delay.

'He's never touched any drugs. He enjoys a few drinks now and then, but that's it. He's more into active yoga than weights. And walking, we do a lot of walking together, miles sometimes, along the coast. We're planning to do the Pembrokeshire coast path in the spring when the weather's better.'

She seemed satisfied with my answer, quickly moving on, asking her next question, building her picture one jigsaw piece after another. 'What was James wearing when you last saw him?'

I'd seen him only hours before, but that time now felt so long ago. My life had changed so very much. 'Straight blue jeans, Levi's, 501s, I think, a little faded with button flies, a white cotton shirt, and a dark green wool jumper with a round collar. There's a small hole in one of the elbows. I keep trying to get him to throw it away. But for some reason, he loves it.'

'And his shoes?'

'Um, brown leather, laces, made in Italy, a pair I bought him for Christmas, size nines. He said they're the most comfortable shoes he'd ever worn. I'm planning to get a pair myself.' Why the hell did I say that? Why didn't I stick to the pertinent facts?

'Any distinguishing marks, scars, birthmarks, tattoos, that sort of thing?' she asked next.

I flinched, folded my arms across my chest, hugging myself tight. I knew exactly what the question implied. Such things might be needed for identification if my lovely James couldn't do that for himself. If he couldn't speak. If he couldn't even utter his name. The fear truly set in at that point. I took a deep breath, resisting the impulse to cry again. I'd already shed so many tears. What use were more? If I started again, I feared I might never stop.

'He hasn't got any tattoos or scars, but he has got a small birthmark in the shape of a human heart, about two centimetres in diameter, on his left buttock close to the cleft of his bum.' I thought for a second and then added, 'Oh, no, there actually is a small scar on his right knee. I almost forgot that. It's hardly visible. It's from a childhood accident. He told me about it one day a few months after we met. He fell from a tree in a London park when he was seven. The resulting injury needed stitches.'

I asked myself if I was giving too much information again, saying things that weren't helpful. But PC Whitlock said nothing to support my anxious hypothesis. She made some final notes and then stood, pushing her glasses to the top of her nose with the first finger of her right hand.

'Okay, I think I've got everything we're going to need for now. You head off home, I'll make a report, have a quick word with the duty sergeant, and then we'll progress from there. Your car is still at the service station, yes?'

I nodded.

'Have you got the keys?'

'James had them.'

'A spare set?'

I screwed up my face. 'Maybe at the cottage, but I don't think so, I think we only had the one.'

'Okay, no worries, we can always open it. But if you do find a second set, let me know.'

I rose to my feet, staring at her, not looking away. 'What exactly are you going to do to find him?'

Her expression softened, and I like to think she understood I needed the details. 'We'll circulate your husband's description and when he was last seen, contact all the hospitals in the area, and notify you of any relevant information as soon as we receive it. I'll make a start on all that now, as soon as I've spoken to my sergeant. A more senior officer will decide who's allocated the case in the morning. Whoever that is will make further enquiries. It may be me, but it might not be. That's not my decision. I'm sorry I can't be more specific than that.'

I looked at her with pleading eyes. 'You will find my James for me, won't you?'

She frowned. 'Most missing people are found safe and well. Try to stay hopeful. You've acted quickly and you did the right thing reporting James missing. As of now, you need to get some rest. There's no more you can do.'

I followed her as she approached the door, my dad a step or two behind.

'You said *most* missing people are found safe and well; that means not all of them.'

She pressed her lips together. 'No, Daisy, not all of them, but I promise we'll do all we can to ensure James isn't one of those unfortunate people.'

11

My father played a classical music CD as he drove the eight miles from Carmarthen to our Ferryside village home, Vivaldi, I think, but I can't be sure. It sounded quietly in the background as we talked, me looking for reassurance and my dear dad offering it as best he could. He tried his hardest, but nothing he could ever have said would satisfy me. Kind words didn't change anything, however well-intentioned. My husband was still missing, and I couldn't be sure when or even if I'd ever see him again. Those were the stark facts. It really was that simple. Dad switched the music off as we approached our estuary village, driving past the garage on the right, over the small humpback bridge. I knew he was about to say something. And it wasn't long until he did.

'I was surprised to hear about the baby.'

'We were going to tell you and Mum in person this evening, until James... well, you know the rest.'

He sighed. 'When did you find out?'

'On the day of the wedding.'

He slowed, pulling in to the side of the narrow road, allowing a car to pass in the opposite direction. 'Is it good news?'

I placed a hand on my belly. 'I want this baby.'

'And James?'

I felt my gut twist. 'He said all the right things. I think he's pleased. No, no, I *know* he's pleased. He hasn't run off for fear of being a father, if that's what you're thinking.'

Dad drove off again, keeping the speed low. 'I wasn't thinking that for a moment.'

I made a face. 'Glad to hear it. I don't want to talk about this any more, not now.'

'No problem at all, *cariad*. Whatever you want.'

I insisted Dad take me straight to my beloved cottage before heading to my parents' bungalow. A part of me was in denial. I was hoping James might be there waiting for me, that the lights would be on, shining bright, illuminating the garden as they had so often in the past. But, of course, he wasn't there. It was a desperate fantasy rather than reality. All was darkness. The cottage was obviously empty, just as we'd left it a week before. I couldn't face going in. My dad pulled up, and I quickly told him to drive on. Just for a fleeting moment, it seemed as if I'd lost my James all over again.

I reflected on events as Dad drove towards the bungalow, thinking things couldn't get worse. But then it dawned on me, James's parents still knew nothing of their son's disappearance. I fidgeted with my seat belt, tugging it at my waist. I didn't know what else to do with my hands. Oh God, they had to be told.

'Dad, we need to tell Margaret and Roy what's happening.'

He frowned hard as I turned my head towards him. 'Um, don't you think it can wait till morning?'

I could tell from his tone he was hoping the answer was yes. 'What if it were the other way round?' I said. 'What if I was missing? You'd hate it if they kept something so important to themselves. And what if the police ring them tonight? That would be awful. They need to hear it from me. James is their son. They love him, too. I've got to tell them myself. They have a right to know.'

Dad still didn't seem convinced. 'What if I give them a ring when we get to the bungalow after a nice cup of tea? We could talk to them face to face tomorrow. I'm just thinking of you, *cariad.* You look exhausted. You've already had a long day.'

He had a point. It was a long day that was about to get longer. 'No, no, absolutely not,' I insisted. 'Please drive straight there now. They deserve that much. I've always thought they've got a low opinion of me. I don't want to make things worse. It's not something we can avoid.'

And so that's what we did. I stood next to my lovely dad as he knocked on my in-laws' bright red front door in the light of a winter moon now partly shrouded in cloud. Oh God, it was so awful. I can't stress that enough. I dreaded the door being answered as an owl hooted somewhere in the far distance. And I could clearly see from the look on Roy's face that he knew something was very wrong as soon as he opened the door. His quickly vanishing smile became a deep scowl as his shoulders slumped. I feared his legs might give way as he leant against the doorframe. Even in the half-light, I could see his face sag. The blood seemed to drain away. I think my expression and body language rang alarm bells. No, I *know* they did. How could they not? I must have looked ashen. Roy uttered just two words which said so very much.

'Where's James?'

Dad retook the lead at that point, for which I was grateful. Good old Dad, the man was a star. 'Let's go inside, Roy. There's something we need to discuss with you both.'

'What is it? What's happened?'

Dad spoke up again, every part of him conveying his distress. 'Come on, Roy, in we go, mate. Let's not do this on the doorstep.'

And so the four of us talked, me, Dad, Roy, and Margaret seated on two tan leather sofas in the comfortable lounge. Or, to be more accurate, I did most of the talking while my in-laws listened, asking intermittent questions at critical points, no doubt hoping for different answers to those I was obliged to provide. I think it's fair to say that it was one of the most challenging conversations I've ever had. Giving bad news is never easy, and it wasn't that night. It wasn't just the telling; I was so upset and already grieving. Roy also asked if James and I had argued, and, of course, I said no. That made things worse for him and Margaret, too, one avenue of hope extinguished by one simple reply. It seemed James had disappeared for no good reason. There were no explanations that made any sense, none at all, not to them or me.

All four of us cried as we talked, even Dad. And Margaret wept, I mean *really* wept, as I had earlier in the evening, her chest heaving as she gasped for breath. And then, at one point, she said something that truly surprised me through her tears. She turned to her husband, glaring, almost venomous, spitting out her words as if she desperately needed to expunge them from her mouth. 'What was the point of coming here? It didn't achieve anything. We may as well have stayed in London. I told you that at the time. I blame you!'

I knew she was upset. And people sometimes say strange things when distressed. They hit out, go on the attack, looking for anyone but themselves to blame for the situation in which they find themselves. I'd experienced that at work more times than I cared to count. But, oh my God, Margaret's statements hit me hard. I'd always had the feeling that she didn't like me that much. She'd always been polite, but never warm. And now this, those hateful words, which seemed to confirm my fears. As Margaret sat there seething, I asked myself if she resented me and my marriage to James. If she was expressing her true feelings for the first awful time. Her words hurt, but I kept my mouth shut. I was quick to forgive. I bit my tongue. Margaret thought she might have lost her son. I recall Roy glaring at her, quick to reply, his tone harsh, which I put down to the situation, nothing more. He didn't seem nearly as ready to forgive her as I was.

'For goodness' sake, Margaret, shut up. Engage your brain before your mouth.'

Dad and I gave each other a meaningful look. What the hell was that all about? Roy's reaction seemed so inappropriate, so out of the ordinary and over the top, however upset he was. Neither of us knew where that conversation came from; no idea of Roy's true meaning or the future implications for me. We put it down to the stress of the news we'd had no option but to impart. People react differently in a crisis. We rationalised and put it in that context. Shock can affect people in strange ways, particularly when a loved one is concerned. Margaret and Roy were both very obviously and understandably upset. I could easily have acted out of turn myself, and I thought I understood. I think it's fair to say I gave James's parents the benefit of the doubt, as did Dad.

The four of us talked of the investigation after Roy's outburst when things calmed down, Dad again taking the lead, valiantly breaking a pervasive silence that for a brief few seconds seemed never-ending. Dad spoke up, stressing the efforts the police would make to find James, wherever he was. He was trying to emphasise the positives. I know that. I knew it then, and I know it now. But he wasn't convincing anyone. After a minute or two, it seemed Margaret could take no more, the truth too much, the burden too great, Dad's declarations not sufficiently persuasive. I get that. I can relate. I felt much the same. Margaret stood on unsteady legs, hurrying towards the kitchen, where she closed the door against the world. She slammed it shut so very hard that it shook in its frame. The sound of it seemed to echo throughout the house as if bouncing off the walls. It did at least bring our interaction to a timely close. I couldn't wait to get out of there. Dad and I stood to leave as Roy made his impassioned apologies, his emotions bubbling to the surface, threatening to explode. I didn't mention the baby, not even once, that would come later. The time wasn't right. There'd been enough drama for one night. Talking about anything except James seemed entirely inappropriate. Dad must have thought much the same because he said nothing, either. Sometimes silence is best.

Dad only told me where my lovely mum was after we'd left the house and travelled the short distance to the bungalow at the other end of the village, revealing another problem to accompany my own. Life's like that sometimes; crises come in bunches, keeping us in fear and beating us down. It felt as if some great unseen puppet master in the sky was pulling my strings, taunting me, playing with my ragged emotions for the entertainment it gave. I could have screamed. I could have torn my world apart and smashed everything in my path. It was undoubtedly the most challenging day I'd ever had the misfortune to suffer. I didn't know it then, but my problems would soon worsen. In a short time, I was to face the most challenging time of my life. Roy's reaction was a red flag of sorts. If only I'd known back then.

12

I didn't go back to work the day after our return to Wales as initially planned. I couldn't face it. In truth, I was falling apart. I'd slept fitfully in my childhood bedroom, often waking, one nightmare after another until the morning sun finally crept over the far horizon, illuminating the countryside in soft winter light. Mum was back from her hospital vigil by that time. She hugged me tight and offered kind words of reassurance before making me breakfast, supporting me as best she could. I drank the peppermint tea on offer but couldn't face the toast. Eating seemed beyond me. I had no appetite at all. I sat at the kitchen table with Mum for twenty minutes or so, and then I spent most of the morning pacing around the bungalow, not knowing what to do with myself. I'd already posted several emotional appeals for information on social media as soon as I got up, Twitter, Facebook, and the like. I hoped that might best complement what the police were hopefully already doing to help find my love. And it was a lot better than doing nothing. A great many people commented. A lot of people shared my posts. And most were sympathetic, but nothing was gleaned that helped. No one had seen James, and no one had heard from him. Or, at least, not that they were telling me about. One idiot suggested aliens might have abducted James. That's about as helpful as it got.

Janice Hoyle, my senior ward sister, rang my mobile just before twelve that afternoon, asking where I was. She'd been in a meeting until then, and given my focus on James, I hadn't thought to ring. Remiss of me, but I guess forgivable in the circumstances. I remember jumping at the sound of the ring-tone, desperately hoping it was James, or at least news of James, the disappointment crushing when I heard Janice's familiar voice at the other end of the line. I cried as I told her my tale, and she was sympathetic, conveying what seemed genuine empathy. She was nothing but supportive. It seemed she understood. I think she was the nearest thing I had to a friend. But then, I guess, support was all part of her role. It's what she was trained for, after all.

'He's been missing now for over sixteen hours,' I said.

'Oh, I'm so very sorry to hear that, Daisy. I can't begin to imagine how awful that must be for you. As far as I'm concerned, you're on sick leave from today. Don't rush back until you're ready; please take as long as you need. You focus on yourself, James and your family. And do let me know if there's anything I can do for you, anything at all. I'll give you another ring tomorrow to see how things are. And please contact me if there's any news.'

I thanked her profusely, my reaction genuine; they weren't empty words. I knew my boss was well-intentioned, but again it didn't help, not really, not deep down where it mattered most. Yes, work was one less thing to worry about. But I wanted James back; I wanted to hold him, cling on, and never let go. Nothing less than that was ever going to make me feel any better, not then. Time did soften the blow, but only slightly. The pain never truly went away. It's still with me to this day.

I began pacing again when the call ended. I couldn't relax, not for a second. I was on full alert, desperately hoping for good news that didn't come. I rang the police three times that first day. PC Whitlock wasn't on duty, her shift had ended, and DI Kesey was apparently unavailable, doing I don't know what. But the detective inspector finally returned my call at five past three that afternoon. I answered my phone, grabbing it as soon as it rang to hear her speaking in nasal Brummie tones I found a little difficult to decipher, monotone, bordering on melancholy. I've gotten used to her voice since. But that first time, it was a bit of a struggle.

'Hello, Daisy, Daisy Earl?'

I confirmed my identity, rushing my words. James had told me the detective had moved to our area from Birmingham, and so I realised who she was before she introduced herself. She told me to call her Kesey, that everyone else did. There was no need for formalities. That made the conversation just that tiny bit easier. Something else I was grateful for – every little helps.

'Is there any news?' I said. The obvious question. The one I had to ask.

'I'm sorry, Daisy, we haven't found James yet. But I wanted to update you on the case. The switchboard told me you'd rung.'

More disappointment, another blow. I cleared my throat before speaking again. 'What's happening?'

'PC Whitlock circulated James's details to all UK forces last night with the photo you gave her and a full description. I know James from the leisure centre. I don't know if he ever mentioned that.'

'He did.'

'I'll head up the investigation personally. I want to do all I can to help.'

I took that as good news. I was pleased, although perhaps relieved would be a better word. It was what I'd hoped for, something I'd mentioned in my prayers. And Kesey seemed genuine. I liked her for that.

'Thank you,' I said with gratitude. 'I can't believe what's happening. It's a total nightmare. I really do appreciate your help.'

'We've contacted all the various hospitals in the area but with no news. And James hasn't used the bank cards from your joint account. Not since you were in Lanzarote. And that was only a small withdrawal of fifty euros, no large amounts.'

I remembered it clearly. I could see the two of us standing there, James using a cash machine. I wanted a sun hat, straw with a yellow ribbon. A nearby shop only accepted cash. 'Yeah, I remember, Teguise, the bank on the square.'

'I've sent James's phone for urgent forensic examination. There might be fingerprints if someone grabbed it off him. I'll need one of my officers to take your prints for elimination purposes. Could you call at the station sometime today?'

I thought, try stopping me. 'What time?'

'Is 4 p.m. convenient for you?'

I tensed my jaw. Any delay seemed unhelpful. 'I could come straight away now. Surely, the sooner, the better. I can borrow my dad's car and be there in twenty minutes.'

There was a moment's silence before Kesey spoke again. When she did, she said exactly what I wanted to hear. 'Ask for me in reception. Whoever's on the desk will be expecting you.'

'Thank you. I'll be on my way as soon as we end the call.'

'I've read through PC Whitlock's notes. Is there anything else you can tell me that you think may be of help?'

Nothing came to mind. Although perhaps it should have. I should have mentioned Oliver. But hindsight is an exact science. It didn't seem nearly so obvious at the time. 'No, no,' I said. 'I think I told her everything.'

And then a strange question, one I hadn't expected. 'Do you know anything of James's background before he moved to Wales?'

'Um, I know he grew up in London. He moved here with his parents when he was sixteen. That's when we met here in Ferry-side. That's about it, really. Why do you ask?'

She was either keen to change the subject or simply wanted to move things along. I gave it no thought at the time.

'I'll see you as soon as you arrive, Daisy. We'll get the prints done and then wait for the results from the lab. And I'll make sure we get them quickly. Right now, finding James is my number one priority.'

And with that, she ended the call. I've given our conversation a lot of thought while writing this chapter. Why did Kesey ask about London? Did she know more than she was saying? Or was she simply doing her job as a good detective, searching for a piece of the jigsaw as described by PC Whitlock? To this day, I still don't know the answer. Maybe she knew nothing at all. But if there were things concerning her, I think she should have told me. Because had I known then what I later found out, future events could have taken a very different turn. I'd have made better decisions, acted very differently with different results. But sadly, it didn't work out that way. I can't rewrite the past. I can only tell the rest of my story as it happened.

13

I rang police headquarters every day after providing my fingerprints, speaking either to Kesey or, if she was unavailable, to DS Raymond Lewis, her second-in-command. He seemed a decent person, as she was. Both detectives seemed to care. The officers were friendly, polite, and receptive to my concerns, but they had no significant news to raise my spirits. If anything, what they told me made things worse. My car had been taken from the service station for forensic examination, but nothing noteworthy was found. And there was only one set of fingerprints on James's phone other than mine, which, of course, were his. Nothing offered any clue as to where he might be or who, if anyone, had taken him. I tried my best to remain optimistic, but that became more difficult with each hour. I read online that the chances of finding a missing person safe and well decrease with time. Whether that's true or not, I can't say. It may even have been an American website. But reading it hurt. I shouldn't have looked. The internet isn't always helpful. I wished I hadn't seen the article at all.

The days passed so slowly with constant tension, making it

impossible to relax for a second or even think about anything but James for very long, whatever the distraction. Whenever the phone rang or there was a knock on the door, I jumped, praying it was my soulmate with every part of my being. But to my huge disappointment, it never was. Each time, that disappointment was a crushing body blow that hurt me deeply. The pain was physical and emotional, as if my heart was being torn from my body by some unseen demonic force out to destroy me. Nothing had ever been harder, ever so challenging, and I struggled to hold it together, often weeping, plummeting into the depths of despair. Mum was attentive, saying kind words, desperately trying to relieve my angst even slightly, but nothing she said was ever going to help. After a time, I think she realised that herself. She didn't stop trying, but her words offered more consolation than hope.

My mum sat me down over a cup of tea in her spacious kitchen three days after James's mystery disappearance and said we needed to talk. I could tell it was more than a chat by her tone and the expression on her face. And I think I half-guessed what was coming next. To Mum, I was still her little girl. She did care about James. But I'm certain it was me she was most worried about. My distress was tearing her apart. And, of course, she was concerned about the baby. I understand that now.

I sipped my hot drink, nibbled at a gluten-free Digestive biscuit with very little enthusiasm, looked Mum in the eye, and waited for her to start talking as I knew she inevitably would. I remember she sighed deeply as we sat at the breakfast bar before uttering her first word, more a groan than a breath, one of the saddest sounds I'd ever heard. It seemed a commentary on my situation, summing it up perfectly. I could have groaned, too, and never stopped. In my mind, no words were necessary. But I resisted my impulse to be dismissive. I've no doubt my mum's initiative came from a good place. And I knew that listening to her was the right thing to do.

'I'm worried about you, Daisy,' she began. 'I know you're fretting; we all are. But you've hardly eaten since getting back from your honeymoon. You've already lost weight, that's obvious – I can see it on your face. And you were slim to start with. It's weight you can't afford to lose.'

I focused on anything but her. Not because I resented her words but because I knew she was right. Food seemed unimportant. I had to force it down, even in small amounts. I lifted the biscuit to my mouth, taking a small bite, making it obvious for her benefit. I didn't want the conversation, but I was sure my mum wouldn't let it go. 'I know, Mum, I will try, but I haven't got any appetite. And everything tastes terrible. Even the things I used to love.'

She smiled but the expression quickly left her face. 'You need to start looking after yourself, and especially now you're pregnant. If you don't eat for yourself, do it for your baby. It's what James would want. If he were here, he'd tell you that himself. I know he would. He loves you so very much.'

I dropped my head. 'But he's not here.'

She was quick to reply, reaching out and touching my hand. Her fingers felt cold on my skin. 'No, he's not, so you need to stay strong for both of you and the baby, too. Hopefully, we'll get some good news very soon.'

I pounced on her positive words. Any offer of hope was more than welcome. I craved it, sought it out. I knew false hope was no hope. But back then, I still believed the police might find James alive. I wasn't prepared to consider any other outcome. 'Do you really think so?' I asked, looking for more positive encouragement.

'The police are doing everything they can. You've said this

yourself. And your social media posts are getting so much attention. I saw one of your tweets had over a thousand shares. Someone must know something. I'm certain it's only a matter of time.'

I nodded twice, wanting to believe her, desperate to agree. 'Yeah, that's right. And Kesey said finding James is her number one priority. That's got to be good. I'm so glad it's her in charge. Sergeant Lewis said she's one of the best. And James likes her. He considers her a friend. She was the one who recommended the villa. He told me that himself.'

It was nothing I hadn't told Mum before. But she sat there, taking it all in as if hearing it for the first time, no doubt searching for the right thing to say next. Talking to me must have been a little like walking on eggshells.

'Well, there you go then. There's every reason to stay positive.'

Was there? Was there really? I wanted to think so, but there was always a nagging doubt at the back of my mind that wouldn't let up. 'I will try, promise.'

Mum smiled again, more warmly this time. 'Glad to hear it. Now eat the rest of that biscuit. There's not much left. Do it for me.'

I lifted the Digestive to my mouth, took a small bite and chewed, forcing myself to swallow, washing it down with a slurp of tea.

'Do you fancy going to the Cabin for lunch?' she asked. 'Just the two of us, my treat? They do some lovely meals. Me and your dad went there last week when you were away.'

I placed the half-eaten biscuit on the table next to my mug. 'Oh God, no, I can't face going out, not yet, maybe in a day or two if I'm feeling stronger.'

She made a face. 'It's a lovely sunny day. Why don't we go for a nice walk together as far as the beach? We could dress up warm.'

I shook my head, jumping to my feet and rushing towards the lounge as my mobile rang on a wall-mounted shelf to the left of the sofa. I felt a sudden adrenaline rush as I lifted it to my face. I recognised Kesey's voice as soon as she spoke.

'Morning, Daisy, it's Laura Kesey. Have you got five minutes?'

What a ridiculous question! I couldn't wait to hear what she had to say. 'Yeah, I have, as long as you need.'

'I wanted a quick word about what we're going to do next.'

'Is, is there any n-n-news?' I stuttered. 'Have you found anything out?' I think I knew what she would say before she even replied. Had there been positive developments, she'd already have told me. It's the first thing she'd have said.

'No, I'm sorry, there's nothing significant. There was one potential sighting in Llanelli, but it turned out not to be James. And that's why I've rung. I think it's time for a press conference. We'll get the local newspapers and Welsh TV involved. It's time to ask for the public's help.'

I perched on the edge of the nearest armchair, my phone now on speaker as Mum joined me in the lounge. I wanted her to hear Kesey, too. It was another beacon of hope, although a part of me was irritated it had taken the police so long. Why hadn't they done it before? 'When?' I asked. 'I think the sooner, the better. There must be someone who's seen something. Someone must know where James is. He hasn't disappeared into thin air.'

The detective spoke slowly and calmly, so unlike me. 'I'm planning the conference here at headquarters at 2 p.m. tomorrow afternoon. I'll be there, Ray Lewis, and I'd like you to be there, too. I think your participation would make all the difference.'

I asked what, for me, was the obvious question, the first one that came to mind. 'What about James's parents?'

Kesey was silent for a beat before I heard her voice again. When she did speak, she sounded a little reticent. 'I have spoken to Mr and Mrs Earl. I thought it would be helpful for you to have the full picture. I wanted a full list of participants before speaking to you. But they've declined to attend.'

I jerked my head back. Why the hell would they do that? James was their only son. It didn't seem to make any sense. '*Really*? That seems crazy. Are you sure?'

'They think it's something that you would better do. I did try to persuade them it would be a good idea for them to be there, too, but they said no.' Kesey paused and then continued as if surprised by the situation herself. That's an assumption on my part, but I think a correct one. I could hear it in her voice when she spoke. 'I'd like you to make a direct appeal for information. It's a method I've used before, a strategy that often gets good results. You're James's wife. You were only recently married. The public will relate to you. The appeal is more newsworthy that way. And we want as much publicity as possible. We can talk in advance about the things you'd need to cover. Is that something you think you can do for me?'

I didn't need persuading, not one little bit. 'Yes, *absolutely*, I'll do it. What time do you want me to be there?'

'I suggest we meet in reception at half one. That'll give us plenty of time to talk. I can coach you on what to say, and you can ask any questions that come to mind. I find that's the best way of doing these things. Does that work for you?'

I could hardly contain my excitement. I could feel the sensation rising in my chest. 'Yeah, I'll be there. That's fine with me.'

'Okay, that's good to hear. I'll look forward to seeing you

tomorrow, Daisy. Is there anything at all you want to ask me before we end the call?'

I very briefly considered asking again about James's parents, but what was the point? They weren't taking part in the conference, and no questions I asked would change that fact. I felt more angry about what the detective told me than disappointed, although there was a disappointment. Whatever Margaret and Roy's reasoning, I was determined to make up for what I saw as their failings. And I did see them as failings. I liked them a lot less after that. I felt they'd let both their son and me down. I was upset, but there was a new determination too. I knew in that instant I had to focus on what I could achieve, with or without other people's help. It was my only way to cope – the only way to retain my sanity. I asked Kesey the only other thing that came to mind. Another question that, in truth, I think I already knew the answer to. I suspect I was seeking confirmation more than anything else, attention to detail, dotting the i's, and crossing the t's. 'Was the man in Llanelli definitely not James? Are you completely certain? Is there even the *slightest* possibility it could have been him?'

'The man was seen by a local officer and spoken to; he looked a little like James, but no, it wasn't him. He was a local man, a supermarket worker. Let's see what comes of the press conference. Nothing is guaranteed; it never is with these things. But I've had good results before. There's no reason to think we can't again.'

I was determined to look on the bright side as Mum hugged me tight at the end of the call. She said she felt as optimistic about the press conference as I did, and I think she really did. They weren't empty words; she meant them, every one. I realise the press conference was a fishing exercise more than anything else, the police casting the net wide, hoping for a break. But it offered hope, which I clung to by my fingertips. It was all I had.

Mum and I talked of Margaret and Roy's refusal to participate in the conference as we separated from our warm embrace. I guess that was inevitable. It wasn't all about the positives. And Mum seemed as shocked as I was. That didn't surprise me. She's always been on my side.

'Do you think I should speak to them?' I said, looking my mum in the eye.

She shook her head determinedly, from left to right and back again. 'I don't think that's a good idea,' she said. 'I can't see it achieving anything. You'll be there. That's what matters. Focus all your energy on that. If Margaret and Roy don't want to take part, to hell with them, that's up to them. You could ask Dad what he thinks if you like, but I don't think he'll say any different.'

In truth, I quickly decided I couldn't face a conversation with James's parents, whatever my dad thought. I might have told them exactly what I thought of them. There was more than enough to deal with without that. I needed to focus on the conference, on saying what I wanted. My mum was correct about that. 'Yeah, I suppose you're right.'

'You're doing brilliantly, Daisy, in tough circumstances. I'm so very proud of you. And James would be, too.'

'Thank you, that means a lot.' And it did. It seems words can sometimes help after all.

As I placed my mobile back on the shelf, plugging it in to finish charging, Mum suggested she cook a lentil casserole with brown rice for lunch, one of my favourite meals. And to my surprise, I said, 'Yes, that would be lovely.' The words came out of my mouth almost before I realised what I'd said. They were as much of a surprise to me as it seemed they were to her.

Mum smiled warmly, no doubt relieved. Suddenly, I felt like eating for the first time in days. I even committed to a much-needed shower later that afternoon. Washing my hair and body, being clean, mattered again. Hope can do that. It gives life purpose. It energises. If only it had lasted longer than it did.

Dad was as shocked as Mum and me about Margaret and Roy's refusal to participate in the conference when he arrived home that evening. I can't remember where he'd been. But I do recall he rang them on the landline after our evening meal despite Mum's insistence to the contrary. He spoke to Roy, trying to change his mind, but without success. Dad became increasingly angry as the call continued, but it didn't get him anywhere. In the end, he slammed the receiver back on its cradle, ending the call, red in the face, swearing loudly and crudely, so unlike him. It was a side of my dad I'd rarely seen. He spent about ten minutes in the back garden after that, pacing the lawn, standing alone in the dark, shifting his weight from one foot to the other before finally returning to the bungalow when Mum called him in for the third time.

Dad did his best for me out of love. I appreciated his efforts on my behalf. But I'd already accepted that the press conference was something I had to face alone. I was certain James wouldn't hesitate to take part were I missing, however much he loathed public attention. I had to do for him what I believed he'd do for me. It was the very least I could offer. I'd have crawled over broken glass had it meant finding him alive and well. And I'd have done it willingly without hesitation, however bloody, painful, and deep the scars. Nothing mattered more than getting my husband back. Maybe the conference would achieve that. All I could do was hope. And I'd finally found some courage. Whatever happened, I had to stay strong.

14

Two officers, one of whom I knew from school, returned my Nissan early on the morning of the press conference after the police obtained a replacement key. I suppose I should have been pleased the car was back. But its sudden appearance did little to raise my spirits. If anything, its arrival outside my parents' bungalow was another reminder of the man I'd lost. I did consider driving to meet Kesey later in the day, but as it turned out, that wasn't necessary. I left it where it was.

Dad dropped Mum off at the local hospital before driving me to police headquarters, having left Ferryside at just after one that afternoon. I was concerned about my grandmother, of course I was, but the conference was at the forefront of my mind. I could think of little else. It seemed such a potentially crucial event – a pivotal time in the efforts to find my love.

Dad then drove the Volvo into the large police car park in plenty of time for my meeting. He parked in one of several available spaces in front of the large modernist building, close to an impressive smoked-glass entrance reached by a series of wide paved steps with a disability ramp to one side. I could feel myself shaking with the apprehension of it all as Dad turned in his seat to face me. He glanced at his watch.

'Okay, this is it,' he said. 'You've got five minutes before meeting the inspector. Do you want me to come in with you? I've put a shirt and tie on just in case.' And then something no doubt intended to lighten the mood. 'I'm even wearing clean underpants and matching socks. I'm ready if you need me. All you have to do is say the word.'

I'd thought that was probably why he'd dressed up. He was usually more casual, in jeans or cords, a shirt and jumper. I couldn't remember the last time I'd seen him wearing a tie, the wedding apart. Maybe it was at my paternal grandfather's funeral the year before. Yes, I think that was it, not black but navy blue.

I forced a quickly vanishing smile, as much as I could manage. 'No, you're all right, thanks, Dad. This is something I've got to do myself.'

My dad looked back at me with a pained expression I've no doubt was born of love. I think he was feeling almost as anxious as I was. Events mattered to him as they did to me, although, like Mum, I suspect he was more concerned for me than James.

'Are you sure, *cariad*? It's absolutely no problem if you're not. I'm certain DI Kesey won't mind if I come in with you.'

I prepared to leave the car, shaking my head determinedly before opening the door. I tried to sound a lot more confident than I felt. 'No, I'm good, thanks, but nice of you to offer. Stop worrying. I'll be fine.'

He gave me a reassuring look. 'Okay, as long as you're certain. I'll be here waiting for you when you finish. You're going to do great, I know you are. Just be yourself. That's all you need to do.'

'I can give you a ring when the conference finishes if you

want to go to the hospital. I've got no idea how long this is going to take. It might be ages.'

'I'm going nowhere. Now deep breaths. Get in there and do your stuff. I'll be here for however long it takes. Your mother will be fine without me. She'll be glad of the peace.'

I ran a hand through my hair. I was so lucky to have such a supportive father. I know not everyone does. 'Do I look okay?' I asked with a frown.

'You look perfect, you always do.'

I forced another smile, thinking this was it. The time had come. And, oh God, it seemed all the responsibility rested on me.

It was chilly despite the winter sun shining brightly as I climbed the grey stone steps, full of nervous energy, apprehensive but keenly anticipating what the afternoon would bring. I was pleased to see Kesey was already waiting for me when I entered the spacious reception area. She smiled warmly as she approached me, dressed in a smart black trouser suit with a white blouse and shiny leather shoes that looked as if they'd been recently polished. She had a look of white-collar, managerial efficiency. That was my first impression. I think that sums up her appearance. She reached out to shake my hand a little more firmly than I'd expected, and said hello in that Brummie accent with which I was now so very familiar due to our various conversations. She was friendly but professional, as I like to think I was at work when interacting with patients. There was reassurance in her voice, its pitch and tone. And there was an easy confidence about her, too, as if she was comfortable in her own skin. If she was nervous about the press conference, it didn't show, not one little bit. She was in her domain, a lion, not a mouse, seemingly entirely in control.

'Welcome,' she said. 'I'm glad you're on time. If you follow me, we can talk in my office. We'll take the lift. It's a little quicker than the stairs.'

I followed the detective through a light oak door with a rectangular glass pane, and down a brightly lit corridor, to a lift that took us to the first floor at the press of an illuminated button. Within a minute or two, we entered a modern office with a large picture window with a view of the car park below. I could clearly see my dad sitting in the Volvo's driver's seat before I sat myself down at Kesey's invitation. She sat at the opposite side of an overly cluttered desk piled high with files of various colours and several sheaves of loose papers. There was a framed photo of her, another woman of similar age, and a young boy of about six or seven years. She apologised for the mess before offering me tea or coffee.

I glanced at the clock on the wall above the detective's head, white numbers on a red background. Time was passing quickly, the conference fast approaching. 'Not for me, thanks,' I said. 'I haven't long had lunch.' It was a half-truth that served a purpose. In reality, I'd had a single slice of brown toast and half a glass of filtered water, and only then at my mum's insistence. Much-needed sustenance was the last thing on my mind. I was even more nervous than I'd anticipated. My gut was doing somersaults. It seemed the courage I'd so recently found was melting away like an ice cube in the hot summer sun.

Kesey relaxed back in her chair, looking every bit the confident professional. My nervousness, in contrast, must have been blatantly evident to her as she tried to put me at my ease.

'It's important to remember that this afternoon is all about finding James. I've already spoken to several journalists I know well, and they're interested in your story. They want to help. And it's newsworthy, as I've said before. That's something we can take advantage of; the more press and media coverage we can facilitate, the better. We need to get the word out, much as you've been doing on social media. Do you understand?'

All she'd said seemed glaringly obvious to me, but I guess she felt she had to say it. Maybe it was something she said to everyone in similar circumstances. I wouldn't be surprised if it was. Or perhaps she thought she had to calm my nerves.

'Yeah, I get it.' That's all I could think to say.

Kesey smiled without parting her lips, nodding twice. 'Good, that's good.' She glanced at her watch. 'In a minute or two, we'll head to the conference room to make a start. I'll speak first, introducing you, Ray and myself to everyone, and then I'll talk about James. And I'll allow you to speak directly to the journalists. I need you to say how much you miss him, how worried you are, and how much you'd appreciate the public's help. And don't be afraid to show your emotions. Don't hold back. If you feel like crying, let the tears flow. There's absolutely no need to hide your upset. Let people see how you really feel. People respond well to that kind of appeal.'

I nodded but didn't say anything in reply. I sat there, opening and closing my mouth to no good effect like a goldfish in a bowl. The words seemed to stick in my throat.

Kesey leant towards me, maybe silently questioning my ability to come up with the goods. A supposition on my part, no more than that.

'How does that all sound to you, Daisy? Is that something you feel comfortable with?'

I fingered the small green jade beads hanging on a string around my neck. I don't think I'd ever felt less comfortable in my life. But there seemed little point in saying that. I didn't want to admit it. Not even to myself. 'Not a problem,' I said. 'I've given a lot of thought to what I'm going to say.' I'd actually practised alone in front of a bedroom mirror that morning after my car arrived, but I kept that detail to myself. It all seemed much more manageable then than now, sitting in the detective's office looking her in the eye.

'It's good that you're prepared. That's always a good idea. Some people like to wing it, but most not.'

I was desperate to turn the focus away from me. 'How quickly do you think we'll get some publicity?'

'There should be something on the Welsh TV and radio news this evening and then in the papers in the morning. I'm confident the local press will get on board, and the *Western Mail*. They're always great, but less so the nationals. We may get some UK-wide coverage if we're lucky. It's an unusual case, and you were a young couple returning from honeymoon, so there's every chance they may be interested. In truth, it often depends on how much other news there is on any particular day. These things are never an exact science. All we can do is our best.'

And then a question that really mattered to me. I was thinking less about my anxieties now and more about James, which is precisely what I should have been doing all along. 'What do you think the chances are of someone contacting you with relevant information?' I asked, praying for a positive response.

Kesey uncrossed her legs, rested her elbows on the desk in front of her. 'There's never any guarantees. But there's every chance. After the media coverage, we will get some nutters ringing in with all sorts of crazy claims. We always do. But they're easy to spot, so we won't waste any time. And there may be that one crucial call that tells us what we need to know. Sometimes that's all it takes to make a significant breakthrough. Bottom line, there's everything to gain and nothing to lose.'

I looked at the clock again, followed by my watch. Time was rushing away, tick tock, minutes passing in what seemed like seconds. It wouldn't be long before the press conference started. There was just over five minutes to go.

Kesey rose easily to her feet. 'Are you ready to do this?'

I felt so hot, so sweaty. My mouth, in contrast, felt parched as I said yes. I had a great deal of hope invested in that conference. It seemed my best chance of getting James back. And I would. That day would come, but not in any way I expected.

15

Kesey led me into the conference room to be met by camera flashes and lively journalistic chatter. She'd prepared me well, but it still came as a surprise, particularly the large TV camera held by a strikingly tall man with short-cropped brown hair positioned to my right. I stood stock-still for a second, frozen in indecision as I took in the scene, a little taken aback, before quickly pulling myself together and following the detective to our seats behind two adjoined tables covered in pristine white cloths. A man I correctly assumed to be DS Raymond Lewis was already seated and waiting. He looked a good few years older than Kesey, overweight and world-worn, dressed in a tweed jacket that looked well past its best, much like him. His grey hair was receding, flakes of snowy dandruff were on his shoulders, he badly needed a shave, and his tie was pulled loose at the collar. Not exactly a picture of sartorial elegance. I remember hoping he was a lot more efficient than he looked. He turned to face me as I settled in my seat, introducing himself and calling me love. 'Nice to meet you, love.' He actually used those words. He was old-school, a bit of a dinosaur. That came as a surprise too.

Kesey sat in the middle seat, with me and her DS to either side, each of us no more than two feet apart. There was some kind of projector on the table to the left side of Lewis and a large West Wales Police logo on the white-painted wall behind us. All that detail stuck in my mind and more. I can see the room now as if I was there only hours ago. The ceiling was high, the windows large, with plenty of illumination from the low afternoon winter sun and the bright fluorescent lights above our heads. I took repeated deep breaths as I sat there waiting for the conference to begin. It felt like I was the centre of attention. As if a spotlight was shining on me. It wasn't a feeling I liked, but I was glad I was there.

Kesey rose to her feet at precisely 2 pm., waiting a few brief seconds for the chatter to subside before uttering her first words. She then addressed the room without the need for notes. I liked that; it impressed me. She was a woman who knew what she was doing. You could have heard a pin drop. All were silent as she began speaking. She held the room in the palm of her hand. For the first time, I noticed her Birmingham accent was tinged with just a hint of musical Welsh.

'I'd like to start by welcoming you to West Wales Police Headquarters. Thank you all for coming. It's very much appreciated, and I'm sure we'll have a very productive afternoon. I can see a few familiar faces, but for those of you who don't know me, my name is Detective Inspector Laura Kesey, the senior investigating officer for the case we're here to discuss. Also present are Detective Sergeant Raymond Lewis, my second-in-command, and Daisy Earl – the wife of the missing man, James Earl. I intend to start by giving you the facts of the case, and then I'll invite Daisy to share anything she wants to say. I'd ask that you keep any questions until the end of that process. I usually find that works best.'

Kesey then walked around to the front of the adjoined tables, standing no more than six feet or so away from the first row of seated journalists and looking directly into the lens of the only TV camera in the room. All of Wales was in that lens. I'm certain Kesey realised that. She knew she had to connect. It was the best chance we had.

She turned her head, looking back at Lewis, who was already doing something to the projector, I think switching it on.

'If you could put the first image on now, please, Ray.'

I took a sharp breath as a large photo of James's handsome, smiling face, at least ten foot by six foot in proportion, was displayed on the white-painted wall behind me to the side of the force logo. I was momentarily transfixed. My gut twisted as I averted my eyes. In some strange way, seeing my lost love looking back at me big, bright and bold made my sad situation seem all the more poignant. It was a brutal reminder of something already at the forefront of my mind. I focused back on Kesey as best I could as she spoke again, still staring at the camera lens. Unlike me, she hadn't lost her focus at all. She was the very picture of resolute efficiency – a woman at the top of her game.

'James was last seen by Daisy at approximately 8.45 p.m. at the Glyndwr Service Station on the M4 on 10 January. And it's the details of his disappearance that make this case very different from others I've dealt with over the years. Daisy and James had flown into Cardiff Airport earlier that same evening after enjoying a week's happy honeymoon in Lanzarote. They hadn't argued. James had a slight headache but was otherwise well. They were both looking forward to getting back home and getting on with married life. All seemed well. That's what makes this case exceptional.'

I dabbed at my eyes with a paper tissue as Kesey turned to

Lewis again and nodded. Another familiar image replaced the first, this time a photo of our black Nissan car taken when parked at the service station exactly where we'd left it, but in daylight, not darkness. I assumed the photo was taken by the police the following morning when searching the car park. You could clearly see the front number plate. I share that simply because it came to mind.

Kesey reached out, pointing toward the image with a jabbing digit before speaking again. I could see that several journalists were interested, no doubt looking for the next big story. Once again, that gave me hope. As Kesey had said, the more publicity, the better.

'Daisy left James standing by the car in the service station car park on that fateful evening. He wanted some fresh air before joining her in the café. She waited, but James never came. She searched both inside and outside the building but without success. She did, however, find James's badly damaged phone on the ground under their car, but there was no sign of him. We have Daisy on camera at the service station but not James. He never entered the building. The CCTV does not cover the area of the car park where James was last seen. As of now, we have no information that goes any way towards explaining what happened to James that evening or since. We are concerned about his safety and well-being. His disappearance is unexplained. We need to find him as a matter of urgency.'

Lewis reached stiffly towards the projector, displaying the third image without needing to be asked. As soon as it appeared on the wall, I recognised the police switchboard telephone number, large black numbers against a white background. Kesey briefly glanced back at it and then continued.

'Someone must know what happened to James Earl. Someone must know where he is. I want to make a direct appeal to the public for help. If you have any information that may be relevant, anything at all, please get in touch with the police immediately. You can ring the number on the wall behind me twenty-four hours a day, or if you'd prefer, you can ring 101 or contact your local police station. Someone will be ready and waiting to take your call, whichever option you choose. Now, unless any questions can't wait, I'll ask Daisy to share anything she wants to say.'

No one said a word, and I suspected they were saving their questions for me. I felt the centre of attention again, even more so than at the wedding, and not in a good way. It seemed every eye was focused on me, unblinking, never looking away. I took a deep breath and then stood on unsteady legs, my eyes bouncing from one part of the room to another, searching for a friendly face. I chose a woman about my age with short ginger hair, focusing only on her, finding comfort in that one act. I know my speech was hesitant when I finally began speaking. Despite my preparation and determination, the situation's emotional impact was too much to bear. I felt inclined to crumble, to collapse back into my chair. But I stood there nonetheless, resisting the impulse to weep, and I did my best. I leant slightly forward, the palms of my hands on the table, fearing my legs might give way at any moment. But thankfully, they didn't. I somehow held it together for just long enough to say what was necessary in a faltering voice resonating with raw emotion.

'I'd, er, I'd like to s-s-start,' I stuttered, 'by thanking DI Kesey and her t-t-team for everything they're doing trying to find James. And I'm grateful to all of you, too. My husband's d-d-disappearance was a total and utter shock to my family and me. It's the most terrible thing I've ever experienced. James and I were o-o-only married on 2 January, and now he's gone. I know if he could, he'd, he'd have c-contacted me long before now. If

anyone, if anyone knows anything, I'm *begging* you not to hesi-
tate to get in touch with the police as a matter of the utmost
urgency. It would m-mean so, so very much to me if James is
found.'

Kesey gave me a reassuring look as I glanced in her direc-
tion, asking myself if I'd said enough or needed to say more. She
quickly stood again, gesturing to me to sit with a subtle nod and
hand gesture. I was glad that part of the conference was over,
although I felt sure I'd need to speak again.

Kesey invited questions, and as I'd suspected, most of them
were directed to me. I'd spoken to groups before at university,
but the conference was very different. It was so personal and
meant so much to me, with such a massive potential impact on
my life, and so the pressure proved horrendous, so much more
than I'd envisaged. And worst of all, one of the journalists, a
pencil-thin, middle-aged man with receding dark hair swept
back in a midlife crisis ponytail, seemed to doubt almost every
answer I gave. That may or may not be true, but it was certainly
my impression. I was sure I could see it in his eyes as he made
his scribbled notes in the front row. And for some reason, I still
can't explain, once I looked in his direction, I couldn't look away,
as if his was the only face in the room. The red-haired young
woman no longer existed; it was just him and me with his
accusatory glare. It felt almost as if I was on trial, standing in a
witness box. As if I was at fault, bearing at least a degree of guilt
for James's disappearance. The odious man's final question was
the worst of all.

'Do you think there's any chance James left of his own voli-
tion?' he said, with what seemed a smirk.

I could take no more. I lost my composure completely at that
point, shouting out, 'Don't be so ridiculous. You're talking
nonsense.' And then I held my hands to my face and cried.

Pathetic, really, I let myself down, and James, too. I should have done so much better than I did. I'm confident James would have in my place. He was braver than me, more accomplished, and a more effective communicator. Although I like to think I've grown since.

Kesey took over at that point and I silently sang her praises. To my huge relief, my contribution was over. She succinctly summarised everything that had been said, repeated her request for the public's assistance, and then brought the conference to a swift and timely close as I dropped my shoulders, making myself smaller, trying to sink into my chair.

I felt a strange mix of emotions as I left the building minutes later, Kesey having said her goodbyes to me at the conference room door. She tried to be reassuring, but all I heard was criticism. My mind was racing as I crossed the car park to join my waiting father in the Volvo. I was discouraged about my performance but still hopeful that the press interest would give the police the break they hoped for. And it did; their fishing exercise would hook a witness. But the information gleaned wouldn't be anything I'd expected. It was so very far from that. Life can be full of surprises; not all are welcome.

16

I spoke to Laura Kesey most days following the press conference. And to give her the credit she deserves, I no longer had to chase her; she rang me. But it was never good news, nothing I wanted to hear. The story of James's unexplained disappearance received a good deal of media coverage, at least partly due to my obvious distress as I publicly poured out my angst. My sobbing performance quickly gained over 100,000 views on YouTube, with the majority of comments supportive, but others not so much as the trolls played their destructive games. I think of them as the playground bullies of the internet. Such people can be cruel, and they were, inadequate, feeding their fragile egos. But for all the attention, well-intentioned or otherwise, nothing useful was gleaned. I found it harder to remain optimistic with each day that passed. In all honesty, pessimism crept in, swimming up, snapping at my heels as I began to think the police initiative had failed. I still blamed myself to a degree, although I'm now not so sure those feelings were justified. Perhaps I could have said more at the press conference. Maybe I could have held it together better than I did. But looking back, even if I had, I'm far from sure it would have made any significant difference to the outcome. A less emotional performance might even have resulted in less coverage than was achieved.

I waited, counting the hours with hope and trepidation, desperate for good news and fearing bad. And then, on 22 January, just when I'd reached a point of almost total despondence, Kesey rang again. And this time, she sounded different. There was an upbeat urgency to her tone, an energy. I could tell something had changed. For good or bad, I couldn't wait to hear what she had to say.

'We received a telephone call from a witness late last night, Daisy, and then I interviewed him this morning here at police HQ. He's a lorry driver, HGV, long distance. He's been on the continent for a few days and only realised he may have seen something we needed to know about when he got back to Wales.'

I swallowed hard and sat in the nearest seat for fear of passing out. My entire body was tense, every muscle, every sinew. I could feel my temperature rise and my heart beating in my throat. 'What, what did he tell you?'

'He was in the service station car park that evening when James went missing.'

Oh my God, oh my God! Was this it, the moment I'd been waiting for? A part of me was scared even to ask. 'What, what d-did he tell you?'

There was a second or two's tense silence before the detective finally spoke again. To me, time almost stood still. That silence seemed like an age. And when Kesey did speak, there was a slight hesitancy, as if she was tempering my heady expectations in the interest of my coping.

'The witness was parked a fair distance from your car, approximately 50 metres, and it was dark. A nearby light was faulty. And he did say he didn't have his glasses on; he'd taken them off to rest his eyes. But despite all that, he claims he did see a man who he thinks matched James's description talking to a second person wearing a large, dark padded coat with a hood up close to where your car was parked. Our witness thought the second person was probably male, but he couldn't be certain, not 100 per cent.'

I pulled my head back. 'I find it very hard to believe a woman could be involved.'

'I'm just telling you what he said. We've got to keep an open mind. But this is where it gets a little strange. He said the man we think was probably James appeared very drunk. He was staggering as the second person led him away by the arm.'

I asked the obvious questions, confused by what she'd said. 'What? What do you mean 'led'? Led him away to where?'

I thought I heard Kesey sigh at the other end of the line.

'I'm sorry, we don't know. The witness had lost interest by that time. He didn't see anything more. He'd closed his eyes to sleep.'

'Shit, no, no, no!' So close and yet so far. My rising hopes were crushed at that moment. Kesey ignored my outburst. I'm sure she'd heard worse.

'I have to ask, Daisy, had James been drinking? You were driving. A lot of lads like a beer on the plane... Is there *anything* you haven't told me? Can you make any sense of what our witness says he saw?'

My head was spinning, one unanswered question after another bombarding my troubled mind. None of it computed; it made no sense at all. What the hell? What on earth was going on? Drunk? Absolutely no way! Maybe it wasn't James at all. 'There is no way James was drunk; he'd had *one* glass of wine with a sandwich, that's all.'

And then a question I resented, a query that stung.

'Did James ever use drugs? If he did, you need to tell me. It would be best if you were totally honest with me. Now is not the time to hold anything back.'

I swore silently under my breath, more upset than angry, but there was anger too. I didn't shout, but I did bark out my reply. 'No, no, never, I've already made that clear. Why are you asking me the same thing again? Drugs aren't James's thing and never have been. I can't be any clearer than that.'

Kesey didn't sound entirely persuaded. I could hear it in her voice, the tone. Something had changed. 'And he wasn't ill?'

Oh, for goodness' sake! Hadn't I already said all that and more? Her line of questioning was infuriating. It was as if I was back in the conference room with that doubting journalist spouting his nonsense, as if Kesey questioned every word I said. I realise now she was simply doing her job, being a good detective, but it didn't feel that way at the time. I remember I started to cry, something I'd been doing a lot in recent days. It felt as if she was questioning my integrity.

I swallowed hard before speaking. 'No, Laura, James wasn't ill. Nothing I know of would have caused him to stagger in the way your witness described. And what about his phone? It didn't smash itself. If it was James the lorry driver saw, maybe the second man did something to him. Have you thought about that? Or, or perhaps it wasn't James at all.'

Kesey was quick to respond, her voice softening. 'It's a potential lead, Daisy, the first we've had. I've got to explore every avenue and leave no stone unturned. Is there anything about James's life you haven't told me? Anything at all that may give us some clue as to who the second person was? If we find them, we will likely find James. At the very least, they're a person of interest we need to identify and interview.'

'Do you think if I knew anything, I wouldn't have already told you? There's nothing. None of this makes any more sense to me than it does to you. What about a description? Didn't your witness describe the person he saw? The person who may have taken James away.'

'The coat and hood made it difficult for our witness to provide any useful detail. We've got an approximate height and build, but that's about it. I pushed him for more information, but that's all we've got. He was far from specific. It's not ideal. But it does give us an avenue of enquiry.'

I let out a long, deep, audible breath.

'Ah, okay, shit, one door opens, another closes.'

All went silent again, and for a little longer this time, maybe up to five seconds. I thought the line might have gone dead before hearing Kesey's voice. When she spoke, she asked about London again, as if our prior conversation on the subject had never happened.

'How much do you know of James's life in London before his move to Wales?'

I thought maybe she was looking for more detail. Details I didn't know. All I could do was tell her what I could. Although I thought it unlikely anything I could say was of any relevance. Not exactly a waste of time, but close. I wondered why she wasn't asking James's parents rather than me.

'Um, he was very closed about his past. It's only recently dawned on me how little he talked about it. I don't know a huge amount, to be honest,' I said. 'I know James lived in the Blackheath area with his family, close to Greenwich Park and the river, but that's about it. He promised to take me to see the place sometime, but it hasn't happened. There was always something else we needed to do or other things that needed paying for. I suggested going a few times, but he never seemed keen.' I cried again, coughed twice, and then added, 'Maybe now it'll never happen at all.'

I so wanted Kesey to contradict me, to say something positive, to raise my flagging spirits, but for whatever reason, she didn't. I guess she's a police officer, not a social worker. It wasn't her job to make me feel better. She had other priorities, that's my rationale, and maybe I was expecting too much.

'I'll contact you when we find out more, Daisy. That's a promise. I'll be straight on the phone. You'll be the first to know. If you do think of anything you haven't told me, let me or Ray know.'

She often used my name in conversation, I think more than the norm. It was Daisy this or Daisy that as if she needed to remind herself or me of who I was. I'm probably overthinking things again, reading too much into the little details, things that really don't matter at all. But I did ask a final question that day that really did matter, something crucial, a question that went to the very heart of the matter, the thing that mattered most.

'Do you think you'll find James alive?'

'We'll do everything we can to achieve that end. Some of my best officers are on the case.'

Not exactly the wholehearted optimism I'd been looking for, but I suppose it was the best an honest detective could offer. I almost asked again, hoping for a different, more certain reply, but I thought better of it. It was time to end the call. 'Okay, thanks, Laura. I'll wait to hear from you; speak soon.'

17

I next saw Laura Kesey in person four days later, at ten past twelve on a windy, wet winter afternoon that will be etched on my memory until my dying day. My grandmother had been discharged from the hospital by that time, moving to a Carmarthenshire Social Services rehabilitative home for the elderly for a period of a few weeks, and I'd finally returned to the cottage. It was something I felt I needed to do. To behave like a grown-up rather than continue living in my childhood bedroom, although I still hadn't gone back to work. Life had far from returned to normal. James was still missing. How could it? Such things weren't possible. I was, by that point, on extended sick leave, signed off by my GP and taking prescribed anti-anxiety medication suitable in pregnancy twice daily, morning and night. In truth, it was as much as I could do to cope day to day without the heavy demands of nursing. Almost every thought was about James. Meaningful employment was the last thing on my mind.

I remember sitting on the double bed in our bedroom, staring at my wedding dress hanging on the front of the wardrobe door, when the doorbell rang once, twice, and then a third time. I leapt up, startled. Everything made me jump, the slightest noise, any distraction. I crossed the small landing on my bare feet and rushed downstairs, descending the staircase two steps at a time until I reached the small red-tiled hall at the bottom. When I opened the door with a trembling hand, I prayed it would be James standing there full of apologies, offering love and affection, but deep down, somewhere in my subconscious, I think I already knew that wouldn't be the case. Kesey had a dark expression on her otherwise ordinary face as she stood there in the cold. That look said so much, and none of it was good. I knew it was bad news before she even opened her mouth to speak.

'Can I come inside, please, Daisy? There's something I have to tell you.'

I clenched both hands into tight fists, digging my nails into the palms. 'What is it?'

She screwed up her face. I really think she was close to crying herself. She reached out and touched my arm just above the elbow. 'Come on, let's go in out of the cold; we can talk inside.'

My legs gave way as I turned towards the lounge. My world became an impressionist blur, I fell to my knees, and everything went black. I don't know how long I lay there on the hall tiles. But Kesey was kneeling at my side when I came around. She'd taken off her coat, folded it up, and placed it under my head as a pillow. After a minute or two, she helped me back to my feet, led me to the lounge, and sat me on the sofa. I didn't ask the reason for her visit. I didn't ask a thing. I was too terrified of the answer. But deep down, I knew she'd tell me anyway. There was no avoiding it. That's why she was there.

'Is there anything you'd like me to get you, Daisy, before we talk? Or perhaps you'd like me to contact your parents. I can ring them for you if you like.'

I was certain it was terrible news. What else could it be? I was utterly convinced. Kesey's whole approach screamed it and told me so much. I dry-gagged once, then again. But I knew it couldn't be put off any longer. Whatever she was there to disclose needed saying. 'Look, whatever it is, j-just tell me. Nothing could be worse than my imaginings. Please say whatever you're here to... to say. I need to know.'

Kesey's shoulders slumped as she looked me in the eye. She let out a short breath. I'm sure she'd imparted bad news before, but such things are never easy. Not that I considered her feelings at the time. My emotions were far too raw. My pain was far too significant a burden without hers too.

'I'm so very sorry to have to tell you that a body matching James's description was found washed up on Pendine Beach just after nine this morning by a local woman walking her two dogs. I wish I could give you better news, but I can't. The body has been taken to the mortuary at West Wales General. I've spoken to the coroner and a consultant pathologist. There's no easy way of telling you this; there'll be a post-mortem either today or early tomorrow morning to establish the likely cause of death. There always is in suspicious circumstances. There's no avoiding it. It's crucial to the investigation.'

I gripped one hand with the other, my mind in turmoil. I was searching for any semblance of hope, a light at the end of a very dark tunnel, however dim, however distant. All this talk of death was too much to bear. How could my lovely young husband, so full of life, with so much youthful promise, be dead? I forced the question from my mouth, desperate to deny it, pleading to God, fearing the reply. 'Is it, is it *definitely* James? Is there e-even the slightest possibility it could be someone else?'

'There will need to be a formal identification at the mortuary before the post-mortem. A close relative will have to do that for us. And then there are the dental records. But I think you need to prepare yourself for the worst. I have every reason to think it is James. I don't believe there's any reason for doubt.'

Even then, I wasn't ready to accept the truth. People made mistakes, didn't they? Maybe Kesey had it wrong. 'I want to see him,' I said, clutching at straws.

Kesey's eyebrows bunched as she emitted a heavy sigh. 'I don't think that's a good idea, Daisy. I've spoken to James's parents. His father has agreed to do it. The body had been in the water for some time. Best to remember James as he was in life. I'm not sure it's something you could cope with.'

I'd read somewhere that the sea isn't kind to corpses. I tried to push the mental pictures from my mind, blinking them away. The thought of seeing my vibrant James in that state was repugnant to me. I quickly decided that leaving the identification to Roy or Margaret was one less burden for me. Grief was enough without that, too. 'Okay, if you think that's for the best,' I said, now only too ready to agree.

Kesey nodded her head. 'I'll keep you fully informed as things progress.' She paused and then added, 'Now, do you want me to ring your parents for you? Probably best not to be on your own.'

I mumbled my response through my tears. 'My, my mum, ask my mum to come. And please tell her to bring my green cushion with her, the, the one I had as a child.' I'm not sure why I said that, the last bit. I guess the cushion was a comfort blanket of sorts. Ridiculous but true.

Kesey used her mobile, conversed, and then told me my mum was on her way. 'She'll be here in five minutes, Daisy. If you like, I'll hang on till she arrives. Is there anything I can get you? A cup of tea or coffee, maybe?'

I realise the detective was trying to be kind, but it was lost on me at the time. I was in pieces. It was as if the world had closed in on me, nothing but darkness and despair. And I think it was only then that shock truly set in. Suddenly, I was cold, sweaty, slightly dizzy and panting like an overheated dog in need of water. I stared into space, not seeing Kesey at all. 'That w-would be appreciated, thank you. There's some brandy in the... in the kitchen c-cupboard to the right of... of the sink. I could, er, I could do with some, please. You're allowed one drink a week when you're pregnant, right?'

Even now, that conversation still haunts me. Sometimes it's the first thing I think of when I wake from sleep. I wish I could turn back time and eradicate all that was bad. But that isn't possible, not in this world, but maybe in the next.

James's body was formally identified by Roy later that same day. Kesey notified me by phone. And they'd checked the dental records. I had to face reality, however awful. And soon there was more to come. Other things I'd have to deal with. Entirely unexpected new challenges that would further tear my life apart. It was an avalanche of trauma. One thing after another, beating me down.

18

Kesey contacted me again at around ten in the morning two days later, again by phone. Mum took the call as I lay in bed, exhausted and broken-hearted. She'd stayed at the cottage, sleeping in a spare room, reluctant to leave me alone with my sorrow after I refused to return to the bungalow I'd left only days before.

Mum knocked on my bedroom door, then pushed it open without waiting to be asked. She reached out, handing me my phone and saying it was DI Kesey, as I moved my winter quilt back, sitting up in bed, my eyes still half closed as the morning light shone through a gap in the curtains. Even then, after everything that had happened, a small part of me still clung to denial. I desperately hoped Kesey would tell me there'd been a mistake, that James wasn't dead after all, that some other young man had died in his place. But that was no more than a fleeting fantasy. What she actually said was so very different. This time there was no small talk. She got straight down to business. And that may seem harsh, but I've decided brutal honesty is sometimes best, avoiding ambiguity when there's no obvious way of softening the blow.

'There are some questions I need to ask you, Daisy.'

I closed my eyes tight shut. There she was with my name again, Daisy this, Daisy that. I didn't need reminding. I knew exactly who I was even if, at that precise second, I wished I was somebody else – someone not dealing with loss. Anyone happy with their life, as I'd been not so long before.

'What do you need to know?'

The detective cleared her throat. And then she gave a slight cough as if she had a cold. A lot of people did. A virus was doing the rounds. I'd had a few sniffles myself.

'I've had the preliminary results of the post-mortem,' she said. 'There's nothing in writing yet, no formal report, but there are things we need to discuss based on what the pathologist has told me.'

I was fully awake now, my head aching as it had that morning we travelled to Lanzarote. But this time, I already knew there was no good news to ease my pain. 'What? What did they say?'

I heard the sound of Kesey blowing her nose and then another cough. Her voice was a little hoarse when she spoke again, deeper in tone. 'I know we've talked about drug use before, and I realise what you've told me. But a needle mark was found on James's right arm about ten centimetres above the elbow. And a sedative drug sometimes used recreationally was found in his system, enough to explain the staggering appearance described by our lorry driver witness. I have to ask you again, Daisy. Do you think there's even the *slightest* possibility that James administered the drug himself? If it was James that was seen by our witness that evening, which now seems very likely to me, I need to know if the second person was helping him or if they were doing the opposite. Your answer will inform our investigation from here on in, so I need total honesty, nothing less will do.'

I was angry now, furious and upset. But then, all of a sudden, some things started to make sense. My mind raced, one thought after another, mental pictures playing behind my eyes. James was drugged and abducted. Someone had done that to him. Oh my God, I'd never been more certain of anything in my life. I recalled a dream where I'd imagined something similar nights before, but the memory was veiled, vague at best.

I pushed my shoulders back, feeling more determined than ever to drive my point home. It was as if I was bursting with indignant energy as adrenaline flooded my system, flight or fight but with nowhere to run. 'I'm sick of saying this, Laura. James didn't use drugs, ever! He didn't have a syringe and he didn't inject himself with a sedative or anything else. I know I'm a nurse, I know I'd have access to that sort of thing. But I *never* took anything to do with my work home, if that's what you're wondering. If there was a drug in his system, someone else put it there. Some sick, twisted bastard stuck a needle in him, drugged him and took him away. I need you to understand that. I don't ever want to have to repeat myself again.'

There was a brief silence, no more than a second or two before Kesey spoke again with what sounded like a conciliatory tone.

'Okay, that was what I was expecting you to say. It's nothing personal, I don't doubt your word, but I had to be certain. I've already spoken to Chief Superintendent Halliday, the head of the Criminal Investigation Department. As of now, this is a murder investigation. It's my opinion that our witness very likely saw James's killer.'

'Murder?'

'There's the unexplained disappearance, the needle mark, the sedative, and James had some bruising to his body when he was found on that beach.'

My fingers touched parted lips. 'Bruising?'

'There appeared to be grip marks on his upper arms which must have been inflicted before his body entered the water.'

I knew exactly what she meant. I lifted patients at work. It was one revelation after another, each a body blow, each a shock. Someone had killed my James. There was no longer any room for doubt. Horrible mental pictures played in my mind. I knew I'd dream about that, too.

'Did... did James drown?'

Kesey was quick to reply.

'No, I wondered that myself, but the pathologist said not. He was already dead when his body entered the sea. There was no saltwater in his lungs. It appears his heart gave out due to the excessive dose of the drug. I suspect the killer wasn't expecting the body to turn up, or at least not as quickly as it did. It wasn't weighed down in any way. Had it been, it could have been a very different story.'

For some reason, the fact that James hadn't drowned came as a relief; I'm not sure why. He loved swimming and adored the sea. And I'm sure there are worse ways to die. 'What... what happens now?' I asked, keen to focus on anything but his death.

'It's more of the same, to be honest, Daisy. I was already treating the case as a high priority. But DCS Halliday has allocated more resources and a generous overtime budget, so the investigation can pick up pace. Several additional officers will be dedicated to the investigation.'

I lowered my legs over the edge of the bed to the floor, looking up at my mum, who'd been standing there in silence the entire time, close to tears herself.

'Will you be talking to the media again?' I asked, focusing back on my call.

'It's already done,' Kesey replied. 'I made several calls and released a new press briefing earlier this morning. I'm confident of getting some additional coverage later today.'

I blinked repeatedly, scratched an itch on my arm. 'Why... why would anyone hurt my James? He didn't have an enemy in the world. He was gentle, kind, a lovely guy, one of the very best.'

'I'm so very sorry, Daisy, that's what I'm trying to find out. Maybe it was a case of him being in the wrong place at the wrong time. Or perhaps there's more to it. We'll only know when we establish the facts.'

In that instant, anger was my dominant emotion as I gritted my teeth. How dare someone do such a terrible thing, tearing my life apart? Why do some feel the need to spawn nothing but destruction? I gripped my phone a little tighter as I held it to my face, spitting my words with an unfamiliar snarl that seemed out of place even to me. 'I want you to catch the bastard, whoever he is. I want him locked up to rot for the rest of his stinking life.'

19

We all deal with loss at one time or another. Some cope better than others, and some not at all. Initially, for me, denial was replaced by anger and then by a profound sadness that left me unable to sleep and with no appetite, as eating became an unwelcome chore. Dark depression quickly became my prominent emotion as I popped more prescription pills than was sensible, a chemical cosh to numb my troubled mind. Mum told me repeatedly to stop the medication, for me, for my unborn child, and I eventually did, but not nearly as quickly as I should have. That took time. I regret that now and always will.

Mum returned to the bungalow at my insistence the day after Kesey's call. I'd had enough of her company by then, enough of what I called her nagging. I know she meant well, and everything she said was correct, but the attention was too much. I needed to be alone with my grief in my cottage home. Alone with my memories. And alone to talk to James, too, mostly without reply. Although I sometimes thought I heard his quiet voice encouraging me on.

I'm willing to admit that my emotions often got the better of me in those dark days. I was increasingly despondent that James was gone and his killer hadn't yet been caught. I detested that unknown person, whoever they were, with a burning strength of a type I'd never experienced before. I'd never truly hated until then. I hadn't known the true meaning of the word, that feeling of intense loathing that became an intrinsic part of me for a time. I was desperate for the killer to be arrested, prosecuted and imprisoned, repeatedly fantasising that they'd suffer as no one had ever suffered before. I wanted the monster of my imaginings lost in a sea of despair as I was, dreading waking each new day as they inhabited their version of hell.

My thoughts were focused as much on brutal revenge as justice. In my mind, they became intrinsically linked, each becoming the other. And I think my thought process was understandable and entirely reasonable given the circumstances. Why wouldn't I indulge in such fantasies? Why wouldn't I want to make them real? I'd been robbed of the future I'd planned and, to some extent, had taken for granted. The very person I'd loved the most had been snatched away by some mystery assailant. I experienced a burning rage at times, an intense fury. I shouted, screamed, and smashed things – cups, bowls, plates and the like – sometimes hurling crockery at one wall or another in an explosion of relentless grief. There was no room for forgiveness. It was far too soon for that. My emotions were too raw.

I still spoke to Kesey or Ray Lewis most days, but now, it was mostly me who rang them rather than the other way around. I don't for a second think they'd lost interest in the case. They seemed no less dedicated than before. I suspect it was simply that they had nothing new to tell me and were tired of repeating what had almost become a mantra. Despite their efforts, the police investigation into James's disappearance, abduction and murder didn't seem to get anywhere despite the further publicity Kesey facilitated. It was hugely frustrating, massively disappointing, eating away at my peace of mind day after disheartening day. A major investigation was ongoing as I dealt with my angst, but it seemed to have little positive effect. There were still so many unanswered questions. The mystery killer remained an enigma. It was all so difficult to compute, so impossible to comprehend. We were just an ordinary loving couple returning from a honeymoon in the warm Canary sunshine. Why us? Why James? Happiness became sorrow in the blink of an eye. Who would do such an awful thing, and why? It seemed no one could answer those questions. I didn't have a clue, and neither did the police. I kept asking without a resolution.

I'm happy to acknowledge I was an emotional and physical wreck as I faced my new reality. Grief can do that, particularly when combined with injustice. There's no point in hiding the truth. Life seemed almost worthless at times without my lost love. If it hadn't been for the unborn child inside my womb, that part of James still living, I think I might well have harmed myself. But suicide is never the answer. My baby saved me, the distant light at the end of a very dark tunnel. I clung to the hope that one day I'd somehow find a semblance of happiness again, for my little one. Life can be cruel and brutal, and it was then, for me, each day as bad as the one before. But for all that, I couldn't simply wallow in my sorrow. There were things I had to do, responsibilities that come with death. That's how it is when someone dies. It's complicated.

There's a great deal of red tape procedure to deal with, as well as grief. It's a cruel reality that can't be avoided. I'd never realised that before then. It's not something I'd even thought about, but now I knew the truth. The coroner finally released James's body to a local funeral director of my choice when it was no longer required for the investigation. Mum and Dad suggested a local service based in Kidwelly that'd facilitated other family funerals with sensitivity, tact and efficiency, so I accepted their recommendation with good grace. Roy offered to make the necessary arrangements, but I was keen to do it myself. I felt it was my duty, my responsibility, the least I could do for the man who'd meant so much. I even chose the coffin, a light oak veneer casket with brass-coloured furniture that I don't think were metal at all.

Both my parents were there with me at the time. I was grateful for their involvement. It isn't something I would have wanted to do alone. But despite all their support, it was undoubtedly one of the lowest points of my life. Discussing the details of the funeral brought reality into stark focus. James's parents were less involved, but I kept them fully informed, usually by phone; never an easy conversation. They were keen to pay for the funeral, some four thousand pounds. He was their son, after all. And so I said yes without hesitation. And, to be honest, the cost would have been beyond me. I was grateful for their help. It was one less burden. There was enough to cope with without further debt. I already had more than enough of that.

James's funeral took place at the Narberth Crematorium in the beautiful coastal county of Pembrokeshire at 11 a.m. on 16 February, a surprisingly mild winter morning three weeks after his body was found washed up on that nearby beach. James made his final journey on this earth in a black Ford hearse, while I travelled from Ferryside with Mum and Dad in the Volvo, all three of us clad in sombre-coloured clothing we thought suitable for the occasion.

I clearly recall a bright rainbow, an arch of beautiful colours over the estuary as we drove through our coastal village, something I still like to think was a sign intended only for me. I told myself it was my soulmate's way of telling me he was okay in whatever world he now inhabited. It gave me a degree of comfort in tragic circumstances. His soul was looking down on me with love and affection. Some others may think my viewpoint ridiculous, pour scorn even, as some have online. But I still believe that to this day.

The entire morning of the funeral was a surreal experience for me, almost as if it was happening to somebody else. That's the only way I can explain it, even if it makes little sense. We arrived at the crematorium a short time before the hearse, about ten minutes before the funeral was scheduled to start. Dad parked in a quiet spot with a view of the well-tended gardens, quickly exited the car, and then walked me arm in arm towards a small glass-walled waiting room directly opposite the modern building's main entrance. Margaret, Roy, two of my nursing colleagues and some of my relatives were already waiting, but once again, as in the case of the wedding, there were no relatives on James's side of the family, just his parents. I again found that strange, considering it only briefly. Oh, and Tom turned up, the guy from the leisure centre who'd acted as best man. But he didn't seem in the least bit upset, smiling inappropriately, seemingly happy with life. As if James didn't mean anything to him at all. As if my love was worthless. I didn't like that and it bothered me. I experienced unexpected feelings of rage which I managed to suppress. There were other things to think about. More important things. So I pushed the resentment from my mind.

I watched in tears as the hearse arrived and stopped immediately in front of the entrance, directly between the waiting room and the crematorium. I walked hand in hand with Mum, following the coffin as it was taken into the small chapel on a chrome-coloured trolley to the sound of 'Everybody Hurts', a moving REM track that was one of James's favourite songs. Roy and Margaret walked close behind us, all of us then sitting at the front of the small chapel room as the other black-clad mourners filed in behind us to take their seats in the wooden pews. I remember thinking the room was cold. Although, whether it was or not, I can't say. It may just have been me.

James was a spiritual young man, a believer in a creative universal force he sometimes called the Source or the Mother Father God, but he didn't follow any organised religion. And so the song I'd chosen seemed perfect instead of a hymn. Or, at least, it did to me. I can't say if the other attendant mourners thought the same, and to be honest, as I must, I don't particularly care. I looked behind me as the song ended to see Kesey and Ray Lewis entering the chapel room a couple of minutes late. Their timekeeping didn't bother me a great deal. They were busy people. It was good of them to come. It told me James still mattered to them.

The relatively brief service, no more than half an hour in total, was conducted by a non-religious funeral celebrant rather than a priest or vicar. I found the local middle-aged, dark-haired woman online, living in an alternative community in the Preseli Hills, and I like to think that's what James would have wanted. She was warm, friendly and approachable, making the service a celebration of James's life, saying things which touched my heart. It was almost as if she'd known him herself. James's father spoke from the raised pulpit, and I did, too, extolling my love as my tears freely flowed. Given my heightened emotional blubbing, I'll never know whether the small congregation could understand a word I said. I like to think they did, but whether they did or not, I'm sure they got the gist. And I know James knew exactly what I said as he looked down on me with love. Of that I have no doubt.

Jodie Whittaker's charity version of Coldplay's melodic

classic 'Yellow' played as the service ended, another of James's absolute favourites, and as it happens, mine too. We once danced to the track, holding each other close, smiling, in happier times that now seemed so far away.

In truth, writing this chapter hasn't been easy, engendering some memories that a part of me believes were best left in the past. It's as if I've re-experienced events. As if I've attended that funeral service all over again. And in doing so, I'm certain the most challenging time of that morning was the curtains closing, hiding the coffin from my sight before it made its way on rollers into what I correctly assumed to be the crematorium's furnace. I watched with unblinking eyes, unable to look away as images of dancing blue-yellow flames played in my mind. But as my mother held my hand, squeezing it tight, I consoled myself that my lover's soul had left this earth long before his body entered the fire. Funerals are for the living. The dead have already passed.

Mum continued to hold my hand as she led me from the chapel room and outside through a smaller second door to our immediate right. It had started raining by then, and no more rainbows, but a slate-roofed, open-sided structure offered shelter as we stood in the fresh Pembrokeshire air, thanking the mourners for their attendance as they left, offering their condolences one after another.

And then it happened, there he was again – Oliver, standing in the car park close to the Volvo as Mum, Dad, and I made our weary way back to the car. I recognised him immediately. He was wearing that same ill-fitting suit he'd worn at the wedding. However, his long hair was still dyed blond as on the island, rather than brown as it had been. I remember thinking his unexpected arrival strange in the extreme as he slowly walked towards us, expressing profound sadness on his boyish face. I let go of Mum's hand as Oliver got nearer.

Margaret and Roy appeared to stand and stare at Oliver momentarily before suddenly turning and rushing away, Roy tugging at Margaret's hand. Roy glanced back once on approaching his car. Oliver, in contrast, appeared to ignore the couple's presence completely as he began speaking, focused only on me.

'I hope you don't mind that I came, Daisy,' he said in that same English accent. 'James was a very good friend to me at university. I'm so very sorry for your loss. He was a lovely guy. One of the nicest I've ever met. I'm going to miss him terribly. I hope you can accept my condolences.'

Really? Good friends? James and him? I thought it but didn't say it. Oliver had expressed himself with such apparent conviction and feeling. There were tears in his eyes. Could it be anything but the truth?

Mum and Dad both stepped away, hurriedly entering the Volvo to escape the rain, leaving Oliver and me to talk after I'd quickly made my introductions. Mum had given me a small, black, pound-shop umbrella taken from her handbag, which I held above my head to little effect as a drizzle continued to fall, seemingly coming from every direction at once, soaking everything in its path.

'I, er, I didn't see you in the chapel,' I said, still surprised to see him there at all and even more surprised by his warm words.

Oliver lowered his head momentarily, his chin almost touching his chest. 'No, I listened to the service just outside the door. I wanted to say my final goodbyes to a good friend I'll miss. But I realise today's a time for family. I didn't want to intrude. I hope you don't mind me turning up like this. I almost left before you came out, but I wanted to tell you how much James meant to me. I got to know him so well in that first year at university. He told me so much about you.'

Really? That question again. Why would he say such things if not true? Had James and Oliver really been that close? There were so many things I wanted to ask him. Why and when they'd fallen out. Was it really about me as James claimed? Or was there more to it? Things that James hadn't chosen to share. Standing in the crematorium car park, I quickly decided it wasn't the time for clarification. And what did it matter anyway? James was gone, and nothing was going to change that. No amount of curiosity on my part or anything else.

'Um, would... would it be okay if I kept in touch?' he asked as I was about to turn away. 'If there's anything, anything at all, I can do for you, do please let me know. All you have to do is ask.'

Keep in touch? What on earth could I say to that? His request was so unexpected. That was the last thing I'd thought he'd say. But for some reason, I felt comfortable in his company, however briefly. And his kind words seemed genuine, not some meaningless platitude people say in such pained circumstances because they can think of nothing else. It seemed to me Oliver was a connection to James, and so I said yes without much thought before finally opening the car door. Despite the rain, Oliver stood there waving as my dad drove off as he had at the wedding. That made me smile despite myself. I'd liked him at university and I still did. He was unlike anyone else I'd ever met. That surprised me too.

We returned to my parents' bungalow after the funeral, where we were joined by several members of the congregation to drink tea, eat cake and chat. Roy and Margaret, however, chose not to join us. I left after an hour or so to be alone with my thoughts. People were friendly and supportive, saying all the right things, but there's only so much a girl can take. For all the good intentions, I needed to escape. The bottom line – no words could help. It had been a long day, and I needed rest.

I didn't hear from Oliver for some time after that, although I have to admit he did occasionally come to mind. But he did eventually get in touch again, just like he said he would. He found me on Facebook, which is not difficult given my public profile, and sent a friend request. So much changed after that. It was the start of another chapter – the next part of my story. A tale I'll soon tell.

20

Ray Lewis rang me on 24 February. I was back at work by then and taking a much-needed break in the staffroom, chatting to a colleague and enjoying a fast-cooling mug of camomile tea to help calm my nerves. I recognised the sergeant's gruff voice as soon as he said hello, rough and low in pitch, and I was glad he'd got in touch. It likely meant he had something to tell me, perhaps something significant; hopefully, the breakthrough I prayed for every night had finally come. Catching the killer had become my predominant wish. I wanted the bastard caught and punished. In some ways, focusing on that outcome kept me going. Hate can be a powerful motivator. Nothing mattered more.

'What's happening, Ray? Any news?' We were on first-name terms by then.

I heard what sounded like a groan at the other end of the line. 'There is something we need to talk about, love. But don't get excited. The DI thinks there may be something in it, but I can't say I agree.'

I gripped my mug tightly, apprehensive about what he might

say next. I'd got used to him calling me love by then. I took it as a term of affection, something I suspect he said to most females he encountered, no more than that. There was nothing sexual in it. When I spoke, I tried to sound as assertive as possible, keen to hear more, hoping my tone didn't betray my anxiety. 'Whatever it is, I need you to tell me.'

The sound of another groan, Ray blowing out the air, not exactly filling me with confidence.

'We've got another witness, love, a young woman who *claims* to have seen James in the service station car park that night. I've taken a written statement. She claims she doesn't watch TV, listen to the radio or read the papers, but she finally came forward after seeing one of your social media posts, the one with a photo of James sitting on the beach in Ferryside near the yacht club.'

I knew exactly which photo he meant. I remembered taking it the previous April before the two of us went swimming from the jetty. And despite Ray's caution, what he said raised my hopes. But he'd placed a heavy emphasis on the word *claims*, which confirmed to me he had his doubts. I needed to know more. I asked an open question, encouraging the detective to talk, as I would with a patient. I often find that's best. Although, given his years of experience, I suspect he knew exactly what I was doing, reading me like a large-print book. 'What did she tell you? Please tell me everything.'

He paused for a beat before speaking again. I imagined him shaking his head, his brow furrowed, a scowl on his unshaven face. 'She knows James from university. She was at the service station that night, that much is true. We've got her on camera in the building. But as for the rest, I don't think so. She *claims* she saw James getting into a two-seater convertible Mercedes sports car with a young woman with long blonde hair, a short skirt, high heels, and expertly applied make-up. She said she was certain it was James, gave me a detailed description of the woman, and even told me the colour of the car, silver. But how would she see all that detail in the dark? The car park wasn't even lit up as it usually is. Some sort of electrical problem. Laura's insisting on putting out a new press release and dedicating resources to finding the car and driver. And that's why I'm telling you all this. It'll be all over the news soon enough. You're bound to see something. But to be honest, love, I think it's all a waste of time and effort. I think the whole story is bullshit. She's an attention seeker. I've been in this job a long time. I don't believe a word of it. I've seen her type before.'

I'd never felt more conflicted. Ray seemed so adamant, but everyone made mistakes, and maybe Kesey was right. I didn't know what to think. I wouldn't say I liked the idea of James going off with some mystery woman. And my immediate instinct was not to believe it. But that tiny element of doubt was still eating away at me. I wanted the detective to convince me those nagging doubts were wrong. 'Okay, you say you don't believe her story, but why so sure?'

He spoke in hushed tones now, as if wary someone might overhear. I could only just hear him myself. 'If I tell you this, it's in confidence, yeah? It's for your ears only. You remind me of my daughter. I'm telling you because I think it's the right thing to do. But I don't want it shared with anyone else. It's more than my job's worth. Have we got a deal?'

I knew he was bending the rules. 'Just tell me, Ray. Whatever it is, it won't go any further. You have my word.'

'The witness, I know the woman. We lived on the same estate years back when I was still married. She was my daughter's friend for a while, although they fell out in the end. She even came to the house a few times.'

I still didn't know where he was going with the conversation. None of what he'd said negated her evidence, not yet. Although, James getting in a car with some mystery woman? Really? My mind raced. It still seemed highly unlikely to me. But what if I was wrong? Kesey seemed to think so. And those we think we know so well can sometimes surprise us, shock us even. Could I really be so sure James hadn't betrayed me?

'Okay, so you know her,' I said. 'What's the relevance?'

I heard what sounded like a door closing before Lewis spoke again. 'She's a bright girl with a high IQ, but she was in a residential psychiatric unit for a few months as a teenager. She's got a history of drug abuse and related mental health problems. She went right off the rails for a while. She says she's sorted herself out, but I'm not convinced. She still looks like a user to me. She said she met James in his first year at university before you joined him. She... er... she even claimed they had sex a few times before you turned up on the scene.'

I was close to puking, a sinking feeling deep in the pit of my stomach as his words rang in my ears, assaulting my sensibilities. How dare she? How dare she say such a terrible thing? It had to be lies, dirty, filthy, rotten lies, every stinking word. I said all that to myself and more. But just a tiny part of me questioned if it could be true. The lipstick came to mind. The stain on James's collar. Maybe I shouldn't have been so ready to believe him. How well can we ever really know someone, however much we love them? We all have our secrets. Just for a moment, I wondered if James did too. There it was, that insecurity again. It still occasionally plagues me. It always has and probably always will. What if he did get in that car? What if the mystery woman was a better catch than me?

'Was this witness *definitely* at Swansea University? Is that bit true?'

He cleared his throat. 'Yeah, she was studying sociology, but don't go reading too much into it. I spoke to her face to face, up close and personal. I've got an instinct for these things. I don't think she saw anything at all. It's a fabrication, fiction. She's in it for the attention, no more than that.'

'Can you tell me her name? I may know her. I could tell you what I think. I could even talk to her myself.'

This time he was quick to reply. 'No, I'm sorry, love, that's a step too far. Laura would hang me out to dry. I've said too much already.'

I wasn't surprised by his answer. I was professionally bound by rules of confidentiality too. He'd already put his career on the line in my favour, and I was grateful for that. With every thought, another question came to mind to fire at the sergeant, but when it came to it, I froze. I was emotionally fragile. I'm not sure I was even thinking straight. I was whimpering slightly, feeling utterly conflicted when I finally found my words. I trusted the big detective, but my insecurity was getting the better of me again, as it had many times before. I was torturing myself with doubts.

'If you're telling me what you think I want to hear to make me feel better, then please don't. I want to know the truth.'

I thought he sounded irritated when he responded, probably losing patience. I can hardly blame him for that. I know I can be frustrating; I drive myself nuts with my constant rumination, so why not others?

'For goodness' sake, girl, I couldn't have been any clearer. I've told you what the woman claimed she saw, and Kesey thinks it's worth following up. And she's the boss, so it will be. It's a top-down profession. That's the way the force works. But don't get your hopes up when you see the reports on the news. That's all I'm saying. For me, this witness isn't credible. She's pointing us in the wrong direction. The lorry driver's evidence is a much better bet. I still think it likely he saw James's actual killer. We need to look for that man.'

Despite all that Ray had said, my imagination was still running riot. I pictured my James getting into a flash, expensive sports car with a glamorous, super-sexy temptress far more attractive than me. I asked myself if this mystery woman had killed my James, if that was a possibility. How ridiculous is that? I wonder what's wrong with me sometimes. I drove the image from my mind, resisting the impulse to scream.

'Come on, Ray, tell me who she is. It really would help me to know.'

'No, love, I can't tell you. I thought I'd made that clear. Don't make me regret telling you what I have.'

I knew when I was beaten, so I moved on, still looking for reassurance but taking a different tack.

'And you are still looking for the guy seen by the lorry driver, the one in the coat?'

'Yes, love, I'm still focused on finding them. That hasn't changed.'

I decided to take that as good news, although I realised there were now two strands to the investigation, one driven by Kesey and another by Ray.

'Are you any closer to finding out who it was?'

'Not yet, enquiries are ongoing, that's the best I can say.'

There were still so many unanswered questions.

'Will you ring me again when you find out anything new?'

'Of course I will, love, no problem at all. I'll be straight on the phone.'

I raised a hand to my face, two fingers touching my chin. 'You will catch the bastard, won't you, Ray?'

'No guarantees, but I'll do my very best, that I can promise you. I won't let you down for lack of trying.'

Was that really the best he could offer? I concluded it was. I was certain he'd said nothing but the truth as we ended the call. I believed he'd expressed his genuine opinions out of kindness, no more and no less, and I was glad he had. There was no avoiding that story as he'd so accurately predicted. I saw it on the BBC Wales news early that evening and again before going to bed, with an appeal for information.

I pondered long and hard about who the new witness might be for days after that, but no one came to mind. A part of me still wanted to speak to her face to face, to question her myself. I thought I might ask Oliver if he had any ideas who she was if he ever got in touch, although, for whatever reason, I didn't contact him myself. And I didn't contact any of James's other friends either. It may simply have been indecisiveness on my part, a lack of confidence, or perhaps a combination of both. To be honest, I'm not sure. All I can say with certainty is that insecurity can be terrible. I'd lost James, and now a small but insistent part of me wondered if he'd loved me as much as I'd loved him. I'd heard Ray Lewis, I knew exactly what he'd said, and all logic told me the idea of James getting into that sports car was unlikely at best. So why did I torture myself with the thought he might have? Why did I dream about it? Why couldn't I let the idea go? It would have been so much better if I had. Things aren't always what they seem. One thing can lead to another. Things can run away with themselves, and they did for me.

21

I next heard from Oliver on St David's Day, 1 March. I'd stopped taking the anti-anxiety medication by that time. Mum's wise words finally had an impact. And work was going reasonably well, despite occasional tears. Those were the positives; it wasn't all doom and gloom, but there were negatives too. Sadly, the police still weren't getting anywhere with the investigation. The information given by the second witness led nowhere, as was the case with the first. James's killer remained unknown, with no significant new evidence or breakthroughs with which I could console myself. And so, all in all, things weren't great, although, as I've said before, the new life inside me gave me a reason to carry on. I think I lived more for my unborn child than for myself for a time. To some extent, I still do. She provides inspiration to survive.

I sat in the hospital staffroom that lunchtime, distracting myself with my iPad as I nibbled less than enthusiastically at a homemade peanut butter and Marmite sandwich I'd packed in a plastic lunchbox along with two gluten-free *Free From* biscuits bought in Tesco the previous weekend. I was still regularly posting about James on social media, asking for help, and holding onto hope, although the responses had slowed by that time. It seemed people had already moved on. His disappearance and murder were old news. The importance of the case had faded in public minds far too quickly. That was incredibly disappointing, but I did everything possible to keep the interest alive.

I looked at my Twitter page first that lunchtime, then at Instagram, and finally Facebook, and there it was, not just another friend request – I got quite a few – but a message from Oliver, wishing me well, and with an accompanying photograph of James and himself standing outside a Swansea University library building I recognised as soon as I saw it. They were both smiling warmly in the photo. And they each had an arm around the other's shoulder. It seemed to me their relationship appeared far closer than James had ever admitted. Or, at least, that's how it looked to me. I wondered why my love had played down the connection as I pondered whether or not to accept the friend request. I'd become increasingly doubtful regarding James's explanation as time passed. Not that I'd given it a great deal of thought. But that day, as I stared at the photo, studying the two young men's expressions and body language, such things were at the forefront of my mind. I cast my mind back to mine and James's conversation as we travelled back from that wild Lanzarote surfers' beach, almost hearing his words as he said them in the rental car that day.

Almost ten minutes passed as I wondered whether to accept Oliver's friend request. I still don't know why it took me so long. As I said, I liked him. But it seems I was racked with doubts about anything and everything, my already fragile confidence crushed as life's many demands beat me down. Even the simplest of decisions could sometimes prove difficult, what to wear each morning when a uniform wasn't required, what to eat for lunch, or even whether to eat at all. But as I sat there, I asked myself what possible harm accepting a Facebook friend request from someone I already knew could possibly do.

Oliver wasn't one of those slimeball men who sometimes got in touch. Women will know the type I'm referring to – the men I block immediately after viewing their profiles. I thought of Oliver's kind words at the funeral. Oliver was fine, just an ordinary lad. That's what I said in my head to reassure myself. And so I accepted his friend request with a gentle touch of my finger. I responded to his message, too, commenting on the photo he'd sent, thanking him for sharing it, and asking when it was taken. He didn't reply until that evening, shortly after 7 p.m., although I know he'd seen my response to his original message long before. Maybe he was busy, or perhaps he was playing it cool. I think the latter is a more likely explanation. The sort of thing he sometimes did. I read his message as soon as it appeared on my smartphone:

Hi there, Daisy, lovely to hear back from you. Glad you liked the photo. I hoped you would. I can't remember exactly when it was taken, but it was definitely in James's first year before you joined him in Swansea. How are you doing? Any news your end? The last time I saw you was at the funeral. XXX

The funeral, oh my God, yes, like I needed reminding. I thought of it often. I put the TV off, focusing on my screen, surprised to find myself glad Oliver had replied despite his unwelcome reference to one of the worst days of my life. I was both lonely and curious; that's the reality. I was still missing James terribly, wanting to know more of his life and how and why he died. And being in contact with Oliver again did at least allow me to ask more about their relationship when the time seemed right. That and other things, things I needed to know. It was almost as if my new connection with Oliver was a connection to James.

I recall staring at my phone for what must have been minutes while repeatedly tapping a foot against the floor. I remember the tension, the pressure I felt as my head began to ache. I'd thought a lot about what Ray had told me recently. About the alleged female witness he'd said he so doubted. And now seemed the obvious opportunity to find out who she was. I thought maybe that knowledge would help still my nagging doubts. Her mention of that mystery glamorous blonde sometimes played on my mind, particularly at night when I lay alone in the dark. Should I ask Oliver my question? Should I wait or dive right in? Yeah, what the hell, go for it. The opportunity had presented itself, so why not take full advantage? I'd only end up regretting it if I didn't, wouldn't I? I looked down at the small screen and began one-finger typing.

Did you know any of the girls on the sociology course at uni?

A few minutes passed before Oliver replied. I was hoping I hadn't frightened him off.

Yeah, a couple of them. We were all in the same building for lectures. Why do you ask?

I almost didn't ask my next question, but then I did, typing as quickly as possible before changing my mind. All of a sudden, I wasn't nearly so sure I wanted to know the answer. My thoughts weren't as clear as they should have been.

What about James? Did he know them, too?

Yeah, I guess so. But why?

Now I'd asked that much, it seemed I couldn't stop. I typed with a fast-moving finger as each new question came to mind. It must have felt a bit like being interrogated on the other end of the torrent.

How well did he know them? Was he close to any of them? A girl with drug issues, maybe? Someone Welsh like me?

What's this about, Daisy????

It seems like an ordinary enough response on the face of it. But I didn't see it that way. I couldn't still my mind, my thoughts rushing one after another, making me wince. I asked myself if Oliver was being obstructive. Was he avoiding answering my questions because he thought I wouldn't like the answers? Or was I being ridiculous? Maybe, I was being stupid. I really wasn't certain one way or the other. There was no going back now. I decided all I could do was ask more.

Can you think of the girl I described, Welsh, drugs, mental health issues? Someone James knew pretty well, someone he liked?

I could see that Oliver was typing again as I awaited his response, tenser by the minute, sweating, and my mouth dry. Why was I torturing myself? I really don't know. I grimaced as I read his reply.

I can think of one girl it might have been. I think her name was Lily or maybe Lottie, I'm not sure. But if it is the one I'm thinking of, it was her who liked James, not the other way around. She was always giving him the eye, trying to chat him up, very hands on.

I rolled up my sleeves, loosened my collar. And now, a question that really mattered to me. If I knew who she was, I could contact her, ask her what she thought she saw, and so much more.

Can you remember her surname?

LOL. IDK. I'm not even sure I got the first name right. And why are you so keen to know?

Please think hard.

A quick response this time. Was I that obvious? It was as if Oliver had read my mind.

I think it may have started with an E, Evans maybe, or Edwards. But why do you want to know? James wasn't interested, if that's what you're worried about. She's a good-looking girl but you're the one he wanted.

Oh God, yes, I now thought I knew exactly who the witness was. Why hadn't I thought of her before? I wasn't entirely sure of her name either. Evans or Edwards, it was one or the other. But I could picture her in my mind. Overly tight clothes, large breasts, heavy make-up, hair tied back, hoop earrings and loud. It seemed I'd answered one question. And there were other things to ask while I had the chance. I was ready to move on.

It's just something the police said. She may have seen something.

They put out a press release asking for information without identifying the witness.

What???

I quickly decided it wasn't something I wanted to discuss.

You didn't see anything on the news?

I must have missed it. What did she say?

I wrote my following message as much for my benefit as his.

Oh, it's nothing important. The detective I spoke to said she's full of crap.

Tell me about it. I'd like to know.

I was keen to change the subject.

Do you mind if I ask you something else?

This is a bit like being on Mastermind.

I've started, so I'll finish.

Ask away!

I'd like to know more about you and James. Were the two of you very good friends?

Oliver sent a yellow smiley face and a red heart emoji followed by text.

Well yeah, the best. James was the closest friend I've ever had.

But James said he didn't invite you to the wedding. You just turned up. And then there you were on our honeymoon and at the funeral too. I can't make sense of all that. What happened between the two of you?

He took a minute or two to respond this time; I guess, considering his answer, maybe choosing his words with care. A part of me feared I might have asked too much. I thought he might not reply at all as the seconds ticked by.

I've been surfing in the Canaries quite a few times. I get a budget flight from Gatwick, stay somewhere cheap, a youth hostel, a tent, something like that. I didn't know we were in Lanzarote at the same time until I saw your posts on social media. It was a crazy coincidence, although James and I had discussed a trip there one day before we fell out. We'd even talked about going in January. The waves are better at that time of year. I was gutted I wasn't invited to the wedding, but I felt I had to be there. It was just too big a deal to miss. The same with the funeral, but then you already knew that. I hope that explains everything well enough. I always thought me and James would be mates again before he died.

I wasn't sure I entirely believed Oliver about the honeymoon. But I decided on the benefit of the doubt. And I appreciated his full explanation about everything else. It all seemed to make sense. He had me engaged by then. I already felt as if I could ask him almost anything. Which I'm now certain is exactly how he wanted it.

I hope you don't mind me asking. What happened between the two of you?

He replied immediately as if he didn't need to think about it. Maybe he'd been expecting the question. Perhaps he had an answer prepared in advance.

Oh, it was just some stupid shit that got way out of hand. What are you doing with yourself these days? Are you working?

I was sure he was deliberately changing the subject, but I quickly decided to push it anyway. It was something I'd been thinking about for what felt like a very long time.

What sort of shit?

Oh, crap, do you REALLY want to know? It's all in the past. Can't we forget it???? It was just nonsense, blokes' stuff.

I do want to know. I NEED to know. Come on, enlighten me.

I waited with bated breath as he typed again, time passing slowly.

You may hate me after this.

I wondered what was coming next, more interested than ever. And I hate to admit it, but I think a part of me was fishing for compliments as I sat alone in the cottage lounge. That is so pathetic! I feel thoroughly ashamed.

Just tell me, Oliver, please. I won't judge you. I know what you men are like. You said to ask you if I ever needed anything at the funeral outside the crematorium, and this is it. I'm asking you now. You did mean it, didn't you? What happened? It's been playing on my mind.

Really???

Come on, own up. You made a promise. I want to know.

Ah, okay, you've got me, here goes. I told James I fancied you. I should have kept my stupid mouth shut. I said too much. You were his, not mine. He hardly spoke to me after that night. I was totally gutted, apologised, and explained I was pissed, but he wasn't having any of it. I couldn't believe he didn't even invite me to the wedding. That hurt, I was close to tears. I couldn't believe he'd held the grudge for so long. In different circumstances, I would have expected to be the best man. Who did James choose? I've been wondering. I saw him in the church but it wasn't anyone I knew.

James worked with him at the leisure centre, a man named Tom. I don't think he even knew him that well. I don't like him at all.

It should have been me! If I'd kept my stupid mouth shut, it would have been.

I very much appreciated what I saw as Oliver's honesty. Not everyone is nearly so open. I thought it was refreshing. I didn't see any warning signs. It felt good to read his confession of sorts rather than easy denial. I found Oliver's seemingly heartfelt words both pleasing and reassuring. They made me think I could trust him in a way I didn't trust many people other than family. And James's reaction still seemed an overreaction based on what I knew, however crude Oliver's language might have been.

Yeah, okay, thanks for explaining. James told me much the same. I'd been wondering if there was more to it, that's all. And back at uni, I didn't even think you liked me that much. You hardly ever talked to me. Just that one time you bought me a coffee.

I regretted the message almost as soon as I sent it. Was I fishing for compliments again? Looking to boost my fragile self-esteem? I very probably was. I think even then, at that early stage, a relationship was forming, initiated by Oliver, but I played my part. I read his reply with interest, lapping it up.

It was a self-preservation thing. I liked you a bit too much. What are you doing with yourself these days?

I knew he was trying to change the subject again. But this time, I went with it. I thought his explanation was enough. I was flattered. And to be honest, I felt a little embarrassed that I'd encouraged his praise. It seemed almost disloyal to discuss such things with another man so soon after James's death. I don't like myself very much when I think about that now. Everything was moving so fast. I would have liked to have been a better person than I was.

I'm back working as a nurse in Llanelli. I hope to move to West Wales General when a suitable vacancy arises, less travelling.

Oh, wow, how's it going? Is it everything you hoped for?

It's tough since, well, you know, since James passed. But I'm just about coping most of the time. I think that's the best I can say. The work's fine. It's just hard to motivate myself sometimes. I'm still grieving.

Yeah, I get that, but be proud. It's impressive, Daisy, you're doing brilliantly given everything that's happened. You're a total star. Don't ever forget that.

I think I smiled at that point, my face reddening. It was exactly what I wanted to hear. And I lapped it up like the fool I was.

What about you?

I'm still looking for something working with people after my psychology degree. Easier said than done, I'm afraid. I've been doing a bit of gardening until now – anything to pay the bills. But I've seen a couple of jobs advertised in the Carmarthen area that look interesting. There's one support role with Barnardo's and another as a teaching assistant in a school for kids with special educational needs.

Interesting! I didn't realise that's the sort of thing you're into. James never did get the teaching job he hoped for. But I guess that doesn't matter now. Although I still wish he had.

Oliver changed the subject again, something I came to realise he often did as I got to know him better. I think it was his way of directing a conversation. Maybe he asked next what he wanted to talk about all along.

How's the police investigation going? Any important developments? I saw something on the Welsh news some time back, but nothing since.

I took a deep breath. Dredging up any positivity was getting harder. I briefly considered feigning optimism, but I decided to tell the truth. I was under the impression Oliver had, so I decided to do the same.

They don't seem to be getting anywhere. I want the bastard caught. I'm starting to give up hope.

Oliver's response was almost instant, much quicker than before.

Have they no hopeful suspects at all? What about that bloke seen in the car park by the lorry driver mentioned on the news? The suspect with his hood up.

I wasn't sure if the news reports had mentioned the hood, but I thought they must have. How else could Oliver have known? I was close to tears now, my mood low.

The witness couldn't even see the person that clearly. The police are still looking for them, but they haven't got a clue who they are. I'm beginning to think they never will. They don't even know if it was a man or a woman.

Is there no other credible evidence?

I decided again not to mention the claims made by the second witness. Talking about what she'd claimed was just too upsetting. There seemed little, if any purpose to saying anything more. I just typed no and left it at that. I was tired by then. I was ready for bed. Sleep was calling. Welcome oblivion.

He changed the subject again for a final time. And this time, I think he got to the crux of the matter, his primary reason for contacting me.

How would you feel about getting together for a coffee next time I'm down your way? No pressure, I'll understand if it's not something you want to do. But I would love to see you. And we could talk about James.

I'm not entirely sure why I replied yes so very quickly, but I did. Maybe I thought it wouldn't come to anything. Or perhaps, if I'm honest with myself, I quite liked the idea of seeing him again, not in any romantic way but as a friend. I tried to type with my thumbs again but quickly gave up on the idea, reverting to a finger.

Yeah, nice idea. That would be good as long as I'm not at work. Let me know well in advance, and I'll make the time if I can.

Okay, brilliant! I'll be in touch. And I'm looking forward to it already. See you soon! XXX

Oliver sent three red hearts and a blue thumbs-up after that, and that was it; our conversation ended as quickly as it began. I felt in a surprisingly positive mood as I stood in the cottage kitchen making my almond-milk cocoa in a favourite pottery mug. Seeing Oliver again had its appeal; I'll freely admit that. It seemed something to distract me from my sadness for however long a time. Life, after all, had to go on. But be careful what you wish for, that's my cautionary advice. Things aren't always nearly as obvious as they seem. If only someone had told me that at the time. Although I may not have listened even if they had. Red flags aren't always as visible as they seem. Sometimes we don't see them at all.

22

I found Lily Evans on social media with predictable ease. I'd thought a lot about what she'd claimed as I lay in bed that night. I kept picturing her tarty face in my mind, my muscles tense, teeth clenched, the very thought of her preventing much-needed sleep. In the end, at about 2 a.m., I got up, put on a dressing gown, headed downstairs and picked up my iPad from the dining room table. I sat in the lounge close to the fire and perused one social media site after another. She was on all of them, but Instagram seemed her favourite. There were so many images of her in various states of pouting undress. None were wholly nude or overly crude, but sexy, suggestive, and with promises of more to see if you accessed her OnlyFans and were willing to pay. I didn't, and I haven't. It's not difficult to work out what I'd see.

Those mental images played almost constantly on my mind when I finally returned to bed, giving in to exhaustion. I couldn't help but see her and James, their bodies entwined in a passionate embrace in my mind's eye. She'd claimed to have had sex with him. I didn't want to believe it. A big part of me still thought she was full of crap, just as Ray had said. But those doubts, those nagging doubts, they ate away at me. They wouldn't give me peace, not for a second. And if she really did know something about James's death, I had to know.

I was back on my iPad early the following day, having rung into work sick, feigning a migraine. Another thing I'm not proud of, but it's the truth. I was searching for a clue as to where Lily lived. And it wasn't hard to find out. There was a photo of her standing in the open doorway of a Carmarthen terraced house. I could even see the name and number of the property on the wall and I thought I recognised the street. What to do? What the hell to do? I felt conflicted, wanting to challenge her. But should I do anything at all?

I ruminated while forcing down a light breakfast, and in the end, I decided I had to talk to her face to face. I had to look into her eyes, to ask her why she'd told the police what she had. Within half an hour or so, I knocked reticently on Lily's door, my determination and confidence already waning. I knocked a little harder now, urging myself on, but some of me still hoped I wouldn't receive an answer. But then the door opened, and she was standing there, wearing what I can only describe as a school uniform that was several sizes too small for her. I remember jerking my head back, not quite able to believe my eyes as Lily glared at me, hands on hips, leaning slightly back as she tottered on her high heels.

'I've been wondering if you'd show your ugly face,' she said, still glaring at me with angry eyes heavily lined with mascara. 'That copper should have kept his stupid mouth shut. I've got nothing to say to you. Why don't you piss off? I'm busy.'

I took a single step back, swallowed hard but held my

ground. 'Why did you tell Sergeant Lewis you saw James get into a car with another woman?'

She smirked. 'Maybe he did. Take a good look at yourself. You're not all that, girl. He might have needed another woman. One like me with a bit of life to her.'

I shouted now, unusual for me. 'You're a liar! You clearly made the whole thing up. Not even the police believe you.'

And then she laughed, a mocking cackle, and I'd never hated anyone more. 'Believe what you want to, love. I couldn't give a toss. Means nothing to me.'

I could see she was about to close the door. Should I ask? Did I really want an answer? 'Why did you say you had sex with my James? He wouldn't have been interested in the likes of you.'

She smiled sardonically. 'He screwed me hard. Lots of times. The whole way through uni, really. Couldn't get enough of it. Said you weren't up to much.'

I clenched and unclenched my fists, yelling as she went to slam the door. 'I don't believe a word of it. You're a lying bitch. You're sick in the head.'

My mind was racing as I drove away from Lily's house in tears. The visit served no useful purpose. I wished I'd never seen her at all. If anything, I gave her the attention she craved. Ray had said her story was total nonsense from start to finish, that she was looking to insert herself into the narrative and was enjoying the drama she created. And I concluded that was very probably true. But there were still doubts; with me, there are always doubts. Maybe the police were correct in following up on the lead, or perhaps they were wasting their time. I hoped Ray would never find out I'd stuck my nose in. I knew it wouldn't go well if he did. But as it happens, I don't think Lily ever told him. Or, at least, not that he told me.

I tried to push Lily's taunts to the back of my mind as I

returned to the cottage after my Carmarthen visit. I had more than enough to worry about as it was. And this is the first time I've ever mentioned Lily to anyone since, although I've thought about her more than once. She still sometimes comes to mind. Why did I let her get to me? Why torture myself? I just can't help thinking there was more to James than I know.

23

I applied online for a bank loan early on 5 March. I know the date is correct because I found the relevant emails still archived in my Gmail account. I'd been putting off the application process with one lame excuse after another but finally accepted it had to be done that day. My credit card was maxed out, and my current account was already close to being overdrawn. I urgently needed to borrow £5,000, not to buy anything special or to treat myself in an effort to cheer myself up as I was some-times tempted, but simply to pay some outstanding bills and consolidate debt. The entire amount and more was spent before I even received it. That LPG gas delivery I'd discussed with James was now well overdue; my car badly needed servicing, and paying the cottage's monthly rent was proving challenging. I was desperate to keep the cottage. It meant so very much to me. And the idea of losing it was hard to take. I'd tried to talk James into taking out life insurance at the villa after I told him I was pregnant, but he argued we were young, heathy, and didn't have a mortgage, and so the money could be spent on better things.

I was earning what I thought was a reasonably good salary as a nurse, but I still felt the financial strain following James's untimely passing. The household income had dropped by at least 30 per cent, and maybe more. I've never worked out the exact figures. I lost James, his love, friendship, emotional support, and practical contribution. My parents were always generous when I asked for help. They never made it difficult. But I didn't think it was something I could keep doing. They weren't wealthy, far from it. They were just ordinary people living modestly. I knew they'd help again if I asked, but they had their bills too. And they deserved some of life's luxuries, holidays and the like; they both loved travelling. Asking them for money time and again just didn't seem fair.

I concluded keeping busy was best as the morning progressed, offering a welcome distraction and stopping me from overthinking as I still tended to do. Doing practical things was a survival tactic of sorts as I somehow faced the future, preparing my nest for my baby's eventual arrival at the beginning of September. Having been provisionally accepted for the bank loan at what I thought an exorbitant interest rate, I forced down a light lunch at around midday, just organic Italian vegetable soup from a can and a glass of filtered tap water that didn't need chilling. I'd decided to start sorting through James's clothing later that afternoon, packing some in large black plastic bin bags for delivery to one charity shop or another and putting the best items aside for sale on eBay. I read somewhere that our lives all end up in plastic bags, and it seems it's true. I was truly dreading the task but told myself it had to be done. I couldn't face going through his paperwork or emails. That somehow felt like an intrusion. I committed to do that at some unspecified later date. One thing at a time.

I must have stood staring into space in the bedroom for at least ten minutes before I finally built up sufficient courage to open the wardrobe doors. I was crying when I eventually reached out to pull the doors towards me, tears rolling down. I held a familiar men's blue cotton shirt to my face, enjoying the touch of the soft cloth on my skin, taking in the emotive scent. And then I stuffed the shirt into a bag quickly with a shaking hand, followed by everything else, one item after another, my white wedding dress included. I just couldn't stand the sight of it any more. It seemed to bring my loss into even sharper focus, my grief still painfully raw.

I kept nothing back for selling as I'd planned, not a single thing despite my financial situation. Silly, I suppose, but that's how it was. I wanted it over with. I packed everything, all his clothes, shoes, and more. I did it in a frenzy of fevered activity over which it seemed I had little, if any, control. I packed and wept, sweating, overheated, and red in the face, working through my angst until all was done. I filled seven large bags in total, each packed to the brim and tied in a knot at the top. I struggled downstairs with one load after another, my legs aching and complaining when I eventually completed the task at about 3 p.m. that afternoon.

I sat on the bottom of the ancient wooden staircase and looked at those seven bags piled up around the front door, my chest heaving, my red eyes sore, and I decided I had to finish the job I'd begun. I couldn't stand to see them there mocking me for a second longer than I had to. They seemed to taunt me, a painful reminder of the glorious happiness I'd lost. I slipped twice on the icy ground as I carried each bag to the car, placing some in the boot and others on the back seat once the boot was full. And then I drove straight to Carmarthen, an eight-mile journey I completed in about twenty minutes, no longer than usual due to the recently salted roads. I dropped all the bags off at the same place, the Salvation Army charity shop on Lammas Street. Another customer helped me carry the bags from the car, for which I was grateful. There are good people in this world of ours as well as bad. The grey-haired man's kindness that afternoon was a welcome reminder of that. It was a brief flash of light in a world that had become all too dark.

I listened to an operatic compilation on my return drive to Ferryside, reminding me that there is still beauty in the world if we choose to acknowledge it. We're capable of such creative genius but such horrors too. Why do people like the one who killed my lovely James exist? It would be so much better if they didn't. I thought it then, and I do now. They offer nothing but misery; pain is their only contribution.

I was thinking much along those lines, trying without success to focus on a soaring female aria that filled the car with sound, when I drove past Margaret and Roy's impressive village home. I glimpsed at their detached property once, then again with a rapid turn of my head as I drove on by. I thought I might have imagined what I'd seen, or maybe I was mistaken. It couldn't be a 'For Sale' sign, could it? Really? I braked, quickly reversed, switched off the diesel engine with a turn of the key, and stared, open-mouthed. The house was indeed for sale. Neither of James's parents had said anything of the planned move to me, not a word. And they hadn't told my parents either, I confirmed that later that day. I considered knocking right then to find out what was happening, but it was a conversation I couldn't face. I'd seen very little of my in-laws since the funeral. We spoke on the phone, but only when absolutely necessary. That's how I told them about my pregnancy. Then, of course, they'd avoided the press conference for whatever reason, which left me seething. The more I thought about it, the more I didn't want to talk to them at all. If they were going, that was up to them. I still thought they'd let James down in a way I never could. And if even the knowledge I was carrying their son's child wasn't enough to make them keep me informed, then screw them! That's something I found hard to forgive.

24

The weeks passed, March became April, I'd had my first scan, I knew my baby's gender, and spring beckoned with all its new life promise. West Wales is particularly beautiful at that time of year. A season of vivid colours when trees come into leaf and wildflowers bloom. But for all that, my spirits didn't rise. Life went on; Margaret and Roy had moved back to London, and my gran was home from the rehab unit, but the police still hadn't made significant progress in bringing James's killer to justice. And that's what mattered to me most. I'd spoken to Ray again by phone that morning, the third of the month, and once again, he had nothing new to tell me.

I could hear that Ray's optimism was flagging, much like my own. It seemed he could no longer hide his growing pessimism, which I could relate to. I'd been going through the motions at work, doing my best but struggling to stay motivated. My patients' problems often seemed less serious than my own. And that proved challenging. I sometimes resented their expectations of my help, despite it being my job. I couldn't offer the best of me, and that just wasn't good enough. I feel bad about that now, although regrets achieve nothing at all. Not if we can't act on them, making for a better person. I think, in reality, I was suffering from depression, which I guess was inevitable given my recent loss. Nothing was diagnosed at the time, not formally, not beyond anxiety, it's my informed hypothesis, no more than that. Is there a notable difference between depression and grief? I'm really not sure there is.

I felt somewhat despondent after my brief conversation with Ray. The killer being caught was still so critical to me. It seemed the natural order of things, the logical next step, the only thing that made any sense. That's what happened in all those detective books I'd read, the bad guy got caught. But I'd realised, if not entirely accepted, that it might never happen in my world of woe. Life isn't always fair. The guilty don't always pay the appropriate price for their crimes. At least not in this life. Sometimes they get away with it. And that brutal realisation hit me hard. It seemed nothing could raise my flagging spirits for very long. Injustice ate away at me, beating me down.

I sat alone in my parked car that lunchtime rather than join the other nurses in the staffroom. They were a good bunch, friendly, intelligent and good-natured. But they didn't know James, not as I had. And that was a problem. For all their training and qualifications, I felt they couldn't possibly understand the experience of loss as it was for me. That may or may not have been true, but it was my truth. It's what I told myself, repeating it in my head without argument. I became increasingly convinced I needed someone else to talk to, a friend about my age, someone who truly understood what a wonderful young man James had been. And as I sat there, deep in meditative thought, pondering my new reality, Oliver came to mind. Now he seemed the obvious person. I asked myself why it took me so long to gradually realise. And I'm sure that's precisely how

Oliver wanted it. He may even have predicted it. Who knows? It wouldn't surprise me if he did. He was undoubtedly clever enough.

Looking back, I think Oliver was playing the long game. Biding his time until I finally contacted him was a stroke of inspired genius. It gave me the illusion of control, which was so very misleading. It couldn't have been further from the truth. Control, who was I kidding? He was pulling the strings somewhere in the background, patiently waiting. Although I'm sure he'd have contacted me soon enough had I not acted first. I'm certain that there's only so long he'd have waited. I walked straight into his trap, an innocent in a dangerous world. He was a predator. He fooled the world and did it well, hiding in plain sight, easy to like until you finally saw his true self. And he did all that because it suited his purpose. The man had needs. Needs he was willing to go to any lengths to fulfil. But I didn't know that then. That took time. But hold on, I'm getting ahead of myself again. I'll focus back on that day.

I waited until I got back to my rental cottage home before sending Oliver a message, reaching out, and using Facebook. That's how we'd communicated before, so it seemed the obvious choice. I made a quick mug of tea, added a splash of almond milk and a teaspoonful of honey, lit the gas fire on low to take the evening chill off, and then sat in the lounge in my favourite comfortable armchair, my fully charged tablet at the ready. I looked down at the bright screen, preparing to type. What to say and how to say it? Come on, Daisy, think. It wasn't an easy decision. I wanted to get the words exactly right because that mattered to me perhaps more than it should have. After a couple of minutes of thought, I began tapping the screen, finally deciding to ask Oliver about his life first rather than diving straight into my problems. Although I knew

what would come next. It was why I was messaging him, the
true reason for the contact. I had my needs, too. Had I known
the reality, I'd have run a mile. I'd never have contacted him
at all.

Hi Oliver, how are things? Any luck with the job interviews? I've been
wondering how it all went.

He replied almost immediately, in seconds, for which I was
grateful. Grateful! That's not easy for me to admit to myself or
anyone else. I feel so foolish. I really was that gullible. And I'd
set myself up. I was such an idiot. I bet the bastard was creaming
his fucking underpants. I bet he had the biggest hard-on of his
life. And I make no apologies for my language as I picture the
scene big and bright. It seems entirely appropriate. I loathe the
F-word, but I hate Oliver more.

Hi Daisy, it's lovely to hear from you again. It's been too long. No luck
with the jobs, I'm afraid. I'm still gardening, busy, busy, but I've got
another interview on Friday afternoon, so fingers crossed! Maybe I'll
have more luck this time. I've got a good feeling about this one. XXX

I was a people pleaser, less so now, but certainly then, not so
very long ago. I felt I had to ask more about him before focusing
on me, as I knew I inevitably would. It seemed like the right
thing to do. I typed one sentence, moving the conversation
along. In truth, I wasn't that interested in his life at all. It was my
idea of a convention, that's all. I could lie too.

Oh, that sounds interesting. Tell me more.

And he did, in more detail than I'd hoped or expected. He

began typing again after about thirty seconds, no more than that.

The interview is at the same school I mentioned before, the Catref Coch special needs place near Carmarthen. I thought the last interview went pretty well, and they've asked me back this time, so it's looking hopeful. I might be joining you in Carmarthenshire soon!!! I think I'd love being a teaching assistant. I'd be contributing something worthwhile. It's more me than manual work. At the end of the day, that's why I studied psychology. I want to work with people. And I like kids, so why not?

I thought his interview good news; more fool me. And it seemed our friendship was growing. He seemed so ready to share his feelings with me, as you would with a close friend. I liked that. I found it refreshing. Although I now think it was simply a tactic he used, sharing personal information, conveying liking, and drawing me in. And it worked; I took the bait. All of a sudden, I was interested. I no longer had to fake it. My feelings changed that quickly.

Ah, yeah, I know the school. It's a few miles past the leisure centre where James worked, on the opposite side of the road near the housing estate. I remember passing it. There's a running track outside and a couple of tennis courts.

Yeah, you've got it. That's the one.

A few seconds passed before he began typing again, but when he did, it was significant. He made his move.

I was thinking, my interview is down your way. How about the two of us meeting up before I head back to Swansea? It would be great to see you again. We could have a proper catch-up. And we could talk about James. I miss him. I think of him often. And I know you do too.

Oliver had me with that last sentence. It was as if he understood. He was smart, considered. I've no doubt he used James's memory against me. I think that was very probably planned. And if it was, it worked; Oliver was reeling me in, playing me like a hooked fish, something he was good at. I've come to realise he was something of an expert, seemingly one thing, and in reality, something very different. Maybe his psychological studies helped him with that. He could spot weaknesses. Drive his advantage home. I was on the hook, but he hadn't landed me yet.

It's a nice idea, but I'm working. What sort of time have you got in mind?

Another immediate reply, no delay. It seemed he could type a lot faster than me.

My interview is at 4. I was there for about an hour last time, but I think this time will be quicker because they already know me. There'll be some questions they won't need to ask me again. So I'm sure I could be in Carmarthen for 5 if that's good for you. I don't mind hanging about for a bit if it means seeing you. No rush. I've got nothing on that evening. What do you think? It would be a shame to miss the chance to meet up.

I drained my mug, head back, savouring the sweet local honey at the bottom, moving it around my mouth for a second or two before swallowing. It was a small indulgence I sometimes allowed myself. And I still wasn't eating as much as I should have, so the sugar hardly mattered. I could do with the calories. It seemed one of the few pleasures I had left. As I placed my empty mug aside, I was surprised to find myself hoping I could meet Oliver at the time suggested despite the obvious anxieties involved. It seemed almost everything made me nervous. Even something as seemingly ordinary as meeting someone I now thought of as a friend. I focused back on my tablet, tapping the screen, watching the letters become words.

Give me a minute. I'll check my diary. I should be able to work something out.

I think Oliver must have been on tenterhooks at that point, stressed, worried, and in suspense, although I didn't suspect that at the time. And it's all informed guesswork anyway. I can't be sure. I couldn't swear to it in court, not beyond all reasonable doubt. I think it is highly likely, that's all. But it still seemed like an ordinary conversation to me back then, amicable, a friendly chat between new friends, no more and no less. I looked at my digital calendar, returned to Facebook, and then started typing again, pleased by what I'd ascertained. I could finish work at five on the afternoon of Oliver's interview. It seemed to me that the timing worked well.

I could be in Carmarthen by about 5.30 if that's okay? I may be able to get there a little earlier, but I can't guarantee it. It depends on the traffic.

Another quick reply. It seems he didn't need any thinking time. I guess he knew I was well and truly hooked. And no doubt he didn't want me slithering off when he was so very close to success. The man was reeling me in one bit at a time.

YAY, that would be perfect. Where shall we meet? Where do you recommend? You know Carmarthen so much better than me. It's only a few times I've been there.

I'm now certain his words, as straightforward as they seemed, were a deception, a carefully constructed deceit aimed at achieving his goal. He was giving me that illusion of control again. *I* could choose our meeting place; *I* knew better than him. He was playing his best cards now, one after another. And I feel sure he knew he was winning. He had me exactly where he wanted me. And I didn't see it coming, not for a second. I began typing again, my enthusiasm growing, lightening my mood.

How about meeting at the nice veggie place in Merlin's Lane? I know the girl who runs it. It's always been one of my favourites, and James loved it, too. We sometimes used to go to an open mic night on a Thursday. Happy memories! I haven't been back, well, since, since he passed. Maybe it's time I did.

Oh, wow, it sounds great! Exactly my sort of place. Maybe we could have a bit of food, my treat. What do you think? Are you up for it? I don't often eat meat myself. I've been thinking of going vegan. If the place is as good as you say it is, it would be a shame to miss out.

That was a lie. I later found out that Oliver was an enthusiastic carnivore, not that that was of any real significance. I guess he was saying what he thought would best ingratiate himself; all part of his game. I wasn't too sure about the idea of a meal as I read his message. I still didn't have much appetite, although I knew I needed to up my calorie intake for the baby's sake sooner rather than later. My mum never stopped telling me and offering me encouragement, which I saw as nagging at the time.

But as I carefully considered my response to Oliver's seemingly ordinary suggestion of eating together, I thought maybe the time had come to act on my mum's guidance. I knew she was right; there was no denying it. And I hadn't socialised even once since James's passing, let alone shared a meal with a friend. Maybe the time had come. It felt like an obligation, unwelcome but necessary if life was ever to return to anything even remotely resembling normality. It was something I had to face at some point. So why not, then? That's what I asked myself. And I committed to a positive response. I dredged up some enthusiasm from somewhere deep inside me, conveying far more positivity than I felt when I started one-finger typing again, keen to seem normal and to feel normal too, for however brief a time. My anxiety was already kicking in again. I noticed my hands trembling as I started typing, despite the room's ambient warmth.

Yeah, why the hell not? Nice idea, let's do that. The food's lovely, and it'll give me something to look forward to. I've not been getting out much. It's time I did. And if you get the job, which it sounds like you're going to, it will be a celebration.

Why did I say so much? I can be so very needy. And vulnerable too. Above all, I was vulnerable. I don't know if he guessed my true feelings or took my message at face value. Perhaps he identified my feigned enthusiasm, my nervousness, or maybe not. I've thought about it a lot but never reached an adequate resolution. Either way, I've no doubt he was glad I agreed. Although, of course, he had his reasons for that. I remember smiling when I read his response. I know now he'd achieved his end. It was all he needed to say.

That's brilliant. I'll see you there. XXX

Oliver always began and ended our message threads with three kisses as he had then, as if he felt genuine affection for me. As if it was more than habit. And that was it. We were to meet for a meal, the arrangement made, the deal done. I'd been swept along by Oliver's subtle eagerness as he directed events with skilled aplomb, pulling my strings and making me dance to his tune. And I hadn't even shared my problems by the time we ended our conversation, not even one. That only hit me a few minutes after I switched off my iPad, placed it aside on a shelf, and planned to charge it later. No, I hadn't told him a frigging thing. The realisation even made me laugh. But that had nothing to do with amusement. It's something I sometimes do to relieve stress.

As I sat close to the warming fire, pondering developments, rocking to and fro in my seat, I quickly decided that it might be better to discuss my concerns with Oliver face to face. And at least now I'd have that opportunity. Yes, that made sense. It could wait until then. Our café meeting was only days away. It would happen soon enough. And a part of me was even looking forward to it despite my social anxiety. Although, unknown to me then, it would have been better if it hadn't happened at all. That's the way life is sometimes. We don't see what's coming our way.

25

Friday soon arrived. I was due to meet Oliver. And I thought about him several times during my working day on the ward, caring for one patient after another. I finished work just before 5 p.m., the sister telling me to go home when I started crying in a corridor, which in all honesty suited me just fine. It had already been a long and tiring week. I was feeling jaded, drained of empathy and ready for the weekend. No, *desperate* for the weekend. That's more accurate. I had very little left to give.

I left Llanelli and then drove to Carmarthen via Burry Port, Pembrey and Kidwelly, not the fastest available route possibly, due to the speed cameras, but certainly the most scenic in my opinion, passing as it does along the coast. I listened to music as I drove, trying to relax, classical, I think, but I can't be sure. I've got eclectic tastes in music depending on my mood.

I remember some things that happened that afternoon very clearly but other things not so much. The music is something of a blur. I've already established that. But as the miles passed, I clearly recall silently acknowledging I was feeling somewhat apprehensive about socialising for the first time since James's death. I think that's understandable and easy to forgive. But it wasn't all I was feeling. I have to admit there was a definite sense of anticipation. In truth, a part of me was quite looking forward to seeing Oliver. There was a certain appeal to our arrangement running alongside the nervous tension. That reality has been filed, locked away deep inside me from then until now. I'm gaining insights as I share my tale, not all of which are easy to accept. I'm so very far from perfect. A confession of sorts and not one I'm proud of. But I'm human, after all, so I'll allow myself that mitigation. We all have our flaws. And some more than others.

My approximately sixteen-mile journey to the pleasant west Wales market town took me about half an hour on quite busy roads. I parked in Carmarthen's King Street close to the iconic Lyric Theatre, exited the car, locked the doors in the interests of security, and then hurried in the direction of Merlin's Lane as a sudden downpour of hail began to fall, small balls of ice bouncing off the road and colouring the wide pavements white with surprising speed. The power of nature never fails to amaze me as it did then. There's a majesty to it, a beauty.

I rushed down the narrow lane on quick-moving feet, keen to escape the frozen rain, arriving at the café's door a minute or two later than planned. I saw Oliver sitting on a black leather sofa close to the serving counter as soon as I entered the orange-painted room with its striking mix of paintings and photographs by local artists covering three of the four walls. He had a beaming smile on his unconventionally handsome face as I slowly approached him, taking off my damp grey coat before sitting opposite him on a second smaller sofa, a low wooden table between us and a cluttered bookcase piled with various books and well-thumbed periodicals to my left. There was a white china cup half full of what looked like a herbal tea of some kind on the table in front of him. Oliver reached out, handing me a menu, most of which I already knew by heart. Its offerings hadn't changed since my regular visits when James was at my side. The place hadn't changed – the décor, the tasty fare, the bohemian ambience, the art – but my life had. That had changed so very much. And that reality came to mind now as I sat there, glancing nervously around the familiar room, wishing I could rewrite the past, searching for any crumb of comfort as my memories surrounded me mercilessly.

'It's good to see you again, Daisy,' Oliver said with an engaging grin. 'I feel we have a lot in common. I've been very much looking forward to seeing you today.'

It seemed like a strange introductory remark, but I didn't read anything into it. I thought maybe we did have things in common. Although why he felt the need to point that out so blatantly, I didn't know. I looked at the menu with a thin smile, more out of habit than anything else. I knew exactly what I was going to have. I'm a creature of habit, always have been and probably always will be. I had the same thing every time I went there.

I remember thinking Oliver had brushed his hair. It looked less tangled than when I'd last seen it. And it had returned to its natural brown. He'd made an obvious effort to look good. I don't know if that was for the interview, me, or both. But whatever his motivation, he looked surprisingly presentable in a sixties beatnik sort of way. Yeah, he scrubbed up well. And I quite fancied him. Not an easy thing to admit.

'Have you ordered?' I asked.

Oliver pointed at his china cup on the table next to a small stainless-steel teapot. 'Just a berry tea. I thought I'd wait for you before ordering food. You know the place. You're the expert. What do you recommend?'

There he was, giving me that misleading perception of control again, encouraging me to take the lead on something of no long-term consequence. As if my opinion mattered even one little bit. Like hell it did! If only I'd realised that then. It was all about him. But he hid it well. I was prancing to his tune. Unaware of his influence as he steered our interactions, first one way and then another, directing the dance of life. He had power. I just didn't recognise it yet. I was thinking of James, the place, the food, my memories flooding back.

'Everything on the menu is great,' I said, feeling a little more confident now, on familiar ground. And then I went into far more detail than I needed to, prattling on, I think, due to nerves. 'I usually have a mushroom burger with a salad and some sweet tomato chutney. It's all organic, freshly made. I'm going to have that with a glass of mineral water. I always used to have a fresh banana almond milkshake with a sprinkling of cinnamon, but I don't fancy one today.'

Oliver smiled again, not as widely as before, but warmly nonetheless. I remember thinking the expression lit up his face. And as much as I hate to admit this, at that moment, he reminded me of James. Not Oliver's look, although I did now see a slight resemblance, the line of his jaw, the shape of his mouth. I'm referring to the persona he chose to present. He had youthful energy, so full of life, almost infectious. I've no doubt it's who he wanted me to see. A warm, friendly, caring individual who was easy to talk to. A character he'd created. A nice guy act that was oh so very convincing.

'I'll have the same,' he said with obvious enthusiasm, I suspect feigned but maybe not. He could be tough to read. 'If it's good enough for you,' he continued, 'then it's good enough for me. I don't think I've ever eaten a mushroom burger before. This is going to be a first.'

That voice, the southern English accent. Was there a resemblance to James there, too? A similarity I hadn't previously appreciated. Could I hear James's voice in his? I shook my head, blinking the thought away, focusing back on our interaction, telling myself to get a grip before I made a complete fool of myself. I was feeling more emotional than the situation justified. I'm sure he saw that. I'm certain it pleased him. My vulnerability showed.

'The mushroom burgers are surprisingly tasty here,' I said, pulling myself together as best I could. 'They're quite meaty. You're going to love them, James did. He usually ordered two. They make them on the premises. This place is called the Good Health Café for good reason. There's none of that processed crap you get in some places.'

Oliver had just placed his menu back on the table when the lovely red-haired café owner appeared from the small kitchen located behind the serving counter to say hello and take our order with a friendly smile. She was her usual cheery, busy self, which didn't surprise me at all. James used to joke she was a bit bossy, but I never thought that myself. Had she been male, he'd have called her assertive. The welcome was always warm. I don't think she'd heard about my loss. I'm certain if she had, she'd have said something. I quickly realised I'd missed the place. Oliver let me do the talking. He sat there in silence, allowing me to take the lead. I'm sure that was deliberate as he watched and listened, never taking his eyes off me, not looking away. I returned my attention to him as soon as she walked away, no doubt to start cooking. She did a lot of the work herself.

'How did the interview go?' I said, thinking I should probably have asked before. Although I'd already surmised he'd likely had good news, given his upbeat mood. It couldn't have been more evident.

He gave another beaming smile, the widest yet, his eyes shining bright. He didn't quite punch the air, but he seemed close. It wouldn't have surprised me if he had. He sat more upright, shoulders back, pushing out his chest, the cock of the walk. 'I got the job!'

He'd said it loudly, clearly enunciating each word, as if announcing his success to me and all the other customers seated at nearby tables. And at that moment, I was pleased for him. I really was, despite my fragile state of mind and swinging moods. It seemed Oliver's life was on track even as mine had fallen apart. I thought he at least would be doing a job that made him happy, something that mattered to him. Although I now think he only took the job because of me. I'd argue it was the one reason he applied. To get nearer, to draw me in. But I thought so very differently back then. The realisation took time. All of a sudden, I felt a little agitated that Oliver had obtained a job he wanted while James hadn't. But I didn't let it show.

'Oh, that's brilliant, congratulations!' I said. 'I felt sure you'd get it. When do you start?'

He sipped his tea, wetting his lips. He swallowed only a tiny amount. I could see the slight movement in his throat. Everything was done very precisely. He never gulped anything down. Not that I ever saw. He was a far more controlled and calculating man than it appeared.

'It's all happening incredibly quickly,' he said. 'I'll be starting as soon as the safeguarding checks come back. I was told it shouldn't be too long. Apparently, a couple of weeks at most, maybe less. That came as a bit of a surprise. I wasn't expecting it to be quite so soon. But when they asked, I said yes without even thinking. I'm keen to start, and it seems they're keen to have me. That's what the head said, anyway. So I thought, why not start quickly? It's not like I've got any other commitments. I've booked some gardening jobs for the next few weeks, but they're easily cancelled. I'll just have to make a few phone calls. Then I'm good to go.'

'That's great, Oliver. I'm pleased for you.' That's all I could think to say. Social situations still weren't easy for me. One minute I was up, and the next, down. My mood had swung again. I was feeling a little awkward being there at all. I tried to hide it as best I could, but I don't think convincingly. He could read me better than I could ever have imagined. He had powerful instincts to complement his psychological training. He understood what to say and when to say it to his best advantage. He was brighter than me, like James had been. They had that in common too. I don't think I ever stood a chance.

Oliver looked at me with a pensive expression now, seemingly concerned at my change of demeanour but keeping his mouth shut as the café owner delivered our order to the table. He waited until she'd returned to the kitchen before talking, and then he spoke quietly, as if not wanting anyone on nearby tables to overhear. It was so very different from his earlier announcement. He was calmer now, his speech slightly slower, lower in tone, as if he was wary of saying the wrong thing.

'Yeah, I'm pleased about the job. It's a welcome fresh start but not without its complications. I'll have to drive back and forth from Swansea until I can find somewhere to live down this way. It shouldn't be too much of a problem, although I'm a bit worried about the rush-hour traffic. I don't want to be stuck in the van for hours on end, five days a week. Traffic can get crazy busy on a workday morning.'

He was likely setting another trap for me at that stage, setting his plan in motion and casting his net. And if he was, I jumped right in. I made it all too easy for him, far too easy. In some ways, I let myself down.

'What are you thinking of doing, renting or buying?' I asked, back in control of my feelings, looking him in the eye as the remains of my burger cooled on my plate.

He laughed, knife and fork in hand, speaking while eating, clearly relishing the food. 'It's going to be renting for a while yet, and that's if I can find somewhere cheap enough to afford at all.' He laughed again, which seemed slightly forced. 'Though I might even buy somewhere nice overlooking the sea if I win the lottery. I've always liked the beach. Maybe I should start buying a ticket. I might have more luck then. What do you think?'

I looked at him and smiled. 'Yeah, that might be an idea. You've got to be in it to win it. Although I've never won more than ten quid.'

His seemingly good humour meant I was starting to relax again, if only slightly. His chatty demeanour had that effect. I'm sure as intended. I hadn't lost my sense of humour, not totally. He watched me closely, changing the direction of the conversation again, taking his time. He didn't rush things; he was clever. I might have seen through him if he had. It all seemed so natural, such an unremarkable meeting between two new friends getting to know each other a little better in convivial surroundings.

Oliver forked a small piece of tasty mushroom burger into his open mouth, chewed and swallowed, washing it down with a sip of berry tea. He looked directly at me, again not looking away. I remember thinking he hardly ever blinked. Sometimes it felt as if his eyes were peering into my very soul as if he could read my mind at will.

'Enough about me. More importantly, how are things with you, Daisy? Any more news from the police?'

I shook my head forlornly, back in the doldrums, which often happened and still does. He'd emphasised the word *you*, as if me and my feelings truly mattered to him. As if my well-being was as important to him as it was to me. I was becoming increasingly comfortable in his company as the minutes ticked by, and I was only too ready to talk. It seemed a therapy of sorts, as if he were my counsellor, a confidant.

'I spoke to the detective inspector in charge of the investigation again this morning, as it happens, and there's still nothing. I can't understand it. It seems mad. It's as if the killer has disappeared off the face of the Earth. I really don't think the police have got a clue.'

He put down his knife and fork, reached out his right hand, and gently squeezed my arm. It seemed to offer solace.

'Hopefully, they'll catch the bastard very soon,' he said. 'I'd string him up by his balls were it up to me.'

I blinked as warm tears welled in my eyes. I could never forget my loss for very long, whatever the distractions. It ate away at me, making me cry. I know Oliver knew all that. He understood grief. It was my kryptonite, which he could use to manipulate me almost at will. I was back on an emotional roller-coaster, once again speeding towards despair. And then I shared something which had been playing on my mind. Something I'd hardly been able to admit even to myself, let alone anyone else. I shuddered. And then the words poured out of me. I blurted it all out. It was as if a dam had opened. It seemed I couldn't stop. I spoke so fast that the words almost blurred, one blending into another.

'I, er, I haven't even collected James's ashes from the funeral home yet. They're still there waiting for me. I've thought about it so many times, so full of good intentions, but I just haven't been able to face actually doing it. I want to scatter his ashes in the Tywi Estuary at full tide, close to the Ferryside jetty with a view of the castle, near where James and I spoke and connected for the first time. I know some might think it a little strange after James was found washed up on a beach. But I think it's what he'd want. I really do. I know I would in his place. We both loved that spot. It was our special place, his and mine.'

I brought a shaky hand to my forehead, my shoulders curled. 'Oh God, I'm awful,' I said. 'What the hell's wrong with me? Why have I waited so long? I should have done it long before now.'

Oliver reached out, squeezing my shoulder, a look of what seemed pained sympathy on his face. His tone was reassuring. Yes, the rat played it to perfection, an Oscar-worthy performance. Such a devious scumbag. I think that sums him up well enough. But his words were music to my ears. He said precisely what I wanted to hear. And he seemed to say it out of kindness, generosity of spirit.

'You're not awful, Daisy. You're human, that's all. Don't beat yourself up. You don't deserve that, you least of all. You're one of the nicest people I've ever met. You're beautiful inside and out. James was fortunate to be with you for as long as he was.'

I lowered my gaze, still thinking about the ashes, imagining a lonely urn sitting on a shelf.

'It doesn't feel that way to me,' I said, very close to tears again.

He tapped the tabletop three times with the horizontal handle of his knife, drawing my attention like never before. And then another announcement, stated with enthusiasm. 'Look, I've had a thought. And I'll understand if you say, no; no pressure. But how about we do it together, you and me?'

I made a face. It was the last thing I expected him to say.

'What – collect James's ashes?'

He nodded slowly, just once, almost a bow.

'Well, yes, if you like, why not? It's something you need to do, and I'd be happy to come with you if it makes it a little bit easier.

James meant a lot to me. It's the least I could do. All you have to do is say the word.'

I was still in two minds. The idea of holding that urn in my hands wasn't an easy thing to face. Not even with a friend at my side.

'Can I... can I think about it?'

Oliver grimaced, momentarily clenching his jaw. But the expression quickly left his face to be replaced by another smile, less convincing this time but a smile nonetheless. Nothing in his demeanour rang any alarm bells, not for me, although other women might have seen it differently through more experienced eyes. To me, Oliver seemed nothing but pleasant, caring, sensitive, a thoroughly thoughtful man with my best interests at heart. His words confirmed that impression, exactly as I suspect he intended. I doubt he ever said very much at all without a hidden motive. That's how he operated. And he did that now, implementing his plan, so seemingly understanding, non-judgemental in the extreme.

'Of course you can think about it,' he stressed. 'You're in control. Nothing is going to happen unless you decide it is. But please don't hesitate to contact me anytime if you want to go ahead. I'll be only too willing to help.'

'Okay, thank you, I will.'

And then he surprised me with what he said next, knocking me off kilter, sweeping me along like an irresistible tide.

'Collecting the ashes sometime tomorrow would be perfect for me if you decide that suits you. I've got to come down this way anyway. And I think if we did go ahead, you'd be glad you did. Some things are best done quickly. Otherwise, you're going to be worrying about it endlessly. It's always going to be somewhere in the back of your mind. Best get it done, don't you think?'

I thought about what he'd said as we both began eating again, one tasty mouthful after another. They seemed wise words, and there was some truth in them. That's why his initiative worked for him as well as it did.

'Um, I'm... er... I'm not even sure the chapel of rest is open on a Saturday,' I said a little reticently. But he was never going to let it go.

'Why don't you give the undertaker a ring to find out? There's no harm in trying.'

I screwed up my face, pushing up a sleeve, and glancing at my watch. 'What, now?' I said, my voice faltering.

'Best get it over with, don't you think? Come on. You're in control. I know it's what you really want.'

Maybe I did. I thought he was probably correct. I was that easily influenced. I laid my cutlery aside on the edge of my plate, took a paper tissue from my pocket, and dabbed at my eyes. 'Yeah, I suppose you're right.'

'Of course I am; that's the spirit. Come on, where's your phone? You can do this, girl. You're doing great. Make that call.'

I noticed my hand shaking again as I took the mobile from my brown faux-leather handbag. 'The funeral director said to ring if I needed him for any reason, whatever the time. He seemed like a nice guy. It can't be an easy way to make a living.'

'Have you got the number?'

I nodded twice with only slight movements of my head, still hesitant, trying to build up the courage to act as Oliver encouraged me on. 'Um, yeah, yeah, I have. It's, er, it's in my contacts.'

He pressed his lips together, changing the contours of his face before another smile. 'Come on, dial that number. Do it now while I'm here with you. Don't even think about it, don't delay, just do it. You'll be very glad you did. It's not something you can put off forever. Please do it for James. You know you want to.'

And I did exactly that; I rang, speaking to the undertaker on my mobile a few minutes after 6 p.m.. He didn't seem in the least bit surprised or fazed to hear from me. And he was charming and helpful, just as he'd been when arranging the funeral. I arranged to pick up the urn from the Kidwelly chapel of rest at 12 the very next afternoon. And Oliver was absolutely correct. It was a relief to finally make the appointment, even if it was so very soon. I thanked Oliver for his encouragement with genuine gratitude after I ended the call, putting the phone back in my handbag with a relieved sigh. And then it was more of the same. Oliver's apparent support and praise were almost gushing; if anything, it was all a little over the top. He may have risked over-playing his hand just slightly, but he got away with it. In truth, I lapped it up. He got the job done.

'Very well done, Daisy,' he said. 'That call can't have been easy. Good for you. You're a star. I'm so glad I could help. I can't believe how much more relaxed you look. Wow! I can see a burden's lifted. Now, if you give me your full address, I'll pick you up tomorrow morning at 11.30 a.m., if you think that's early enough. We don't want to be late for something so important. What do you think? I can be earlier if you need me to. Just say the word. It's up to you. You're in control.'

He used that final line often, driving his message home. And nothing could have been further from the truth. I gave Oliver my address as he'd asked; he made a note of it on his phone, and I said his suggested time should be fine. Ferryside to Kidwelly is only about a ten-minute journey at most. I agreed because it seemed the sensible thing to do. I was swept away by his influence. He couldn't have known I'd talk about the ashes. How could he possibly? He wasn't psychic. But once I did, he pounced, no doubt taking full advantage because he knew he could. He was an opportunist as well as a planner. He was nothing if not a versatile man, complicated, layered and deep. We all have our talents, and those were his. He played to his Machiavellian strengths, cunning, scheming and unscrupulous. What a total and utter bastard that man truly was.

Oliver and I sat there finishing our meals together after that, clearing our plates, him a minute or two before me. I think it was the first meal I'd actually finished since the disappearance of my husband. I guess that was a triumph of sorts. I was grateful to Oliver for that too. And then he walked me back to my car, insisting he didn't want to leave me alone even for a second until I was safely seated in the driver's seat. It was as if he cared. He was good at making a positive impression when it suited him, and he did on me. I wouldn't go as far as to say I enjoyed our café meeting, certainly not all of it, but I was pleased I'd gone. That was his achievement. He'd accomplished that goal.

Oliver stood outside the theatre in King Street, waving as I drove off as he had at the wedding and funeral, although it wasn't raining this time. The hail had stopped by then, the sky now virtually clear of clouds as an easterly wind blew. He was still waving, his long hair blowing in the breeze as I looked in my car's rear-view mirror, approaching NatWest Bank on my right and then turning left past the Queens Hotel towards my Ferry-side home. I'd finally lost sight of him. But it would only be a matter of hours until I saw him again. And I was glad about that. Glad! I appreciated what I saw as his support. I can't believe I'm admitting that, even to myself. But it's how it was. The scheming bastard! He'd already got under my skin.

26

I looked out of the lounge window at 10.50 a.m. the following morning to see Oliver's rusty white van pull up outside the cottage. There was a green-painted logo on the side of the aged vehicle advertising gardening services, which didn't surprise me in the slightest. I clearly remember the time because I looked at the brass carriage clock sitting on the mantelpiece above the gas fire, a gift from my parents. Oliver was early. I recall thinking that too. I'd slept for no more than two or three hours, tossing and turning, one concern after another, worrying about what the day would bring.

I'd listened to Radio Wales while making breakfast, then performed a few necessary chores, distracting myself, but with only minor success. Collecting the ashes was never far from the forefront of my mind. And now Oliver had arrived. It was happening. There'd be no going back on the arrangement, no putting it off. He'd driven all the way from Swansea. Oh God! I'd be collecting James's earthly remains. The decision was made.

I'd already opened the front door when Oliver began striding up the concrete path towards my rented cottage home.

I noted he was dressed more casually than I'd seen him since our Swansea University days, the wetsuit apart, wearing straight blue jeans, a check shirt and a red needlecord jacket. His hair was pulled back and tied in a tight ponytail. I noticed a gold metal stud in his right earlobe for the first time, which caught the morning light. But what struck me most was his ability to smile with his eyes despite his mouth being still. And he did that now, right up to the time he said hello. I reciprocated on the doorstep, and then he stepped forward to hug me, the first time he ever had. It surprised me, and I think I stiffened.

He held me for a little longer than was comfortable, and I felt a sense of relief when he finally let me go. It wasn't an easy interaction; guilt my predominant feeling. I was silently asking myself what James would think were he looking down from whatever world he now inhabited. My soulmate wasn't even speaking to Oliver at the time of his death, and now here I was, inviting that same man into our home and to collect his ashes. The thought didn't sit comfortably as I turned, leading Oliver through the small hall and towards the lounge, speaking as I went. I knew my voice sounded trepidatious, but there was nothing I could do about it, not a thing. It seemed I wasn't in control at all.

'Come, come on in, thanks for coming, we've, er, we've got time for a quick cuppa if you fancy one? I, er, I wouldn't mind one myself. I didn't sleep well last night. I could do with a tea.'

Oliver nodded enthusiastically before sitting in what had been James's favourite seat, something else I found hard to accept. Oliver seemed to be very relaxed, at his ease, so very different to me. I could clearly see James frowning in my mind's eye. I felt inclined to ask Oliver to move, but, of course, I didn't. I thought he was there to help. I really did. The last thing I wanted was to be unpleasant or rude. I've never been an impolite person. Such things aren't in my nature.

'Black, strong and one sugar, please,' he said. 'I've cut down from two now I'll be stopping the gardening. I don't want to start putting on weight.'

Oliver was rangy and slim. His comment seemed wholly unneeded. I was surprised for a second time when he stood almost immediately after sitting, following me to the cottage kitchen. It seemed overfamiliar, as if he were treating my home as his own. But I pushed the thought from my mind, reminding myself he was there for my benefit, not his. He stood at the sink, looking out on the overgrown garden at the back of the stone building as I switched on the kettle.

'The daffodils are beautiful,' he said, still peering through the glass. 'But the garden needs some attention. I'd be happy to do that for you when I have time. The grass starts growing at a crazy rate this time of year.'

'I keep meaning to do it myself.'

'You leave it to me.'

I said thank you, and I meant it, one less chore. Although I wasn't entirely certain I wanted him coming again. I don't think I really knew what I felt. It seemed to change from one minute to the next.

Oliver turned to look at me as I dropped teabags into two blue glazed mugs made by a local potter. His looking at me made me even more anxious, acutely self-aware, as if a spotlight was shining upon me. Or as if I was an animal in a zoo. Because Oliver wasn't just looking at me, his eyes were scanning my entire body with inquisitive intent, up, down and back again. I'd been wearing loose clothing when I met him at the café, but now as I stood in the light of the window wearing a red dress that had been one of James's favourites, I knew Oliver could see the shape of my body. And it was obviously of interest to him. I could see it in his face. My body wasn't yet showing my baby's growth. But for some reason I still can't understand, I told him I was pregnant.

He focused on my abdomen for what felt like an age before finally raising his eyes to meet my nervous gaze. For the briefest of moments, I thought he looked angry; there was a fleeting tension, a serpent-like coldness, something about his eyes. But I told myself I was being ridiculous, that I must have imagined it as a lopsided grin replaced his momentary frown, his head tilted to one side. I looked back at him, blinking, silently questioning my judgement. Surely I imagined his anger, didn't I? I must have seen something that wasn't there, my mind clouded by lack of sleep. Yes, of course, that explained it. I thought it and believed it, convincing myself of my rationale. It was the only thing I thought made any sense. I was inclined to trust.

'Wow, Daisy, massive congratulations; why didn't you say something at the café? I'm assuming it's James's. You must be over the moon.'

I stiffened again, sucking in the air, blowing it out, and allowing the nearest unit to support my weight. I remember thinking Oliver had spoken out of turn. I think that was his first mistake that day. Maybe the shock of my pregnancy set him off track. 'Of *course* James is the father,' I snapped back, making no attempt to hide my irritation. 'Who else would it be?'

He held his hands up at shoulder level, palms forward, fingers spread as if surrendering at gunpoint. His face was ashen, the blood draining away. His expression conveyed what seemed genuine regret. For a moment, I thought he might start weeping.

'I am so very sorry, Daisy. Of course it's James's. I can't believe I said something so stupid. It just came out wrong. I wasn't thinking – what a ridiculous thing for me to say. Please accept my apologies. I hope you can forgive me.'

My mood softened slightly. But I was hurt. I wanted him to know that. 'It *was* stupid. There's never been anyone else. I love James as much now as I did, well, you know, before, before he passed. Before some bastard killed him and tore my life apart.'

Oliver slumped, his shoulders lowered over his chest, and yet there was something about his face that, just for a fraction of a second, made me think he didn't feel nearly as gloomy as his body language implied. But I pushed the idea from my mind, thinking my thought process was ridiculous, again not trusting my judgement, a familiar theme. Looking back, I'm sure Oliver must have been both pleased and relieved there was no other man on the scene. But if that was the case, he gave me no further clue. He was back in control as he sat on a tall stool at the break-fast bar. I finished making the tea, glad of something to do with my hands. I was relieved to let the argument go; friction was the last thing I wanted or needed. The situation was already stressful enough without that. I offered Oliver a biscuit, a peace offering, a gluten and dairy-free ginger nut, one of my favourites, which he readily accepted with a smile. I could see he'd relaxed again. And to a lesser extent, I had too.

'I'm so happy for you, Daisy. When's the baby due?' he asked, the biscuit in one hand, his mug in the other.

I smiled. Thoughts of my baby always raised my mood. 'Early September.'

'That's brilliant. I can see you're excited. Have you thought of names?'

I blew my drink to cool it and sipped, thinking back to the honeymoon. To talk of baby names. That happy time. 'I'm going to go for something Welsh. Deryn for my girl. It translates as bird. James and I spoke about it in Lanzarote.'

'That's excellent, great choice. And a little girl, wonderful.'

I smiled. 'I'll be happy if the baby is safe and well. That's what matters the most. And I'll tell her all about her brilliant father as soon as she's old enough. I want my child to know what a lovely man James was. He'll never be forgotten.'

Oliver checked his watch, a large white face, stainless-steel case and strap with a red bezel, for diving. I don't know why the watch stuck in my mind as clearly as it did. It was a chunky style James would have liked but not particularly to my taste. Maybe that's the reason.

'James would be very proud of you. You're going to be a fantastic mother.' He paused, finished his tea, and then continued, looking at his watch again, pushing up the sleeve of his cord jacket higher than required. 'Do you think we'd better make a move? Time's getting on. We don't want to be late.'

In truth, I was still dreading seeing that urn. I hated the thought of holding it in my hands. I knew it would bring death back into sharp focus, as the coffin had. James's earthly remains were contained within. How could it not engender strong emotion? But maybe that was the point of it all, one final goodbye before we were reunited in spirit at some future date. I knew it was something I had to face. I raised a hand, fidgeting with my hair, tugging the fringe, feeling flustered. I glanced at the wall clock.

'Yeah, yeah, you're right. Thanks again for doing this with me; it's appreciated.'

'Not a problem at all.'

I began making my way back towards the hall and the base of the stairs. 'Give me a minute. I need to pop to the bathroom and then get my coat.'

Oliver approached the front door and turned the knob. 'Try not to be too long. I'll be waiting for you in the van.' He gave a little laugh. 'I've even given the inside a good clean, hoovered it and everything. The first time since I've owned it. Nothing but the best for Daisy Earl.'

I thought Oliver's light-hearted comments somewhat misplaced, given the circumstances, but I again gave him the benefit of the doubt. I thought maybe I was being oversensitive. I knew I had that tendency, particularly since my loss. He closed the front door after him as I climbed the stairs, glad of a few moments alone, an opportunity to compose myself. I answered nature's call, washed my hands at the sink with vanilla-scented soap, and then looked into the bathroom mirror, my eyes only inches from the glass, studying myself, questioning who I really was as my reflection stared back at me accusingly. Events had taken such a rapid and surprising turn. My mind raced as I stood there, one invasive thought after another. Why on earth was I collecting my dead husband's ashes with a man who, in truth, I barely knew? A man whom James had rejected as a friend. I could have asked my mum to go to the chapel of rest with me, or my dad, I could have asked him. So why Oliver, for God's sake? What the hell? Why him, of all people?

And then it dawned on me, a light bulb moment. Suddenly all was clear. I was going with Oliver because he'd asked me. That was why. It was all happening that very day because of *him*. I hadn't asked him at all. But why did I agree to his offer so quickly? Was it weakness? Should I have refused? Maybe yes, or maybe no. Oh well, it was too late now. I had to get on with it. And perhaps that wasn't such a bad thing. It was well overdue.

I turned away from the mirror and crossed the small landing, still conflicted but accepting of my fate. The old wooden staircase creaked as I headed back down to the hall with a feeling of resigned acceptance. It seemed a *fait accompli*, a done deal. And maybe I was overthinking things – something else I often do. At least I was going. Surely that's what mattered most.

I pulled on my coat, grey and waterproof with a hood, and then headed down the path towards the van while attempting to still my troubled mind, my ruminations no longer in overdrive. Oliver leant across the passenger seat to open the door for me as I approached. And then I got in, quickly settling in my seat, thinking the inside of the vehicle much cleaner than the outside. The cabin appeared faded and dated but surprisingly immaculate as I looked around. I couldn't help but notice the smell of bleach or something similar as Oliver started the diesel engine on the second turn of the key. I think he'd sprayed some kind of pine or floral air freshener to try to mask the stink, but if anything, it made it worse. I considered asking about the unpleasant odour but, in the end, didn't. He'd already said he'd cleaned the van in preparation for the day, and I thought he'd put himself out on my behalf, so such an enquiry seemed impolite. The chemical began to irritate my eyes, making them sting, but I tried to ignore it as best I could.

Oliver reversed a short distance, performed an efficient U-turn in the quiet road, pressed his foot down on the accelerator, and we were on our way. He chatted about one thing or another as he drove up the steep hill out of the village toward Kidwelly, but I wasn't in the mood for conversation. I had other things on my mind. I remember thinking the smell seemed to be getting worse. And I think Oliver must have thought the same because he switched on the fan and opened a window, which helped.

I felt physically sick as Oliver pulled up outside the chapel of rest a short time later. Not because of the smell but due to the task at hand. I had a sinking feeling as he switched off the engine, pulled up the handbrake and turned towards me, swivelling slightly in his seat.

'Do you want me to come in with you?' he asked, a sad, sympathetic look on his face.

Why was I there with him? Of all people, *him*! I asked myself that again before replying.

'No, this is something I need to do myself. I'd be grateful if you didn't come in. I hope that's okay.'

He pressed his lips together and nodded. 'I'll be waiting here. Take as long as you need. There's no rush at all. We'll do this however suits you best. You're in control.'

I was always in control, according to him. Like hell I was! It couldn't have been further from the truth.

'Thanks, Oliver. I appreciate your help.' And I did. They weren't empty words. What a naïve fool I really was.

I left the van, entering the chapel of rest to be greeted by the undertaker, who was his usual sensitive and supportive self. The man really was good at his job.

'Are you ready?' he asked. 'Do you need me to give you a moment?'

'I'm okay, thanks.'

'Have you got someone with you?'

And, of course, I did. Oliver had made certain of that. He'd made it happen. But at least he wasn't standing at my side. 'Someone is waiting for me outside,' I said.

The undertaker fetched the urn, handed it to me, and asked me if all was well. And I said it was, the reality not nearly as traumatic as I'd feared. He was kind, making an emotional situation as easy as possible. I appreciated that too.

Oliver asked me the time of the full tide as we drove back to Ferryside a short time later. I think he further involved himself in the day's events, worming his way in, ingratiating himself, and making himself increasingly indispensable, things he did well. I'd already checked the tide times online that morning. The full tide was at 4 p.m. that afternoon. The sun was shining, bathing the west Wales countryside in a light, so very beautiful. And as we reached the brow of a hill, approaching my Ferryside home with a stunning view of the estuary, I told Oliver I planned to scatter the ashes that very day. I noticed him swallowing hard. Was that a tear in his eye? It seemed it was. As I've said before, the man knew how to create an impression. He was a master of illusion. Nothing about him was as it seemed.

'Do you mind if I hang about and come to the beach with you?' he suddenly asked when we were only a couple of minutes away from the cottage. 'I'd really like to be there. I'd stay well out of the way at the crucial time if that's what you want. But I'd like to pay my last respects to a special friend.'

Oh, shit! That was something else I hadn't expected or anticipated, another surprise. Not a particularly welcome one, but for some reason I can't understand, I didn't object. Maybe saying yes seemed easier than refusing. I was particularly emotionally fragile that day. So easy to manipulate, so easy to play.

I placed the urn carefully on the cottage kitchen windowsill a short time later, making a light lunch, just brown toast with honey, while Oliver waited for me in the lounge. He was reading one of James's books when I carried a laden tray into the room, tears still welling in my eyes. James was back in our home, and yet he wasn't. That seemed a cruel reality as if the urn and its gritty grey contents were mocking me, a reminder of my grief. And now, another man was in his place, sitting exactly where James should have been. And Oliver wasn't even close to second-best. He was a shadow of the love I'd known. He wasn't fit to lace James's shoes.

Oliver stood to take the tray from me after placing the book aside, still trying to seem helpful, no doubt wanting to be liked.

His plan depended on it. He didn't just fancy me. He wanted me for his own. I didn't realise that then. But that time would come.

I couldn't eat. I couldn't face it. But Oliver did; he finished my toast, too, even the slice I'd nibbled before leaving it on my plate. I almost drifted off in my chair after drinking my tea, physically and emotionally exhausted, and my eyes closed as I yawned.

'I'll sort this lot out and wash up,' he said, pointing at the dirty plates and mugs. 'Why don't you head up to bed to get some rest? I'll wake you in plenty of time for the tide.'

I was so tired. It seemed like a good idea. He'd made me feel cared for, supported. 'Are you sure that's okay?' I asked, hoping the answer was yes.

'Of course I am. This is your day. Whatever works best for you.'

'I think I'll take the urn up with me.'

He began loading the tray. 'Good idea. Do you want me to carry it upstairs for you? Or are you going to be okay?'

I didn't want him touching it, not even once. James was mine. 'No, no, I can do it, thanks. But please knock on the ceiling at a 3.45 if I'm not up. Or you can shout up the stairs. I want to be on the beach by five to.'

He smiled, tray in hand. 'Will do, not a problem. Now try to relax.'

'Are you sure you don't mind waiting? You did say at the café there's something you need to do down this way.'

'That's all cancelled. You're my number one priority. Now get some sleep, and I'll read the book. And I'll wake you at the right time. There's nothing to worry about; you're in control.'

27

The beautiful estuary beach and surrounding area were predictably quiet when I carried the urn along the wooden jetty jutting out over the fast-flowing mix of fresh and saltwater at just before four that afternoon. I was grateful it was dry again after an earlier brief shower. I walked cautiously over the slightly uneven wooden planks, acutely aware of the unborn child inside me, small tentative steps, the urn held tightly in front of me with both hands until I reached the jetty's end. And then I stopped, looking to the right and left, taking in the lovely vista, feeling sad but glad to have known my lovely James for as long as I did. I told myself insistently that having loved and lost was better than not having loved at all. I met my soulmate; we were one for a precious time, which is more than many can claim.

I looked out across the wide expanse of wine-dark water at the imposing Norman castle opposite and cried, tears flowing freely down my face, falling at my feet. James and I had always planned to go there together, to take the small ferry from Ferry-side to Llansteffan, to enjoy a picnic and the glorious views, but for some reason, we never did. And now it was too late; he was gone, nothing but ashes left clutched in my hands. I silently cursed his killer and the police for not catching the bastard. Anger swelled inside me, bubbling to the surface from somewhere deep inside, threatening to erupt until I finally composed myself, taking hold of my raging emotions as best I could. There would be plenty of time for anger. Now was not that time. Deep breaths, deep breaths, exhale slowly and count to three.

I said a short prayer of devotion and love, looking up at the sky for a few brief seconds before removing the urn's lid and slowly pouring the gritty grey contents into the dark water to be washed away by the tide to the open sea, with Cefn Sidan's beach to the left and Pendine Sands to the right. I watched, looking down now, as James's final remains disappeared before my eyes. I must have stood there looking deep into the water for at least ten minutes after that. I'm not really sure for how long. I lost track of time. And then, when I could take no more, I returned to the parking area bordering the beach, an area of raised concrete and gravel, where Oliver was standing waiting for me in front of the yacht club. He'd been standing there silently watching the entire time. He did a lot of watching. It was something that defined him.

'Are you okay, Daisy?' he asked, reaching out to gently touch my arm, as was his habit. He'd done it so often that it became familiar, almost expected. The change in my perception really did happen that quickly. And the human contact, the very experience of being touched, sometimes felt good. I didn't always pull away. But I did now, taking a backward step, frowning. I didn't want Oliver's hand on me, not even for a single second, which from the look of surprised concern on his face worried him a lot more than it should have. He looked almost panic-stricken for a beat before forcing a thin smile, looking past me rather than meeting my eyes. I put it down to the awkwardness of the situation, the emotional tension, no more than that. He told me he understood, another tactic he sometimes used to get me onside. And his methods worked to an extent that afternoon as I apologised, explaining my upset, the distress caused by my silent vigil as if it needed saying. As if it wasn't blatantly obvious to anyone with even an ounce of insight. And he responded with what seemed like understanding, just as he always did when it suited his purpose.

But despite Oliver's apparent kindness, support and attention that day, he didn't get everything his way. I was keen to have some time to myself. Although keenness is perhaps an understatement, desperation is a more accurate description of my state of mind. I thought it but didn't say it, which I now know I should have. Why didn't I say it? Why keep my mouth shut? For heaven's sake, I should have made myself crystal clear, if necessary, yelled it in his face until he finally got the point. I appreciated Oliver facilitating the day, God help me, but now there was a lingering sense of resentment too. Not because of anything he'd done or said, I hadn't seen through him, not even slightly, but simply because he was there. It was almost as if he was making my grief his own, encroaching on my personal space in a way that was far from welcome. At that precise moment, as I held the empty urn in my hands, for all his apparent kindness, I wanted Oliver gone. I needed to be alone with my memories. I should have acted on those feelings. I could have been far more assertive than I was. Not that I think it would have had a major impact on his plan, not in the long run. But it may have. Now, I'll never know.

Oliver said all the right things as we walked back towards the cottage. I listened with only passing interest and barely replied. I thought he'd picked up on it, sensitive to my feelings, because when we reached the van, he said he wouldn't come in. And I was grateful, planning a hot bath, calming music, scented candles, a photo of James in a silver frame, and some much-needed me time to reflect and end the day.

Oliver got into his van, driver's side window half open, we said our goodbyes, and I headed up the path towards the front door, thinking he was about to leave. I placed the empty urn back on the kitchen windowsill, made a pot of calming camomile tea, and entered the lounge, glad to finally be alone with my thoughts. But when I approached the window to close the Venetian blinds, the van was still there, bonnet up and Oliver peering at the engine. I watched for a few minutes, half hidden behind the cottage wall, peering through a gap in the blinds, hoping he'd soon be on his way. But it didn't work out that way. And after some time, he closed the bonnet, standing at the side of his vehicle holding his phone to his face, but he didn't get back in. I swore crudely under my breath, feeling obliged to ask him what was happening if he didn't drive off soon. 'Please go, Oliver,' I said out loud now with no one to hear but myself. 'Please go.'

He looked up as I opened the front door, walking down the path towards him. He lowered the phone, returning it to his pocket with a look of despair.

'What's up, Oliver, having problems?' I asked, hoping he'd say something positive. That whatever issue he was experiencing would soon be resolved.

He shook his head slowly. When he spoke, he sounded as irritated as I felt. Once again, he had me convinced. 'The old thing's knackered,' he said despondently.

'Can you not fix it?' I asked, hoping for a resounding yes.

He gave a little laugh and snorted. 'I'm not great with engines.'

I felt my heart sink.

'Are you not a member of the AA, RAC or something?'

'What, with my bank balance? You've got to be kidding. I've got to watch every penny.'

I did question his priorities, given his recent holiday in Lanzarote, but I chose not to comment, thinking it none of my business. I'm not exactly sensible with money myself.

'There are a couple of garages in the village,' I said. 'I'm sure either would be happy to help.'

He held his hands wide. 'What, at this time on a Saturday? Anyway, I've just given a mechanic mate of mine a ring. He can't come today. He's had a few pints, but he'll be here first thing in the morning. Don't worry about it; worse things happen. I'll sleep in the back of the van. It's plenty big enough. Although, if you could lend me a pillow and a quilt or something, that would help. It's going to be a cold night.'

I swore silently in my head. I almost let him do it, I came close, but it's just not in my nature. If only it were. I let out a long breath; no quiet evening for me.

'Come on, in you come,' I said less than enthusiastically. 'There's a single bed in the spare room. I can sort out some bedding. They do takeaway curries at the yacht club if you fancy one. Highly recommended. It's been a long day. I'm not in the mood for cooking. And if you want one, you'll have to get it yourself. I'm planning a film and an early night.'

I could tell he was pleased before he even spoke. 'Oh, thanks so much, Daisy, you're a star. I hope I'm not putting you out. That's the last thing I'd want. Not today of all days.'

The last thing he'd want! Like hell it was. But I didn't know that then. I believed every lying word he said. He got the curry, ate a lot more than me, and we watched *Notting Hill* on Netflix, one of mine and James's favourite films. I still didn't want Oliver there, but I told myself it could have been worse. He was polite, he didn't talk during the film, one of my pet hates, he tidied away after our meal, and he did the washing-up, even drying and putting things away. To sum it all up, he played his role to perfection, Mr Helpful, Mr Nice Guy. I can picture him sitting cross-legged on my sofa, seemingly relaxed and smiling. It's incredible how quickly he made himself very much at home. And he'd be back soon enough; I just didn't know it yet – all part of his plan and only a matter of time.

28

Oliver had already left the cottage when I rose from bed shortly after 9 a.m. the next morning. I'd slept surprisingly well despite an aching lower back. And I was pleased it was Sunday, glad of the chance to recuperate after the hyper-emotional day before. And most of all, I was happy Oliver had gone. Not because I didn't like him, which I still did, but simply because I needed the space. I thought maybe a walk on the beach followed by a light lunch and then a visit to my parents would fill my day well. The sort of things I did most Sundays after James's passing. The little things that kept me sane.

I found a scribbled note from Oliver on the breakfast bar when I entered the kitchen with thoughts of fresh tea. He'd left one of my clear plastic biros next to a sheet of A4 paper intended for my printer. I remember picking the note up and holding it close to my eyes to decipher his scribbled handwriting, not an easy task. He thanked me for letting him stay, said he hoped I'd be okay after scattering the ashes and finished by saying he'd message me soon and that we should get together again. Oh, and there were three kisses, of course. Three large capital Xs. He never missed those.

I enjoyed my tea sweetened with a little honey, glad of the silence, just bird noise and the sound of the wind coming off Carmarthen Bay. And then I ate a single slice of brown wholemeal toast, forcing it down before getting dressed in a casual outfit suitable for my walk. As a last-minute thought, I decided to put a load in the washing machine before heading out, thinking the cycle would be finished before I got back. Practical things mattered, keeping the cottage in order and doing the ordinary day-to-day stuff we do. Keeping busy sometimes helped stop me overthinking and dwelling on my loss, the past.

I stripped Oliver's single bed, collected worn clothing from my bedroom, and then headed to the small utility room via the cottage kitchen, where my wicker laundry basket was next to a combined tumble dryer and washing machine. I bundled all my collected items into the device before delving into the laundry basket, keen to take full advantage of the wash. And as I pulled things out one at a time, it seemed a pair of white cotton knickers I'd worn a few days before was missing. I couldn't be certain, not 100 per cent, but I felt sure I'd dropped them in there with everything else. I had, hadn't I?

In the end, after a few moments of puzzlement, I switched on the machine to walk away. I put my fleeting concerns down to absent-mindedness, thinking I must be wrong, that I'd probably find my knickers in my bedroom, that I hadn't put my underwear in the basket at all.

I gave it no more thought as I pulled on my coat and walking boots in the hall. But perhaps I should have. Maybe the missing knickers told their own story. The more I think about it now, I think it likely they did. I can only conclude Oliver had made his second mistake, another he got away with. It was a clue I didn't spot. A pointer to the type of man Oliver was. A creep who'd steal a young woman's worn underwear without guilt or conscience. I strongly suspect he was sneaking around searching my private things as I lay asleep upstairs, lost to my dreams. I think he took a risk and gambled because he couldn't resist the temptation to snatch what he saw as his prize. And I hate to think what he did with them. I'm trying not to imagine. I'm trying to ignore the pictures in my head.

Oliver was so much more complex than he first appeared, darker, so full of twisted perversions he hid from the world. Yes, he took my knickers. Why did I ever doubt it? Almost nothing about him was as it seemed. I'd learn that soon enough. I think of him as a devil in a human shell. An obsessive curse. A shapeshifter. That monster disguised as a man.

29

I visited my parents again after work on 15 April, arriving at the bungalow just after six. It was their thirtieth wedding anniversary, so the date stuck in my mind. They were preparing to head into Carmarthen by train for a celebratory meal at The Warren restaurant at 8 p.m., so there was plenty of time to talk. I wasn't invited, which didn't surprise me, given the occasion. But it's another of my favourite eateries, so I would have quite liked to have gone. Or at least I would have, had Mum and me not argued as we did.

I gave Dad a card and Mum flowers, a cheery bunch of red, yellow and white blooms bought from Carmarthen's Tesco store on my return journey from Llanelli at a reasonable cost. I was still careful with money out of necessity, watching every penny, and in all honesty, that was a part of my motivation for being there. Not my primary reason. I like to think I'm not that self-focused, but my visit was an opportunity to discuss my ongoing concerns.

Dad disappeared into the family bathroom to shower and shave after about ten minutes, while I talked to Mum in the kitchen over a cup of tea and a *Free From* chocolate digestive biscuit she encouraged me to eat. My rent had been increased, and I'd received an unexpectedly large electricity bill early that morning. It seemed everything was going up in price, inflation rampant, the highest for years. And, in all honesty, once again, I needed help. As I sat there chatting, I knew I'd raise the issue sometime soon. I was preparing myself and waiting until I thought the time was right. Not a nice feeling, but I didn't think I had any other alternative. Although there were other things to speak of first.

My lovely mum dunked a biscuit into her hot drink, took a bite, chewed and swallowed before speaking in her familiar, musical west Wales tones. 'How're things with you, Daisy? Is your appetite any better? You need to eat for that little baby. You do know that, don't you?'

I snapped off half a biscuit and ate it, making a show. We'd had that same conversation so many times before. She never stopped telling me. 'Yeah, yeah, I know, my appetite has improved. You can stop worrying. I'm eating a lot more than I was.'

The frown on my mum's face told a different story. I noticed she'd aged in recent months. Stress can do that; no surprises there. Gravity appeared to have taken its inevitable toll.

'Are you sleeping any better?' she asked. That was usually her second question. I'd got used to the routine. It was as predictable as night and day. I almost always knew what was coming next.

'Yeah, I'm... I'm getting a good few hours now.'

'What about your back?'

'It's still not great.'

She nodded knowingly. 'I had the exact same problem when I was expecting you. It would help if you stretched. That's the best thing. And I used to find a hot water bottle helpful. Not too hot. You don't want to risk burning yourself. Wrap it in a towel or a tea cloth and take it to bed with you. I used to use an old T-shirt sometimes. That worked well. Oh, and don't lift anything too heavy. That's never a good thing.'

I sipped my drink. 'I know, Mum, you said before.'

I knew what she was about to ask when her expression darkened. It was always the same. 'Is there any news from the police?'

I so wished I had something positive to tell her. But all I had was the truth. 'I spoke to Laura Kesey again earlier in the week, but there's nothing new. The investigation is ongoing, as she always says. But they still don't seem to be getting anywhere. I think she's getting fed up with me ringing so often.'

Mum visibly slumped. 'She always seems to have much to say but nothing to tell.'

'Yeah.' That's all I had, that one word, nothing more. I'd almost given up on an arrest by that point. Although, like Mum, I still hoped for a positive development. I prayed for it every night.

There were a few seconds of silence, the two of us sitting there fidgeting, Mum avoiding my eyes. She did that sometimes when she was about to address a sensitive topic. And for once, I had no idea what she was about to say. All I could do was listen.

'One of my friends said she saw you in the village with a young man a few days ago. She said he looked nice enough. Someone of about your age.'

I sighed; it's a small village, and not much goes unnoticed; people talk. I chose not to mention my scattering of James's ashes. I think Mum would have been surprised and disappointed I hadn't involved her. More saddened than anything. It wasn't something I wanted to discuss. It wouldn't have been an easy conversation. And my money issues were still playing on my mind. 'He was a friend of James's at university,' I said, trying to sound as a matter of fact as possible. I hoped she wouldn't ask more. But no luck there.

'And are the two of you friends, too?'

I was quick to reply. 'Just friends, no more than that.'

She helped herself to a second biscuit – such a sweet tooth. 'Ah, right,' she said while eating. 'That's what I thought. I said as much to Mary. I didn't want her gossiping.'

This time it was my turn to pause, considering my best choice of words. Not that there was an easy way of saying it. I'm sure my mum guessed what was coming next. She's not the only one who's predictable. And she knows me well enough.

'There is one thing I wanted to talk about, Mum.'

She shifted in her seat, a pinched expression, eyes slightly narrowed as if she'd tasted something sour. 'Okay, I'm listening.'

I tried to sound as conciliatory as possible. 'I'm really sorry. It's money again. I'm constantly overdrawn. Halfway through each month, and I'm already in the red. I can't take out another loan. I don't even think the bank would give me one. I hate to ask you, but I need help – just two hundred quid. I'm struggling to afford petrol to get to work. I've got no one else to ask.'

She rested her elbows on the table and leant towards me. 'Look, Daisy, Dad and I have been talking—'

Oh, shit! I already knew I wouldn't like what she was about to say next. It had that feeling about it. And I was right; I didn't like it one little bit.

'We're always happy to help you, of course we are, you know that, but it's not a long-term solution. You're living in a three-bedroom cottage. There's just going to be you and the baby now. And if anything, money is going to get tighter after the birth. Why not look for somewhere cheaper? A flat, perhaps, or a two-bedroom terrace. There must be something suitable in the area. Or maybe even something closer to your work. Why don't you take a look online? You had two wages coming in as a couple, and now there's only the one.'

Mum's wise words seemed like a body blow. The last thing I wanted to hear. I know I was being irrational. But it felt like another potential loss. A loss I couldn't face. I wiped a tear from my eye.

'But the cottage was our home, me and James. I still feel his presence there sometimes. I'm hoping I may even be able to buy it one day. I couldn't bear to leave. It would feel like a betrayal. It'll be the perfect home for me and the baby now James is gone. You know I've always loved the place.'

My mum sighed, letting out a long, slow breath that said so much. Looking back, I can understand her frustration. Our conversation couldn't have been any easier for her than it was for me. 'I understand, Daisy; honestly, I do. But you've got to be practical. You can't let emotion cloud your thinking, however hard it is. It would make sense to move now before the baby arrives. Having a child is a massive life change. If you sort everything out now, it will be much better in the long run. I'm talking sense, love. And I know Dad would say the same. I'm speaking from experience.'

I stood and started pacing the kitchen floor, more irritated than the situation warranted, first one way and then the other. Every generation thinks we know better than the last. 'I don't want a flat, and I don't want a terrace. Why on earth would you think I would?'

She pressed her lips together.

'Well, why don't you move back in with us, then? That's another option. Just temporarily for a short time until you can afford somewhere you think suits you best. We'd be glad to have you and it would give you the chance to save, and I'd be here to help you with the baby as needed. Being a single mum is hard. A bit of help wouldn't be a bad thing, particularly at the end of your maternity leave.'

I glared at her, not something I'm proud of. 'I want to stay at the cottage,' I yelled. 'I've made myself perfectly clear. What part of that don't you understand? Do you ever listen to a single word I say?'

I'd said it all with such vehemence, urgent, forceful, as if she was my enemy. My mum didn't deserve that. I'm full of regrets. I could see I'd upset her by the pained expression on her face. I should have apologised. But I didn't. I just stormed out of there like a petulant teenager, my strained emotions getting the better of me, packed to the brim with misplaced indignation. I so thought I was in the right.

And worst of all, I messaged Oliver again almost as soon as I got back to the cottage, long before I had the chance to cool down. If anything, being back home intensified my feelings. I was looking for an ally. And he was the one person I could think to contact, more fool me. I was sure he'd take my side and say everything I wanted to hear. God, I was so utterly stupid. Of course he would. Why was I so needy? I blame myself in a way I never would other victims. I may as well have rolled out a red carpet. I couldn't have made things any easier for the manipulative bastard if I'd tried.

30

I sat in my cottage kitchen, my iPad at the ready, pondering what to write. Thanking Oliver again for facilitating the collection of the ashes seemed appropriate, so I decided to start there before venting my many frustrations with life. I took a slurp of hot, sweet tea before I started typing.

Hi Oliver, thanks again for all you did. It meant a lot, very much appreciated.

I saw he'd read my message almost immediately, and then he replied about five minutes later.

Not a problem. I was happy to help. It was the least I could do for a friend. XXX

Well, I'm grateful.

I dreamt about James last night. I was in two minds about telling you. But I thought you'd want to know.

That touched my heart, leaving me emotionally vulnerable, as I'm certain he intended. Oliver had played his hand to perfection.

Really? What happened in the dream?

James was sitting at the end of my bed. It was so real. It was almost as if he was there, not a dream at all. He told me that you're going to be okay and that you'd find love again. You will find happiness, however bad things seem now.

I shifted in my seat, crossed and uncrossed my legs. To say I was far from persuaded is perhaps the understatement of the year. It was too much, far too emotional. I just couldn't cope with the idea of meeting someone new. I was angry with Oliver for even suggesting that possibility. That was another mistake he got away with. I decided to change the subject, hoping he'd get the message. I didn't want to end our interaction – only that part of it. And I think now, looking back, he'd planted a seed.

Did you manage to get the van sorted?

It's a heap of junk! A mate of mine is going to do a quick paint job and then I'll sell it. I've actually banged the thing. Nothing serious, but it needs sorting. I need something better for work. But whatever I get is going to have to be cheap. It's not going to be anything flash, that's for sure.

I saw that as my chance. An opportunity to talk about my money issues. Oliver couldn't have known that. Or at least, I don't think so. I suspect it gave him a lucky break, that's all.

Is money tight?

Ha! Isn't it always? LOL. How about you? Are you managing? It can't be easy on your own.

I lifted my tea to my mouth, draining the little that was left.

I'm struggling, to be honest. Mum and Dad want me to move somewhere cheaper before the baby's born.

Do you want to?

I gripped my tablet a little tighter.

No, no, I don't. This is my special place. The place I was happy with James. And I've always loved it. Even before I met him. I wish I could stay here forever.

Are you going to be able to stay?

I pushed my empty mug aside.

I don't see how I can for very long.

Oliver didn't start typing again for a few minutes as I sat there waiting. But when he did, he made his move, playing his best card, throwing the dice. I was venting, nothing more. I didn't expect him to offer me solutions. I just wanted a listening ear. But he didn't see it that way. I bet he was laughing his head off.

Look, Daisy, I've had an idea. You need more cash to stay in the cottage, and I'm still looking for somewhere decent I can afford to live within a few miles of Carmarthen. What would you think about me becoming your lodger? I could help with the gardening, and any DIY needed, and pay you a fair rent. And it would solve a problem for you and me. We both get on. We're good friends. What's not to like? I hope you don't mind me raising the possibility. It seems like a great idea to me.

I really wasn't sure. That was my initial response. I didn't particularly like the idea of having anyone else in my home, Oliver included. But I told myself it was worth considering at least in the short term. Sometimes there's no ideal answer to a problem. It's a case of choosing the least worst option and trying to be satisfied with that. I hadn't previously considered the idea of a lodger. But as I sat in my kitchen deep in contemplative thought, it did seem a viable solution. Not one I'd particularly welcome but a better option than losing my much-loved cottage home. The more I thought about it, the better an idea it seemed. Oliver wasn't too bad to have around, and the extra cash would certainly be welcome. But I wasn't ready to commit.

Thanks, Oliver, I appreciate the offer, but can I think about it? This has all come a bit out of the blue.

Of course you can think about it, no problem at all, it's your life, you're in control. But I've arranged to look at a lovely new-build flat in Cross Hands on the 19th at 4 p.m.. If you could let me know before then, that would be brilliant. If I pay the agency a deposit, there's no going back. And the last thing I'd want to do is let you down. I'd hate to think of you moving out of the cottage against your wishes. You mean too much to me for that. And I know James would want you to stay.

I swallowed hard, screwed up my face. I still thought he was trying to help, stating nothing but the truth. Pressure, pressure, everything was pressure.

I'll make sure I get back to you before then.

Thanks, Daisy, you're an absolute star. I'll look forward to hearing from you. And at least I've given you an option. Let me help pay the bills or look for something cheaper. Now it's up to you. I'm only too willing to help if you want me to. Look after yourself. Sending hugs. XXX

31

After a relaxing hot bath, I was drying myself with a large fluffy pink towel when my mobile rang just after 8 p.m. the following evening. I rushed downstairs without getting dressed, urgently grabbing my phone, answering the call with a sideways sweep of my finger, holding it to my face. I was full of hope when I heard my dad's familiar voice say hello. I thought it might be news of James, of the investigation, an arrest maybe, or at least a breakthrough of some kind. Something I hadn't given up on, not entirely. I still prayed every night with whatever energy I had left before sleep, and I now thought that maybe those prayers had finally been answered. I hadn't watched the news that day. I thought Dad might have heard something I hadn't. And I knew he must have something significant to say because he never rang to chat. Mum did, but not him. That wasn't his style. He didn't make small talk.

'Hi, Dad, what's up?'

When he replied, I could tell from his tone that it was something serious, precisely what I'd expected. It was confirmation, no more, no less.

'Did you see the Welsh evening news?' he asked, rushing his words.

I bent down, switched on the gas fire, and stood close, warming my legs and bum, nervous about answering, fearful I might not like whatever he had to say next but still desperate to hear it. 'Um, no, not tonight,' I replied. 'I was late home from work, and then I had a bath. What's... what's happened? Anything important?'

'It's Tom; he's dead.'

I turned the fire up to medium, shivering slightly, disappointed it wasn't news of James. 'Really? Tom?' I asked, somewhat discouraged, my hopes crushed one more time.

'Yes, Thomas Aitken, the best man. I met him at the wedding.'

I fell into the nearest seat. 'Oh yes, Tom, he was at the funeral. Although why he bothered coming, I don't know. It's not like James meant anything to him. What on earth happened?'

'He was out jogging on a quiet country road near Kidwelly last night when he was hit by a vehicle at speed. He was killed outright, with a fractured skull and multiple injuries, but the driver didn't ring for help. Tom's body was found at the side of the road by another driver sometime later, a local farmer. The police are appealing for information.'

'Oh, shit, it's hardly believable. Life can be so very cruel.'

'I thought you'd want to know.'

'Yeah, absolutely; I'm glad you rang. I didn't really like Tom that much, to be honest. And I don't even think James did. God knows why he asked him to be best man. He didn't even organise a stag night. I could never understand why James didn't choose someone else.'

'He must have had his reasons. Perhaps James thought more

of Tom than you realised. Didn't they work together at the leisure centre?'

'Yeah, they did. I suppose you must be right. Although they never met up for a drink or anything like that. Not that I know of. I think they played squash a couple of times at lunchtimes, but that was about it. He's not someone I'll miss. Perhaps he deserved to die. Maybe he did something awful. Perhaps it's karma.'

'What?'

'Sorry, Dad, I haven't been getting much sleep. I'm being stupid.'

There was a brief silence before he spoke again.

'There's something I haven't told you.'

I wondered what was coming next as I moved my chair a little closer to the fire.

'What is it?'

'The police are treating Tom's death as suspected murder.'

'Murder? But I thought you said it was an accident?'

'The chief inspector interviewed on the news said the police have good reason to suspect foul play but that he couldn't give any details at this time. You know what the police are like keeping things to themselves. But if they're talking murder, they must have a good reason. They wouldn't have gone public on it otherwise.'

I remember repeatedly nodding my head, although, of course, Dad couldn't see me. It was an automatic response, more than anything else, a stress reaction. 'I guess so,' I said, now thinking about James, his relationship with Tom, or rather the lack of it. I recalled Tom's wedding speech, a few mildly amusing jokes, some kind words that were vague at best, and not much else. He was only on his feet for about five minutes before sitting back down, including the toasts. I resented him for that too.

'What could the police possibly know to convince them it wasn't an accident?'

I heard Dad blow out the air. 'Look, I probably shouldn't be telling you this and please don't repeat it. But I was talking to Dave next door when we put the bins out about twenty minutes ago. His daughter-in-law works in the operations room at police headquarters. She's been there for years. There's talk that Tom was run over twice as if he was hit full on, and then the driver reversed back over him.'

'Oh my God, who'd do something like that?'

'Let's hope the police find out.'

I had my doubts. And if I'm honest, my primary thought was to hope the investigation into Tom's death didn't distract the police from finding James's killer. I didn't tell Dad that, although I'm sure he'd have understood. He may well have felt the same way himself.

'I remember James telling me Tom still lived with his parents on a smallholding somewhere in the wilds,' I said. 'I'll try to get the address from someone at the leisure centre, send them a card, give my condolences.'

There was another second or two's silence.

'Sorry to be the bearer of bad news.'

'No, I'm glad you've told me. But it's strange, I dreamt about a car crash. How weird is that?'

He sounded more upbeat when he next spoke – I suspect trying to raise my spirits and ignoring my observation.

'Mum told me to tell you she's making a nut roast with all the trimmings Sunday lunchtime if you fancy it? Although I'm sure we'll see you before then. I think she wants to be sure she's got everything she needs. She's also planning a shopping trip to Narberth with Aunty Sara. You know how much they both love the place. It's all those independent shops. And there's a restaurant they particularly like.'

I smiled; I appreciated the invite, which was no surprise but very welcome.

'Tell Mum lunch will be lovely. Is it 12.30 as usual?'

Dad laughed, and I did too, the tension melting away. I was starting to enjoy the conversation. And I like to think he was. The two of us didn't talk nearly as often as I would have liked. Had I known he'd suffer a heart attack so soon, I'd have said so much more.

'Twelve-thirty it is, isn't it always?' he said. 'Your mother is nothing if not a creature of habit. I'll let her know you're coming.'

I thought the apple rarely fell far from the tree. I had my habits too. 'I'll look forward to it.'

His tone changed again, and I pictured him frowning. I recall thinking he sounded surprisingly reticent. 'Have you thought any more about the cottage? Mum mentioned the two of you discussed it.'

I turned up the fire, putting on all three bars, unusual for me, starting to shiver. I recall thinking I should have wrapped myself in a warm, dry towel before heading downstairs. The central heating was off to save money.

'I'm thinking of taking a lodger,' I told him. 'Someone I was in university with, a friend of James's.'

'Really? Male or female?'

I felt the tiny hairs on my arms and neck rise as I snapped back my reply, resenting what I saw as the implication. I think I was perhaps more sensitive than I should have been. I had been since James's death, to some extent, still am.

'What does it matter?' I yelled. 'I need help with the bills. Someone's offered to pay rent, so what's wrong with that?'

'I'm not saying there's anything wrong with it, *cariad*. I was wondering, that's all.'

'He's a *he* if you must know, Oliver, he's going to be a teaching assistant at a school a few miles from where James used to work. He's a nice guy. I don't know what you're worried about.'

'Who said I'm worried?'

'You sound it. It seems pretty obvious to me.'

I heard what sounded like a sigh. 'Are the two of you dating?'

'No, Dad, we are not dating! I can't believe you even asked the question. I said we're friends because that's what we are, friends. I've got a spare room, and he's willing to pay. And I haven't even made a decision yet. I'm still thinking about it. I'm beginning to wish I hadn't told you at all.'

'It's a big decision, particularly with the baby on the way.'

And it was. I knew he was right. But I didn't want to acknowledge that, not really, not even to myself. The cottage meant too much to me for that. In many ways, I chose denial. I didn't give much thought to the potential impact on my life. If I had, well, things might have been different.

'I'd better go,' I said. 'There's some things I need to do before work tomorrow.'

'You know where we are if you need us. And don't work too hard. You need to take care of yourself.'

'Thanks, Dad, see you soon. Give my love to Mum.'

'I will. And try not to worry. Things will work out.'

As I headed back upstairs to dress, I wished I shared Dad's optimism. But I told myself that thanks to Oliver, I did now at least have options. And a lodger wouldn't be such a bad thing, would it? I wasn't finding the decision easy. But time was running out. It was lose the cottage or share it. Whatever way I looked at it, that's how it was. I knew I had to come to a resolution soon. It couldn't be put off for very much longer. And I still liked Oliver, thought the best of him, so what was the problem? I tried not to think about James's aversion to him. He seemed a friend when I needed one most.

32

I was woken by the intermittent sound of a high-pitched engine at 7.40 a.m. on Saturday, 19 April. I really wished the noise would stop, hoping for a lie-in before finally accepting defeat, throwing back my quilt, jumping wearily from bed and opening my bedroom curtains a few inches to either side, letting in the light. I looked out, yawning at full volume, surprised to see Oliver mowing my overgrown front lawn with a red petrol mower. He was wearing knee-length khaki shorts, a loose purple T-shirt, and white trainers, and so I assumed it must already be reasonably warm despite the early hour. I quickly concluded he must have been working for some time because there was a large pile of freshly cut grass in one corner to the left of the concrete path, with no doubt more to come. And I noticed a dark-blue estate car of some kind parked on the road at the end of the garden, which I assumed had replaced his van.

I stood at the bedroom window for a minute or two longer, looking out on the bright spring morning with mixed feelings that I think were understandable in the circumstances. A part of me was grateful Oliver was doing the work on my behalf. It was something James would have done were he alive to do it. Dad had already offered, but I said no due to his dodgy knees. And I'd been putting it off for weeks, full of good intentions. I told myself it was certainly a job that was well overdue. But despite all that, I was irritated. I thought Oliver being there in my garden without even asking me first was something of an imposition. And arriving so early on one of my days off was far from welcome. I silently cursed him under my breath as I turned away.

I can clearly remember reasoning that maybe my initial reaction was unjustified as I headed across the small landing to my cottage bathroom. The old saying about not looking a gift horse in the mouth came to mind as I dropped my oversized T-shirt to the wooden floor and climbed into the shower cubicle. I stood there taking sensual pleasure in hot water warming my skin, thinking that maybe I shouldn't find fault with what seemed a generous gesture. It wasn't as if people were falling over themselves to help me, my family apart. As I soaped my body, I thought I maybe needed a friend like Oliver more than I'd realised. You very quickly find out who your true friends are following a tragedy. And I began to think that Oliver was a true friend, possibly the best I had, maybe even the only one. At least he was doing something practical to help me. He was giving up his time, putting in the effort as he had with the ashes. Yes, I really should be glad about that. That's how it seemed.

I quickly washed my hair, dried myself as quickly as possible, and applied light make-up before rushing back to my bedroom to get dressed. I wanted to make a good impression, to look nice. I think I must have been looking for validation again, insecurity getting the better of me as it often did. That's the only sense I can make of it all. Although I do realise others might come to a different conclusion. I'm not even convinced I've got it right myself.

I made two cups of herbal tea before finally opening the front door to shout hello. I dropped in the tea bags, staring fixated at the empty urn still sitting on the kitchen windowsill as the water came to the boil. Once again, I experienced a degree of guilt that I was engaging with a man James had rejected. I even thought for the briefest of moments that I heard my soulmate's gentle voice whispering in my ear. I still did sometimes, but not as often as I had. And then, as I poured the boiling water into two mugs, my feelings of wrongdoing slowly lifted. I felt less burdened and lighter. I told myself that maybe James was telling me that he understood. That he knew I needed help. That Oliver was forgiven, not such a bad person after all.

I had a lingering smile on my face as I loaded a tray, walking towards the front door on my bare feet. I held the tray in one hand, turning the handle with the other, stepping back, and pulling the door towards me to see Oliver switching off the lawnmower, walking towards me and waving.

'I hope you don't mind me turning up like this,' he said as he got nearer. 'I was down this way anyway. I want to do some shopping in Carmarthen before looking at the flat, so I thought, why not sort out this garden for you?' He laughed, head back. 'It was slowly turning into a jungle.'

I sat on the doorstep, laid the tray on the ground, and reached up to hand him his mug. 'Tea?'

He grinned. 'Oh yes, please, very welcome. It smells great.'

'It's fruity organic, from a health food store in town.'

'Ooh, very posh! I am honoured. I'm more used to the cheap stuff. I am going up in the world.'

I laughed, starting to appreciate his company. He seemed so laid back, so easygoing. Always ready with a joke when the time seemed right. It seemed like his mention of the flat was an opportune time to take advantage. I hadn't contacted him as I'd promised. I thought I'd almost lost what I was now seeing as an opportunity.

'Um, I've been thinking about the cottage,' I said, avoiding his gaze. I hate talking about money. 'I'm sure we could agree on a suitable rent if you'd still like to move into the spare room,' I continued. 'I'm paying seven hundred a month plus bills. I thought we could split it 50/50, so about four hundred quid each, if you're still interested. Although, your bedroom would be a little smaller than mine, so maybe I'd be willing to accept a little less if that's a problem for you.'

I could see he was pleased as he sipped his tea. It was written all over his face as he lowered himself easily to the ground, sitting cross-legged on the edge of the freshly cut lawn a few feet from me.

'That is brilliant news,' he said, brimming with enthusiasm. 'I hadn't heard from you, so I'd almost given up on the idea. I thought you'd probably decided to move.'

'Not at all. That's the last thing I want. Sorry I didn't tell you sooner. I do know I should have.'

He took another sip of fast-cooling tea, moving it around his mouth before swallowing, I think, savouring the taste on his tongue. 'How soon can I move in?' he asked.

I thought about it for no more than a few seconds, coming to a quick resolution. I badly needed the cash and maybe the company almost as much. I was lonely. Not an easy thing to admit. And even the occasional sound of James's voice whispering in my ear before sleep wasn't enough to console me. It didn't drive the demons away.

'You can move in as soon as you want to, I guess,' I said. 'We're friends, so I don't think there's any need for anything formal. We don't need a contract or anything like that. I'm not even sure I'm strictly allowed to rent a room under my tenancy agreement. So least said, the better. As far as anyone else is concerned, you'd be here as a visiting guest. My parents would know what's really happening, but nobody else. And I know they wouldn't tell anyone if I ask them not to. We'd need to keep it private. Is that okay with you? I'd understand if it's not.'

He drained his mug with another smile, placed it on the tray and then stood, looking down at me, stepping forward, standing close to my feet. 'That's not a problem with me,' he said. 'I'm happy with whatever works best for you. The last thing I want to do is inconvenience you in any way. You're in control. How about I move my stuff in tomorrow afternoon? I haven't got much. Just my clothes, my surfboard and some gardening stuff. I won't take up a lot of space.'

'Would either tomorrow morning or late afternoon be okay?' I asked, glad it was happening but still a little apprehensive in light of such a significant change. 'I'm having lunch with my parents. Although I can always cancel if absolutely necessary.'

'There's no need for that. How about 3 p.m.? How would that suit you?'

I joined him on my feet, tray in hand, leaning back slightly, my back aching. 'That would be perfect. Thanks for understanding. I'll get you a front door key cut as soon as I can. I've only got the one.'

'Nice one, that's great; I'll just finish up here and then head into town. The lawn shouldn't take me more than another twenty minutes at most. I want to give the edges a quick trim before I finish. Can I leave the mower in the shed when I'm done? There doesn't seem to be any point in putting it back in the car. Although I will if you want me to.'

Oh, so very accommodating; he seemed almost too reasonable, so wanting to please. But I saw that as a good thing. His nice guy act was working only too well. 'Yeah, of course you can,' I said. 'And if you've got any other tools you want to put in there, that's fine too. It's almost empty.'

Oliver restarted the mower, pulling the cord twice, the engine roaring into life, but then he switched it off within seconds, calling after me as I walked away. 'How would you feel about meeting me at the veggie café for lunch? I fancy another one of those mushroom burgers, my treat. And you could take the opportunity to get a key cut while you're in town. Don't worry if you've got something else on. No pressure. We can always do it another time. Although it would be nice to celebrate our agreement with a bite to eat. It's a big day.'

'Um, yeah,' I replied. 'I don't see why not. How does 1 p.m. sound?'

'That's perfect; I'll see you there. And I'll let the agency know I'm not going to be looking at that flat. Living by the sea is going to be great.'

I nodded; he was right about that. The wild, ever-changing estuary is so very beautiful at any time of year.

'Do you want a bit of breakfast before you finish the garden?' I asked him. 'I was just about to make myself some toast.'

He shook his head. 'No, I'm okay, thanks. I ate before coming. But another cuppa would be welcome.' He laughed and added, 'I could get used to this service.'

'Do I owe you anything for the lawn?'

He made a face. 'Of course you don't. Don't be so ridiculous. If I'm going to live here, I need to look after the place for you. Make me a list of jobs. I'm only too happy to help. Anything you think needs doing, I'll do it. I'm pretty handy with most things. You'll want the place perfect before the baby arrives.'

Then I smiled too, more sure I'd made the right decision.

Thinking he'd be an asset rather than a burden. 'Thanks, Oliver, it's appreciated.'

'You're very welcome. And as I said, please don't hesitate to ask if you need anything. I meant every word. I'm here to help, but you're the boss. It's your home. You're in control.'

33

Oliver turned up at the cottage at ten to three on Sunday afternoon, about half an hour or so after I'd arrived back from my parents' place. My appetite had significantly improved by then, occasional morning sickness aside, and I was in a relatively positive mood when I looked out of the lounge window to see him get out of his car and rush up the path. It was raining slightly, just a light drizzle, and he was wearing a parka-style coat with a hood but with no fur around its edge. I owned a similar one myself. At the time, I was focused on his arrival and on getting him moved in. I gave no thought to his appearance, not then, that came later. I saw a friend, just a friend, no threat at all.

I opened the front door and raised a hand to wave in a friendly greeting, welcoming him with a smile.

'I hope you don't mind me being early,' he said, despite it being only ten minutes. 'Is it okay if I bring my stuff in? There's not much. I can leave the shed stuff in the car until the weather improves. It's supposed to be getting better later, according to the forecast.'

'Yeah, yeah, makes sense. Do you need a hand with carrying anything?'

He looked me up and down and laughed. 'What, in your condition? You leave the heavy lifting to me. But a cup of tea would be nice if you're making one.'

I was pregnant, not ill, and surprisingly strong, but I didn't protest. 'I'll put the kettle on. Feel free to take your things upstairs; your room's the door next to the bathroom. I've made the bed, and the wardrobe is empty, so you should be fine. If there's anything else you need, let me know.'

He beamed. 'Thanks, Daisy, you're a star.' He said that a lot.

Within about twenty minutes, we were sitting together in the lounge, drinking tea and talking. He asked about the police investigation. I told him it still wasn't going well. Oh, and I told him about Tom's death, about which he seemed surprised, although looking back, I think there was a glint in his eye. I may be imagining that, but I really don't think so. He gave me a month's rent upfront in cash about half an hour later, despite me not having asked. I was grateful for that, as I suspect he knew I would be. And then he insisted on washing up, not just our mugs but the few dishes I'd left in the sink. He was pleasant and helpful, which I think was him worming his way in. He was the perfect lodger, or so it seemed.

It all felt so bizarre having someone else in the cottage at first. But while there were times I craved my own space, I quickly came to appreciate what seemed to be Oliver's positive impact on my life. He cooked tea that first evening at his insistence while I read a book. And I think that set the scene. In short, to sum it up, he did all he could to make himself seem as indispensable as possible with remarkable speed. He was like a whirlwind, a man possessed. He bought food, shared it with me, planted flowers, shrubs, berry bushes and fruit trees, and began decorating the cottage room by room after I asked the landlord's permission. And all in a matter of days, working every spare hour and sometimes late into the night. Oliver even bought the paint. He did a fantastic job of the third bedroom, which I'd decided would become the nursery. And then, as if that wasn't enough, he arrived back from town one day with a used wooden cot, which he rubbed down and decorated with a lovely pale-yellow non-toxic paint suitable for small children, making it beautiful. Yellow has always been one of my favourite colours. I'd told him that. It reminds me of the sun.

All in all, as May approached, while I was still grieving, I was beginning to think I could face the future and that, in time, my sadness might become less extreme. I was still desperately frustrated that the police hadn't caught James's killer. I was only speaking to Kesey or Ray Lewis once a week by that time, and never a fruitful conversion. And Oliver seemed sympathetic, usually giving me a friendly hug when I talked of my loss. And he told me he'd always be there for me, a listening ear whenever I needed it. It seemed our friendship was growing. And that's how I saw our relationship, as a friendship. I did like him, as I've said before. But I wasn't ready for romance. I still loved James. It was too soon for anybody else. Oliver did sometimes remind me of James, but that wasn't enough. I wanted the man I'd lost.

34

My life took another dramatic turn on 25 April. That was the day I lost my father. A heart attack became a full-blown cardiac arrest. My mum later told me Dad woke early that morning with a crushing pain in his chest and shortness of breath. She dialled 999 and urgently requested an ambulance, but it didn't arrive in time. Mum tried her best to resuscitate him as he lay prone on the bedroom floor, but without success. By the time two paramedics finally arrived at the bungalow, almost an hour later, my lovely dad was dead. The timing really couldn't have been worse, before he even got to meet his grandchild. The cycle of life at its most cruel, and again one of the saddest days of my life. A time I'll never forget.

I was back at the Pembrokeshire Crematorium at 11 a.m. on 3 May, far too soon. Death had revisited my family, the service again bringing our mortality into sharp and unrelenting focus. Mum and I sat at the front of the small chapel, and this time Oliver joined us, dressed in that same suit, I think the only one he owned. He sat in a pew one row immediately behind us rather than waiting outside as he had at James's funeral. And he was supportive, or so it seemed. I remember him placing a hand on my shoulder as the service began with one of Dad's favourite Welsh patriotic songs, a rousing rendition of 'Men of Harlech'. I think I probably thought of Oliver's touch as sympathetic if I thought of it at all.

Oliver walked a few feet behind Mum and me as we made our weary way back across the car park in the direction of our cars about half an hour later, our eyes filled with tears. I drove my car back to Ferryside with my mum seated next to me, repeatedly dabbing at her face with a paper tissue, trying to hold it together for my sake. Oliver had come in his car after telling me he didn't want to encroach on my family's grief. I remember thanking him. That seems crazy to me now. And I invited him to the bungalow for the wake. But he declined, again saying it was a time for family. I didn't argue. Mum still hardly knew Oliver, so I think he was right not to come. Although I now know his seeming sensitivity was nothing of the kind. It was all part of his show.

I next saw Oliver when I returned home to the cottage at about 7 p.m. that evening. I recall a melodic Norah Jones album playing on his laptop in the lounge when I joined him, kicking off my shoes, my feet aching after a long day. He made me a pot of tea and offered me a biscuit, which I declined. And then we talked, really talked, about James, about my dad, and the baby, too. Oliver asked about things that mattered to me. He seemed an excellent listener. And he gave me the distinct impression that what mattered to me mattered to him. Not that it did, but that's what I thought. His every expression, his every word appeared to convey empathy and understanding. He gave me comfort at a time I needed it most. He had that skill. I think he'd honed it. I don't believe he did anything without reason. He always knew exactly what he was doing and why. That's the kind of man he was.

Oliver held my hand at one point during the evening as a particularly romantic song came to a timely end, moving from his seat to join me on the sofa, sitting close, our legs almost touching. He told me I'd had a tough day and that he was there for me; that I looked tired and needed rest. And I fell for it, every word. I placed my head on his shoulder, leaving it there for a few seconds before sitting back up, thinking of our mutual affection as nothing more than friendship. But as I turned my head to face him, intending to speak, he stretched his neck towards me, kissing me full on the lips, his wet tongue in my mouth before I jerked my head back, pulling away, surprised but not hating it. I don't think I should have been surprised at all. But I was. I didn't see it coming. I think he'd made another mistake, his first in a while. Or maybe he'd timed it just right.

'What on earth do you think you're doing?' I said, more upset than angry. I was shaking. My entire body tensed.

He moved away, then jumped to his feet, a flash of irritation quickly replaced by what I now consider a contrived look of regret. He had a hard-on. I could see the prominent bulge in his trousers as he stood facing me. I asked myself how I could have misread the situation so very badly. Did he think I'd led him on?

'Oh, shit, I'm so very sorry, Daisy,' he said. 'I got the wrong idea. I thought you wanted it. It's just that I care for you so very much. I'll never do it again.'

I folded my arms atop my slightly swollen belly, my pregnancy now showing. 'For goodness' sake, Oliver, really? On the day of my father's funeral? I like you. I appreciate everything you're doing for me. If circumstances were different, well, maybe. But they're not.'

He slumped into the nearest armchair, dropped into the seat, quickly covering his erect cock with a cushion. I thought he might start crying. He had that look about him, sorrowful. As if he was both embarrassed and upset by events. He took a deep breath before speaking, looking down at the carpet for a few seconds before finally meeting my eyes.

'Look, I'm in two minds about saying this at all, but here goes. I've always thought honesty is best. Seeing you so upset today was heartbreaking. I've always liked you. And I fancy you; you already know that. You're the most beautiful girl I've ever met. But the longer we've lived here together, the stronger my feelings have become. I think I'm falling in love with you, Daisy. And if you think there's even the slightest chance you'll ever feel the same, I'm willing to wait for however long it takes. And I'd be very happy to help look after the baby if you'll let me, but only if it's what you want. Please tell me you'll think about it. I'm not asking you for an answer now.'

I must admit that as I sat there trembling, Oliver's words touched my heart. I'd already forgiven him for the kiss. It wasn't simply that he fed my fragile ego. I realised I did feel affection for him. I liked what he'd said. It pleased me. But yet again, James came to mind. 'I'm so sorry, Oliver, I'm still in love with James.'

He dropped his chin to his chest. His shoulders slumped, a picture of despair. His voice faltered when he responded. And I think he was genuinely upset. Maybe he saw his plan disintegrating before his eyes. I think he would have said or done almost anything to rescue his intentions. I can see now he gambled when he played his next card. He was such an intelligent man; he must have known the risk. Although he may well have had a backup plan. I'd only seen one side of him then, but there were others.

'Look, I've told you how I feel,' he said. 'I do love you, and not just as a friend. My feelings are deeper than that. But I'm willing to move out if this is all too much for you. And I'm sorry this has all come out today of all days. I'll go tomorrow if you want me to. All you have to do is say the word. I couldn't stand being here if there was any awkwardness between us. I think too much of you for that. It's up to you, Daisy. Just tell me what you want. You're in control.'

Was I? It didn't seem that way. My feelings were still so conflicted, clouded by my recent losses. But at that moment, as I considered Oliver's emotive words, I realised I didn't want him to go. It wasn't only the practical help he gave me, the rent, the DIY. For the first time, I accepted I was starting to develop deeper feelings for him too. I still didn't think I was ready for romance. But for the first time, the idea of a new relationship at some future date held its attraction. I told myself that James had gone and that he wouldn't want me to spend my life alone. I repeated it in my head, trying to convince myself before speaking again.

'I don't want you to go,' I said. And I meant it. I realised it was the last thing I wanted. I knew I needed to love again. And I think, at that point, he knew he was winning.

'Are you certain?' he asked. 'I hope it's not the money. I can lend you some if it is.'

Oh God, and then it was me saying all I could to persuade *him* to stay, which no doubt he intended all along. 'It's not just the money,' I said, almost pleading. 'I'd miss you if you left. I like you too.'

He held his hands wide, pulling my strings. 'I'd like to stay, but I'm not sure it's possible. Do you think there's *any* chance of us being more than friends? I don't think I could stand to stay if there isn't. Seeing you every day, so near and yet so far, it's not something I could cope with for very long. It would be like torture.'

What should I say, yes or no? Was I ready to let him go, another potential loss, the third in a matter of months? I should have been stronger, but I wasn't. I bet he was laughing inside, thinking me a fool. But if he was, he hid it well. Something he was good at. He almost always was.

I'd never been single in my adult life, I was young, a widow and expecting. I wanted to keep Oliver on my terms, to say the right things, which didn't come easily.

'I'm... I'm not... ready for a physical r-relationship,' I stuttered. 'But if you're willing to be patient, we... we can start dating if we take it slowly. I'm not making any promises, but I'm w-willing to give it a go. I think it's what James would want. You've been brilliant. I don't know what I'd do without you.'

Oliver's relief was evident as he looked me in the eye. There was an energy about him, a winner's smile.

'That's wonderful to hear, Daisy. I'm so pleased I said something now. I've wanted to for ages. I was just so worried I'd blow it.'

'Well, you haven't.'

He smiled again, beaming. 'Can I give you a hug?'

I shifted in my seat, reaching out, my arms wide. 'Okay, come on, but no kisses.'

He moved towards me. 'Not even a peck on the cheek?'

I relaxed slightly. 'Okay, a peck, but no more than that.'

He sat alongside me, and we held each other close for a few seconds before he gently kissed my cheek, more than a peck, lingering. I reciprocated, now enjoying his physical touch, allowing myself that luxury, the human contact, the comfort. And then he released his embrace sooner than I wanted, again playing the long game, not wanting to spook me as he had before.

'Fancy a drink?' he asked. 'Or a bite to eat?'

'A cup of mint tea would be nice.'

'I'll get some fresh from the garden. I think it's stopped raining.'

I thought, what a considerate man, just like my James. Just like him. 'That would be lovely, thanks.'

'I adore you, Daisy. I hope you don't mind me telling you that. I think you're wonderful. I have since the first day I saw you in Swansea. It was like a lightning bolt at first sight. That's why James and I fell out. You do know that, don't you? He had you, I couldn't, and I was jealous; I said too much.'

'Yes, you told me. I think we'd best put that behind us. Going over it all again serves no useful purpose. What happened happened, and now here we are.'

'I'll make that tea.'

I stood stiffly, in need of the bathroom. 'Thanks, James, it's appreciated.'

He looked back at me, his eyes wide, showing the whites. '*James?*'

'Oh, shit, sorry, you remind me of him sometimes.'

He nodded but he didn't say anything as he turned away, heading for the hall. It was an awful day of sadness, but I told myself it was ending well. I thought maybe Dad was looking down on me smiling, and perhaps James too. They were my guardian angels. There seemed to be a light at the end of a long dark tunnel. Life was continuing. And maybe, just maybe, one day, I would find happiness again. I was hoping that day would come sooner rather than later. I'd had enough of loss. And I was glad Oliver had told me how he felt. I thought maybe one day I could love him. The spark was there. I only had to let it ignite.

35

Oliver and I first had sex about a week later. And I have to admit it was at my instigation, not his. Although he had been increasingly physically affectionate towards me in the days leading up to the event. So I think we both knew what was coming.

Oliver was so very attentive after expressing his affection on the evening of my dad's funeral, seemingly caring and looking to meet my every need at every possible opportunity. And his initiative worked well, my feelings for him quickly grew. I became more receptive to his hugs and kisses. I'd always found him reasonably attractive, but now there was more than that. All of a sudden, I saw him as a prospective long-term partner, a future father to my unborn child. I didn't feel the intense depth of love for Oliver I had for James, not even close, but there were feelings nonetheless. And, to be honest, I missed a man's physical touch. I was young. It had been months. I was sexually frustrated; that's the truth of it. I don't think that's something to be ashamed of.

Oliver had cooked me a pleasant tea by the time I arrived back from work that early evening, an organic mixed salad with an olive oil dressing, followed by lemon sorbet he'd made himself. We ate the tasty meal together in the dining room, Oliver serving each course, a glass vase of freshly picked flowers on the table. Romantic music was playing. He washed up while I changed out of my work uniform, and then we sat on the sofa in the lounge, watching a mildly entertaining rom-com I think we'd both seen before. All in all, it was a pleasant evening. When the film ended, he kissed me full on the lips, and I knew I wanted more. And, of course, I knew he did too. Unusually for me, I decided to tell him exactly how it was. I was self-conscious about my body as my pregnancy progressed. But he seemed to love my curves. He often told me how beautiful I looked. He was always forthcoming with flattery and praise.

I stood, using the arm of the sofa to assist myself to my feet. 'I'm going to have a quick shower,' I said. 'And then I'm going to have an early night. You can... you can join me if you like.'

Oliver's eyes lit up. 'What, in your room, in your bed?'

'If you want to?'

He licked his lips, first the top and then the bottom. 'Of course I want to. It's what I've always wanted. The greatest gift you could ever give me.'

'Give me half an hour and then come up. I'll be waiting for you.'

'I love you, Daisy.'

It wasn't the first time he'd said it. But it was the first time I'd reciprocated in kind when I told Oliver I loved him too.

36

One day passed after another and still, there was no progress in finding James's killer. But I'd told Mum about my new relationship and it seemed she was happy for me. That was one positive. I still missed James. I hadn't stopped loving him. But I was beginning to experience some happiness again. Something I'd doubted I'd ever feel. And it all happened so very quickly. Oliver and I were now living as a couple, sharing a bedroom, and even planning our future. There was talk of our rental cottage being put up for sale. Hugely frustrating after all the decorating we'd done. But that's how it was. We hoped to buy it with a joint mortgage if my mum agreed to lend us something towards the deposit. She'd inherited everything after Dad's passing. I hadn't talked to her yet, the bank of Mum, but I knew I couldn't put it off for very much longer. And then, on 20 May, in the early hours, everything changed. All my cherished plans were blown out of the water.

I remember being woken with a start at about 2 a.m. early that morning, the room in semidarkness, the pale light of the moon the only illumination. I turned my head on the pillow, looking across at Oliver asleep next to me. I thought of shaking him awake as I heard a sudden noise outside, but instead, I rose from the bed, walked across the bedroom floor on my bare feet, and peered out through the window to see a man I didn't recognise coming out of the shed, his arms laden with tools. I remember being doubly surprised because west Wales is a low-crime area. Thefts in our village were almost unheard of, but there he was, stealing Oliver's property.

I shouted, 'Oliver, Oliver! There's someone in our garden.'

He opened his eyes, blinking. 'What?'

'Someone's stealing your stuff. Quickly, he's getting away.'

Oliver leapt from bed, hurriedly pulled on a pair of underpants that had been lying on the floor, and then ran downstairs and out of the front door, yelling expletives. I watched nervously from the window as the man dropped the tools, sprinting across the freshly cut lawn, hurdling the metal gate at the end of the cottage path, and escaping into the road. Oliver yelled more angry abuse, stopped at the end of the garden, collected his tools together, and then returned them to the shed, I think satisfied that none were missing.

I'd already phoned the police on my mobile by the time Oliver returned, panting, to the bedroom a few minutes later. And then things took another unexpected turn. His reaction was nothing I'd expected.

'The police are on the way,' I said, smiling, thinking he'd be pleased.

He frowned hard. 'You've rung them?'

'Well, yeah, obviously, why wouldn't I?'

'What the hell have you done that for? The bastard didn't get anything. He's gone. This sort of thing happens in London all the time.'

I was just about holding it together. 'But we're not in

London,' I said. 'I still think I've done the right thing. Are you trying to give me nightmares?'

He folded his arms across his chest, his feet set wide, a stiff stance. 'Give them another ring. Tell them they're not needed. That you got it wrong.'

I placed my hands on my hips, more confused than anything else. 'No, Oliver, no, the thief might come back.'

He tried to grab my mobile, but I pulled away.

'What on earth's wrong, Oliver? What aren't you telling me?'

He screwed up his face, I think changing tack as his anger subsided. 'I think we both need to get some sleep, that's all.'

I pulled on a dressing gown and tied it loosely at the waist over my baby bump. 'I'm going downstairs to make some tea. It will be waiting for you if you want it. The call handler said the police were already on their way. I couldn't get back to sleep even if I wanted to.'

He mumbled under his breath before finally speaking, 'Okay... in that case, I suppose I'll see you downstairs.'

Two young uniformed officers, one male, one female, arrived in a patrol car about fifteen minutes later. Both were friendly, reassuring and efficient. They were with us for about half an hour, taking statements from us both, and saying a CID officer would be in touch the next day. And that's what happened. Ray Lewis rang me at 8 a.m. the next morning, asking if Oliver could call at the police station to provide his fingerprints for elimination purposes, as I already had following James's abduction. I said 'Yes, of course, not a problem,' thinking that despite his reaction the night before, Oliver would be happy to help. He was sitting in the kitchen eating breakfast when I told him.

'They want me to give my fingerprints, *why*?'

'I've told you, for elimination purposes. Ray will call to examine the shed sometime today. He said we don't need to be here. You just need to arrange to call to see him at the police station at a convenient time. But don't leave it too long. We don't want to slow down the investigation.'

Oliver pushed his plate aside. 'What's the point? Shouldn't he concentrate on finding James's killer instead of wasting his time bothering with this shit?'

This was a side of Oliver I hadn't seen before. A side of him I didn't particularly like. 'Ray said he's dealing with the case as a personal favour because he knows me. Contact him and make the arrangement; it won't take long. He'll ring you if you don't. I've given him your number.'

He stood, glaring. 'Oh, for fuck's sake, Daisy, what did you want to go and do that for?'

I didn't appreciate the language. 'For goodness' sake, just give the police your fingerprints, and it's done.'

He pushed his seat back, rose to his feet, and stormed towards the hall. 'Okay, okay, I will when I get the time.'

I felt inclined to protest, to tell him to make the time. But I decided I'd already said enough. I didn't appreciate the upset or resulting stress. He'd surprised me, and not in a good way. My head had started to ache. I'd had enough. I thought I'd likely have a bad dream about that too.

'I'll see you after work,' I said. Keen to bring the interaction to an end.

Oliver left the cottage without kissing me first. His way of making a point. I knew all couples argue from time to time, but this seemed strange. I couldn't make sense of any of it. Why was it all such a big deal for him? His reaction seemed so over the top.

37

When Ray rang me four days later, there was an urgency to his voice. It wasn't like any conversation I'd had with him before. He told me straight out that his call wasn't about James and then said there was something he needed to discuss with me face to face, leaving me confused but intrigued. I thought that maybe they'd caught the burglar and I might need to give evidence in court.

'Do you want me to come to the police station sometime today?' I asked. 'I'll be in Carmarthen anyway for a training thing.'

'Do you know the rugby club? The one near the park?'

'Um, yeah, I think so.'

'Can you meet me there at 1.30 p.m.? We could have a drink and a private chat, off the record.'

'What the hell is this all about, Ray? You're starting to worry me.'

'I'll see you at 1.30, love. It's better done in person. I'll tell you all about it then.'

Ray was sitting behind a green baize-topped pool table in

the quiet bar when I arrived at the rugby club that afternoon. He was nursing an almost empty pint of best bitter, cradling the glass in both hands with what seemed great affection despite being on duty. There were three empty salt and vinegar crisp packets on the round table in front of him.

'Take a seat, love. Can I get you a drink?'

I nodded, replying before sitting. It wasn't somewhere I'd ever been before. 'Do they do tea?'

He stood with a slight groan and drained his glass. 'I don't see why not.'

'Black, please, no sugar.'

'Anything to eat? They do some decent pies and sausage rolls if you fancy one.'

I was feeling sick and had been since getting up that morning. Maybe the stress, perhaps my pregnancy, or both. And, of course, I don't eat meat. 'No, thanks, I had a sandwich before coming.'

'Not even some crisps?'

'I'm good, thanks.'

He shrugged and walked towards the bar, laughing along with the middle-aged, bottle-blonde barmaid to some joke or other. Within a few minutes, he and I were sitting opposite each other, me sipping my tea and him slurping another beer, making a slight humming sound before each greedy swallow.

'What's this all about, Ray?' I asked again, increasingly desperate to know.

He looked around him to the left and right, lowering his voice. 'This is between you and me, yeah? Like I told you before, you remind me of my daughter. It's nothing official at this stage. But I want to help you if I can.'

'Is it the burglary?'

'Well, not exactly, but sort of. At least, that's how it started.'

I was feeling more confused than ever. 'Okay, I'm listening.'

He scratched his nose and cleared his throat. 'I've been in this job a long time. I've got an instinct for when things aren't right. It's a gut feeling. Something I rely on that rarely lets me down.'

I felt my jaw tense. 'Whatever's worrying you, please tell me.'

He took another slurp of beer, the pint glass now half empty. 'I've been trying to arrange for your boyfriend to have his finger-prints taken. He's agreed to come into the station three times but hasn't turned up. He didn't even ring to cancel. And recently, his phone's been going straight to messages. He doesn't get back to me. I'm starting to think he's actively avoiding giving his prints for some reason.'

I pulled my head back. 'But he told me he's already done it.'

Ray Lewis shook his head. 'Well, he hasn't, love. I don't want to frighten you. But I think he may have something to hide. His prints may be on record. He may not be who he says he is.'

'Oh, come off it, that's ridiculous.'

'Is it, love? Is it? He's lied to you, he's avoiding me, and there has to be a reason. Best find out what it is. Better safe than sorry.'

My mind was filed with conflicted thoughts. I still didn't know what the big detective wanted of me. 'Do you want me to talk to him?'

Ray looked around again before speaking, his words almost whispered. 'I don't think so, love. Think about it. He's already lied to you. We've no reason to think he won't do the same again. I was hoping you could get me his fingerprints, something he's touched; a glass or cup would be ideal. And then I'll get them checked. If they're not on record, I'll tell you, and he need never know about it. But if he is known to the police, we need to know why. Particularly with that baby on the way.'

I shook my head. 'Oh, I don't know, Ray. Do you really think all this is necessary?'

He nodded twice. 'I do, love, I do. I wouldn't be suggesting it if it wasn't. You may be in danger. Are we on?'

I thought about it for a few seconds but no longer, as the officer waited for my response.

'You'd just need a cup or a glass, something he's touched?' I asked.

Ray drained his pint, head back, drinking every last drop of the brown yeasty liquid. 'That's right, love. It's that simple.'

'And Oliver need never know if his prints aren't known to you? He'd never know we'd had this conversation?'

'He wouldn't ever hear it from me. It would be our secret. You have my word.'

Yes or no? What to say? What the hell to say? Not an easy decision even then. I touched my belly, picturing my unborn child. And at that moment, my decision was made. Oliver mattered to me, but my baby's safety mattered more.

'Okay, I'll do it,' I said, rushing my words, still far from sure I was doing the right thing.

He smiled. 'Sooner the better, and best wear gloves when you handle whatever he's touched. It'll make things easier for us.'

'I'll do it this evening if I can. Do you want me to text you if I get what you need?'

'Let's not risk putting anything in writing at this stage. Just give me a ring when you're alone. You've got my number. I'm available anytime. I'll be awaiting your call.'

And that's precisely what I did a few minutes after 10 p.m. that night, standing in the cottage bathroom, whispering into my mobile with the door locked and the shower on. I'd insisted on washing up that evening, hidden Oliver's glass in my handbag when alone, wrapped in an orange plastic carrier bag.

I delivered the glass to Ray at West Wales Police HQ before work the following morning, feeling guilty for my deception but repeatedly telling myself I was doing the right thing. I did it for my child rather than myself. I doubted the detective's suspicions would come to anything, but I needed to know if there was even the slightest possibility he was correct. I didn't have to wait long for the answer. And it wasn't the conversation I'd hoped for or expected when we met to talk. It was so very far from that.

38

Ray and I again met at the rugby club at his request two days later, sitting at the same round table, downing the same drinks, music playing on the sound system. The clock on the wall read 2.25 p.m.. I think it was a little slow. There was only one other person in the bar that warm afternoon, the barmaid apart, an older man sitting at the other end of the room well out of earshot. My entire body was twitching as I looked Ray in the eye. I'd already concluded he must have something significant to tell me. Why would he have asked to meet me otherwise? And he had the look of someone with something to say and struggling to contain it.

'Hello, love, I'm glad you've come.'

'I had to leave work. I hope this is worth it. I'm assuming you've had the fingerprints checked?' I said, not sure I wanted to hear the answer.

'I'm sorry, it's not good news.'

I rubbed the back of my neck, taking short sharp breaths, the skin bunching around my eyes in a pained stare. It felt as the little happiness I'd rediscovered was about to come crashing down. 'Oh God, no, what is it?'

The sergeant's tired eyes narrowed. 'The man you know as Oliver isn't who he says he is. He's known to the London police, with a history of violence towards females starting when he was just thirteen. There were two rape allegations investigated by the Met, which sadly came to nothing. It happens all too often with the current system. But he did serve a six-month sentence in a youth detention centre for the indecent assault of a girlfriend. He created a whole new identity before moving to Wales. I made a few phone calls. It seems everything's in his new name, clever, really. There's nothing you can't get online if you know what you're doing, birth certificates, national insurance number, fake utility bills, references, qualifications, and even convincing passports in whatever name you want if you're ready to pay. And he'll likely have any number of criminal contacts who could help if needed.'

The detail was convincing. My Oliver was a fraud. I could hardly believe my ears. It was far worse than I'd ever imagined. 'Are you certain?' I asked, already knowing he was. 'He's so gentle, such a good guy. One of the nicest people I've ever met.'

'One hundred per cent certain, love. There's no room for doubt.'

I dry-gagged once, then again. 'Who is he?'

'There's no easy way of saying this. His name's Michael Earl; he's James's half-brother, same father, but different mother. His mother died when he was six, from cancer. James and Michael grew up together after that. Michael was three years older than James. I think Michael must have followed James to this part of the world when the family moved to Ferryside, even going to the same university with that false identity. Very bright guy, it seems. I've had a chat with an officer who knows the case well at the

Met. The family finally disowned Michael when he assaulted his stepmother, James's mother, when he was only fifteen. James witnessed the assault but refused to give evidence, as did his mother, despite dialling 999 at the time. Michael moved to live with an uncle in Lewisham shortly after that, a man named Oliver Lee.'

I just couldn't make sense of it all. I'd heard Ray, taken in every dark word. But the man the detective described seemed so very different to the one I thought I knew. 'That doesn't sound like the man I'm living with at all,' I began. 'I can't imagine him assaulting anyone, let alone a woman. If Oliver is this *Michael*, he's hiding it well.'

'They often do, love, until you cross them. Then you find out *exactly* who they are. His family came here to try to escape him. It didn't work. I suspect that's why the Earls went back to London, to get away from him again. They're still running.'

I shook my head, incredulous, one invasive thought after another troubling my mind. 'Why the hell didn't Roy or Margaret say anything to *me*? They just rushed off back to London! They must have known he was a danger, and the baby, what about the baby? They didn't say a thing. And James, he never mentioned a brother. Not a word, not at university, not at the wedding, not on honeymoon. He hid it too. What the hell was that about? They were all living a lie. I can't... I can't understand what was going on in their heads. It seems insane. It's the craziest thing I've ever heard. Did I ever really know any of them? So many secrets they should have shared.'

'People do the strangest things, love. That's all I can tell you. You wouldn't believe some of the things I've seen in this job. Nothing surprises me any more.'

I sat there silently for a few seconds as reality slowly sank in. The detective seemed so sure of the facts. There was no room for denial. Deep down, I knew he was sharing the truth. 'So, so, what happens now?'

He took a mouthful of beer. 'I've checked the system. Earl's not currently wanted. And his MO doesn't suggest he's potentially in the frame for James's death. All his offences are against females and sexual. The DI's off this afternoon. I'll have a chat with her in the morning, see if we can nick him for identity fraud once we've gathered all the evidence. But as of now, I suggest you get him out of your life. Do it today. There's nothing good to come of the relationship. The man's bad news, he's a danger.'

'I thought I loved him.'

'And now?'

I touched my abdomen, glancing down. 'I'm going to be a mother soon. If he's even half as bad as you're saying, he's got to go.'

Ray's relief was evident, written all over his face. 'Do you want me to be there when you tell him? Best not do it on your own.'

For some reason, despite all we'd discussed, I still couldn't accept there was even the slightest possibility Oliver, or Michael as I now knew him to be, would do anything to harm me physically. I thought he loved me too much for that. 'No,' I said. 'It'll be okay. I'll do it myself. He's been kind to me. I owe him that much.'

The detective looked far from persuaded. 'Are you sure?'

I didn't give my answer nearly as much thought as I should have, my decision more heart than head. How very stupid. I minimised the dangers, that's the truth of it. 'Yeah, I'm sure,' I said. 'He'll be upset more than angry. I know him pretty well by now.'

Ray looked me in the eye. 'You know where I am if you need me.'

I felt unsteady as I stood, the stress getting to me, hardly surprising. Ray took my arm and walked me to my car, calling his goodbyes to the busty barmaid as he went. I sat alone in the car park for about twenty minutes after that until I finally felt ready to drive. I wasn't looking forward to talking to Oliver, far from it. But it was, I told myself, something I had to do. It shouldn't be avoided because honesty was best.

I thought about the information shared by Ray as I drove towards my seaside home, Radio Wales playing on the car's stereo, the cheery combination of music and lively chatter seemingly at odds with my plight. The fact that Roy, Margaret and James had all failed to share what they knew again came to mind, and it rattled me, my eyes glistening. Why the hell didn't they tell me? It seemed so unreasonable, so unfair. I thought about it for a few minutes longer as I drove but then I asked myself if the man I still thought of as Oliver could have been involved in James's death despite Ray's comments. Okay, so maybe his history didn't make it likely, but he could be, couldn't he? No, no, surely the police knew best. As I pressed my foot down on the accelerator pedal, I dismissed my hypothesis as ridiculous. I told myself I was getting carried away and needed to get a grip.

Ray told me he trusted his instincts, and I should have too. Why didn't I listen to my gut? The truth was staring me in the face. It would have been so much better if I had.

39

I began collecting Oliver's possessions together as soon as I returned to the cottage later that afternoon. I wanted everything ready and waiting for him when he returned from work, with no unnecessary delay. It was clear in my mind he had to go, and I wanted to make what I knew would be a caustic experience as quick and easy as possible. In short, I wanted him gone.

I was in our bedroom, collecting his clothes, placing them in a large plastic suitcase one at a time, when it happened. I was folding his suit when something fell from the jacket's inside pocket. I looked down incredulously at a band of gold glinting on the carpet two or three feet from where I stood. I momentarily froze, gasping, my mouth falling open, a hand flying to my chest. Oh God, no. It couldn't be, could it?

I bent down, urgently picking up the ring with frantic fingers, holding it close to my eyes, studying it, comparing it to my own. It was an exact match, the distinct Celtic style, even the hallmark. It was a light bulb moment. In that instant, I knew the truth. It hit me like a physical blow. As crazy as it seemed, my earlier brief and discarded suppositions were accurate. I let out a scream as one thought after another drove home my plight. I'd placed that wedding band on James's finger. And his killer had torn it off. A ruthless killer. A madman who was so obviously capable of any atrocity. It was the only logical explanation. The only thing that made any sense at all. Oliver! Why hadn't I seen it before?

Ray, I had to contact Ray. Quickly, Daisy, quickly. I began striding towards the stairs, rushing down toward where I'd left my mobile charging in the lounge. I almost made it, but not quite. As I reached the bottom step, the front door opened. And then there he was.

An angry frown quickly replaced Oliver's friendly smile of greeting as he stood facing me. My fearful body language betrayed me. He had his instincts too. My mind was a whirl. What to say? What the hell to say?

'I was, er, I was just about to visit my mum. I'll, er, I'll make tea when I get back. You, you needn't bother, just relax.'

'What's the rush?'

I fought back my tears with little success, my face flushing, damp patches forming under my arms. I felt so very hot. 'No rush, I w-won't... I won't be long.'

But he didn't move, standing between me and the front door, staring, studying my body language, arms folded, intimidating like a nightclub bouncer. 'What have you been doing upstairs?'

'Nothing.'

'You haven't been snooping around, have you?'

'No, no, of course not.'

'You look like you're scared to me. You're sweating like a pig. What's going on? I know something's up. I've got a sense for these things, always have had. Don't go thinking you can con me. Something's changed.'

'Nothing, nothing is going on. I'm hot, that's all.'

He locked the door now, removed the key, put the chain on, and then looked me up and down, baring his teeth, a snarl. 'You're shaking like a leaf, Daisy. Do you think I'm stupid or something? Have I got *idiot* stamped on my forehead? What have you found? What are you holding in your hand so tightly? What are you trying to hide?'

I averted my eyes, looking down, my lip and chin trembling, my elbows pressed to my sides. 'I'm not holding anything.'

He laughed now, a cold laugh that had nothing to do with humour. 'You can stop playing your little games. Show me, or you're going to regret it. You've got no idea what I'm capable of if you let me down. I can be nice or I can be nasty. It's up to you.'

I fought to control my fear, remain rational, say the right things. I realised I'd made a terrible error in not accepting Ray's offer of protection. He'd tried to warn me. He'd offered to accompany me. So why didn't I listen? I desperately wished I had. As I stood there shaking, I knew I was seeing Oliver's true colours for the first time. The real Oliver. The one he'd hidden. The one he only revealed when his manipulations were finally failing. It was as if a switch had been flicked. His good guy act had crumbled before my eyes. I'd seen fleeting hints of it before, that anger, but it never truly registered. I thought I was seeing something that wasn't there, imagining it because of my fragile state. But now there was no room for doubt. It was as if he was a different person. A very real threat. Not the man I'd thought I'd known at all. I held out my hand and opened it because I had no other option. And then it seems I said the wrong thing.

'Please, Oliver, it's just a ring. I won't tell anyone I found it. I'm begging you. Please let me go.'

He looked at me with a sneering smirk, as if he'd seen through me and could read my mind. 'Why wouldn't you tell anyone if it's just a ring? You know exactly whose it is. And nothing's going to change that. That's why you were trying to leave. I can see that in your face. I thought you were special. But you're just a bitch like all the others. You've let me down.'

He suddenly drew his right arm back, formed his hand into a tight fist, and punched me hard, bang, right on the point of my nose. I tasted blood as I fell back on the stairs, seeing stars as he glared down at me, yelling. 'You had to go and ruin everything, didn't you, my little darling? You had to stick your beak in where it didn't belong.'

I coughed, spluttering, choking on my blood, but I forced the words from my mouth. 'Please, Oliver, think of the b-b-baby.'

He grabbed my arm, pulling me off the stairs, yelling again as he dragged me towards the kitchen. 'Do you think I give a toss about the brat? James spawned the little runt, not me. You and me could have been happy together. We could have had the perfect life. But now you've gone and wrecked that with your snooping. Everything that happens now is down to you.'

He dragged me through the kitchen door and left me seated against the back wall as he stood in front of me a few feet away, close to the window.

'Did... did you kill James?' I asked through my tears, knowing the answer was yes.

'Of *course* I killed him.'

I forced myself to look at him, refusing to look away. I hoped there might still be some affection for me somewhere beneath the rage. I hoped my soft voice might engender a more reasoned, sympathetic response. Maybe my nursing communication skills would pay a welcome dividend. 'Why, Oliver, why?'

He looked pensive now, as if reflecting, the old Oliver again for a beat, deep in thought. 'I followed James to Wales. We made up in that first year at university. I told him I was sorry, a changed man. We re-established a bond, made friends for a time. But then you turned up and he let me down again. Everything went to shit. I wanted you. He had you. I put a tracker on your car. There was only one way I was going to win.'

'I'm sorry.'

'Oh, so now you're sorry, are you? It's a bit late for that.' He took the almost empty urn from the windowsill, hurling it at the wall above my head, smashing it into what seemed like a hundred jagged pieces. A small cloud of grey dust rose as I recoiled, now avoiding his gaze. I wondered how long I had left to live. I told myself that maybe I could talk my way out of it if I was clever enough and convincing. I had to try.

'I forgive you, Oliver,' I began. 'I know you only did what you did because you love me. We can keep *everything* that happened a secret. We can still have a life together. Let's not waste what we have. It's special. I never loved James as much as you.'

He began pacing the room whilst weeping, moving first one way, then the other. 'I'm not going to prison. I know what that shit's like. Another bitch let me down. If I have to kill you, that's your fault. It's all down to you.'

I pressed myself against the wall, making myself as small as possible, instinctively trying to hide when hiding wasn't possible. I pictured the life inside me, giving me courage. 'No one is going to prison, Oliver. I still love you. I don't care what you did. I want us to have a life together. You, me and the baby. That hasn't changed.'

He dropped to his knees at touching distance, his tears now in full flow. 'Really?' That's all he said, just one word.

I wiped the blood from my face with a sleeve as it ran from my nostrils. 'Come here, my love, hug me,' I said. 'We're meant to be together. Screw everyone else. It's you and me against the world.'

I cringed as he held me close for a short time that felt like an eternity.

'I do love you,' he whispered in my ear. 'I get fixated. I trust people and then they fail me. I do things I don't mean to do. It's never my fault. You do understand that, don't you?'

I swallowed twice, preparing to speak, hating his body's warmth against mine. 'Of course I understand,' I said. 'Now, help me to my feet. I'll brush my teeth, shower, and then show you how much I love you. We can do anything you want to. I'm yours. I always will be for as long as you want me. And I'll wear that perfume you like, the one you bought me, your favourite.'

He stood, reached down, took my hand, and pulled me up towards him, hugging me again once on my feet, holding me close.

I glanced over his shoulder, every muscle tense, every sinew, a sudden coldness in my core, telling myself I had no option but to take my opportunity, however scared I felt inside. I pressed myself against him, reached out, grabbing a steak knife from a knife block on the countertop, clutching it tightly in my hand, hiding it behind my back as he stepped away, finally releasing his grip. And then, as he stood facing me, smiling, I moved quickly, adrenaline pumping, plunging the point of the sharp steel blade deep into his gut, using all my strength and weight. I did it for me. I did it for my child. It was my life or his, kill or be killed. And I'd never hated a man more.

I watched, mesmerised, as the person I'd known as Oliver sank slowly to the kitchen floor, clutching his belly in a hopeless attempt to stem the blood flow, looking up at me with an incredulous expression I'll never forget. I watched as his breathing gradually slowed, his chest rising and falling only slightly as I turned to walk away.

I think Oliver was already dead by the time I phoned Ray

Lewis in the lounge. The sergeant joined me at the cottage within twenty-five minutes, the sound of a siren announcing his arrival, followed soon afterwards by an ambulance and a second police car. A paramedic attended to my facial injuries after confirming Oliver had bled out on the kitchen tiles.

Ray repeatedly expressed his regrets as he drove me to the police station in loosely fitting handcuffs he said he was loath to make me wear. He was as reassuring as he could be in the circumstances, but I could tell something had changed.

'It was self-defence, Ray,' I told him. 'You were right, he was dangerous, I stabbed him because I had to. He'd have murdered me and the baby. I had no other choice. It was our lives or his.'

He focused on the road rather than turn his head to look at me. 'Save it for the interview, love. You're under caution. Wait until you've got a solicitor, that's best. Say what you need to on tape.'

'But it was self-defence, you do understand that, don't you?'

He paused before speaking, the last thing he said in the car. 'He was dangerous. He was a convicted sex offender. And I have no doubt he assaulted you. But he had *five* stab wounds, love. Three in his back. He died curled up on your kitchen floor.'

That confused me but I didn't comment. I couldn't make any sense of it. I'd been fighting for life. It *was* self-defence, as I'd later say in court. But not everything was clear. Not on the day of the killing. Did I black out? Some memories were blurred.

My time at the police station was less onerous than expected. It was stressful, and there's no denying that. But given my recent experiences at Oliver's hand, my arrest, incarceration and questioning paled by comparison.

I was interviewed in the presence of a duty solicitor after about an hour waiting in a cell. Ray brought me a cup of tea and a tomato sandwich while I was locked up. He smiled as he gave them to me. And then, once in the interview room, he asked me the questions himself, not putting me under any undue pressure, letting me tell it how it was. And I did, just like he told me to. I talked of my fear, the threat I faced, and the reasons for my actions, stressing self-defence time and again. But despite all that, at the end of it all, I was charged with murder. Now, that did surprise me. I've had nightmares about it ever since. There's so much injustice in the world. Life can be so unfair.

Ray told me the police would still be looking for James's killer despite my sharing Oliver's confession both verbally and in a written statement. I think it must be a procedural thing, something legal. It seems like a waste of time to me. What was it Ray said before I was taken from the police station? That the police only have my word for it. They will never be able to hear Oliver's confession for themselves. It was all so very confusing and still is. Sometimes I think the world's gone mad.

40

This final chapter is the only one written after my acquittal. My court case went well, and to be honest, which I must be, I expected no less. Karma is a powerful force. The most powerful in the universe. And I feel sure it was on my side. When people do bad things, they're punished. And when they're good, like me, they're not.

I told my story in the witness box on being questioned much as I have in this book, or at least, as far as possible, given the nature of the proceedings. And the judge allowed me to sit down to tell it. I was close to popping. I think that helped. I pleaded my innocence, of course, stressing self-defence. And I came up trumps, despite the prosecution barrister's arguments. The fool even suggested that either I'd had James's wedding ring in my possession all along or it wasn't his at all.

After a seven-day trial, the jury found me not guilty by a majority verdict. It was a close thing, but justice finally prevailed. I recall my sense of relief as I write these words. Soon my life would be back on track, I told myself. The worst was over. Better times ahead.

My mum sat in the public gallery for the entire length of my trial, watching, listening, and sometimes with her head in her hands. She cried when Oliver's wounds were described. But I thought I heard her let out a small cheer when the verdict was announced, and the judge said I was free to go. Now it really was over. All the unhappiness in the past.

Mum was waiting for me when I left the court building, waddling while walking, my baby at the forefront of my mind. She had the car's engine running as the attending journalists shouted questions I didn't answer. And then, I got in quickly, and she drove off as I struggled with my seat belt.

'How are you feeling, Daisy?' she asked, tears staining her face.

I smiled. 'I'm okay; there's just me, you and the baby now, all girls together. And I think we're going to be fine. Not all men are good like Dad. Some let you down. I learnt that the hard way. I've come to realise James was almost perfect, but not quite. And Oliver, well, he was a madman.'

Mum said nothing more for about five minutes as she negotiated the traffic. But then she spoke again. 'I've got some news. I've been going through James's paperwork. It's all at the bungalow. I had to empty the cottage once the police told the landlord they'd finished with the place.'

I was interested now, keenly anticipating what she had to tell. 'So, what's the news?' I asked.

'There was an unopened envelope. James took out life insurance while you were on honeymoon. You'll be able to claim. It'll be security for you and the baby. At least something good's come out of it all.'

I did my best to sound surprised. 'Really?'

'You didn't know?'

'How much?'

'Half a million pounds.'

'Wow,' was all I could think to say.

We sat in silence again for a moment after that until I asked my next question. 'What's happening with the cottage?'

'It's still up for sale. I think they're struggling to sell because... well, you know, because of what happened there.'

'How much are they asking?'

'Four hundred and ninety-five thousand, I think; I saw something online.'

'So I can afford it now.'

Mum didn't sound nearly as happy as I felt.

'But would you want it after all that tragedy?'

I picked up her phone from where she'd left it in the cup holder. 'Can you pull up, Mum? I need to make a call.'

She quickly signalled, braked, and manoeuvred to the side of the road. 'You're not going into labour, are you?'

I laughed. 'Who's the estate agent? I may get a bargain if other people aren't interested.'

There was a surprising look of shock on my mum's face as I turned my head towards her.

'I'm amazed you'd ever want to return to that place,' she said. 'It's the last thing I'd want to do.'

I thought her contention ridiculous, but didn't comment. 'So, who's the estate agent?'

She finally gave me the answer while slowly shaking her head. I rang but only got a recorded message, my mind now drifting, already focused on other things... 'I dreamt about James last night,' I said. 'A recurrent nightmare, awful, me standing at a cliff edge, him falling, falling, and then watching the tide wash his body away.'

Mum was gripping the steering wheel tightly now despite

the car being stationary. 'Did you kill him, Daisy? Did you kill him?'

I shrugged, surprised she'd ask such a thing. 'Oliver? Of *course*, you know I did; you were in court; it was self-defence. The jury said so. He was a sex offender, a predator. He'd been stalking James and then me. He was a bad guy!'

My mum was weeping now, holding her hands to her face, speaking through tears. 'I'm talking about *James*,' she said. 'Did you kill *James*? Was describing your dream some sort of confession?'

My mum asked me that, of all people, *my mother*! Not so lovely now. I turned in my seat, looking away, my mind racing, one thought after another. I'd have the cottage I'd always loved and the child I'd always wanted. And I don't think James had even really wanted the baby. I'd seen him looking at other girls even on our honeymoon! He'd never have been a good dad, or husband. That's what I told myself. That's what truly mattered, whatever my mother thought or said.

I told her to drive on as she sat there sobbing. So I'd dreamt about killing James, so what? I had a lot of dreams, none of them pleasant. Some about James's reaction to my pregnancy, Oliver's many lies and even Tom's callous disregard for my feelings at the funeral. And yes, others about watching them die. I didn't dignify Mum's question with a reply.

Oh, and one last thing. I dreamt about that horrid girl, Lily, who'd obviously lied when she said she'd seen James at the service station, although I didn't tell Mum. Not something I expected, but I think worth mentioning. In my dream I saw Lily cold, blue and mottled on a mortuary slab. Who knows? It could have been a prophecy. Karma playing its games. Stranger things have happened. It wouldn't surprise me if it came true, too, now that I'm free.

ACKNOWLEDGEMENTS

With thanks to my new editor, Isobel Akenhead, and to the rest of the brilliant Boldwood Books team.

ABOUT THE AUTHOR

John Nicholl is an award-winning, bestselling author of multiple psychological suspense thrillers, including The Galbraith Series. These books have a gritty realism born of his real-life experience as an ex-police officer and child protection social worker.

Sign up to John Nicholl's mailing list for news, competitions and updates on future books.

Visit John's website: https://www.johnnicholl.com

Follow John on social media:

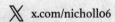 x.com/nicholl06
facebook.com/JohnNichollAuthor
bookbub.com/authors/john-nicholl
instagram.com/johnnichollauthor

ALSO BY JOHN NICHOLL

THE
Murder
LIST

THE MURDER LIST IS A NEWSLETTER
DEDICATED TO SPINE-CHILLING FICTION
AND GRIPPING PAGE-TURNERS!

SIGN UP TO MAKE SURE YOU'RE ON OUR
HIT LIST FOR EXCLUSIVE DEALS, AUTHOR
CONTENT, AND COMPETITIONS.

SIGN UP TO OUR NEWSLETTER

BIT.LY/THEMURDERLISTNEWS

Boldw☾☽d

Boldwood Books is an award-winning fiction publishing company seeking out the best stories from around the world.

Find out more at www.boldwoodbooks.com

Join our reader community for brilliant books, competitions and offers!

Follow us
@BoldwoodBooks
@TheBoldBookClub

Sign up to our weekly deals newsletter

https://bit.ly/BoldwoodBNewsletter